DEADLINE WITH DEATH

TIME-SLIP MYSTERIES, BOOK 1

ZARA KEANE

BEAVERSTONE PRESS

DEADLINE WITH DEATH
(Time-Slip Mysteries, Book 1)

Two Crimes, Two Times…

Dee Flanagan loves Irish history, bad rom-coms, and red lipstick. Dead clowns, injured time travelers, and shoot-outs don't make it onto the small-town reporter's Top Ten list. After the bullets stop flying in Dunleagh Castle's courtyard, it's up to Dee to convince people she didn't imagine a gunfight played out between two centuries.

With the body count rising, and no one willing to believe Dee's time travel theory, she's forced to team up with a man who's either a bona fide fruit cake or a police officer from the year 1919. Using her expert knowledge of the Irish War of Independence, Dee sets out to solve a century-old crime, plus a modern-day murder.

NOTE ON GAELIC TERMS

Certain Gaelic terms appear in this book. I have tried to use them sparingly and in contexts that should make their meaning clear to international readers. However, a couple of words require clarification.

The official name for the Irish police force is *An Garda Síochána* ("the Guardian of the Peace"). Police are *Gardaí* (plural) and *Garda* (singular). Irish police are commonly referred to as "the Guards".

The Irish police do not, as a rule, carry firearms. Permission to carry a gun is reserved to detectives and specialist units, such as the Emergency Response Unit. The police in Dunleagh would not have been issued with firearms.

Although this edition of **Deadline with Death** follows American spelling conventions, I've chosen to use the common Irish spelling for proper names such as Dunleagh Harbour.

ONE

Dunleagh, Ireland

The morning the clown croaked at my feet began with a cockfight and ended with a corpse. Neither covering the fight nor discovering the body was on my to-do list. After five months of juggling my job at the *Dunleagh Chronicle*, a volunteer position at the museum, my history video blog, and looking after my grandmother, I finally had a free day.

Until I didn't.

Courtesy of a virus sweeping through our offices, two of the *Chronicle's* reporters were out sick. With press day looming, my penny-pinching editor was desperate enough to pay me time and a half, and with a mountain of bills on my nightstand, I was desperate enough to agree. I swapped my cozy bed for Mavis, my scarlet scooter, and faced the elements of a rainy Irish summer.

Under different circumstances, a spin through the countryside might've been pleasant. Today's ride was anything but. I steered Mavis through driving rain, gale-force wind, and potholes the size of mainland Europe. The crowning glory was a near collision with a herd of cattle that'd taken up residence in the middle of the road. I seriously should've held out for double pay.

By the time I pulled up outside the tumbledown farm where the cockfight was being held, the organizer had gotten wind that the cops—or Guards as they were known in Ireland—were on the way. In a spectacle of flying feathers and bouncing beer bellies, both the contestants and the spectators were fleeing the coop. I dry-heaved my way through the stench of birds and unwashed men, snapped a few shots of the mayhem, and hopped back onto my scooter. I now had less than an hour to reach my desk and write an embellished account of the non-event, so Mavis and I broke several rules of the road on our return journey.

The clock in the town square chimed ten as I hung a right and chugged up the steep road that led to Dunleagh Castle. In fifteen minutes, the *Chronicle*'s grumpy subeditor would emerge from his lair, demanding to know why my article wasn't on his desk. I swore under my breath and pressed hard on Mavis's sluggish accelerator.

At the top of the hill, the castle loomed, dark and magnificent against the stormy sky. The sight of its gray walls and tall towers never failed to thrill my inner historian, even when I was in a hurry. From its clifftop perch, Dunleagh Castle had cast a menacing glare over the harbor for the last six centuries. While most of the original outer wall was gone, and the outer courtyard had been repurposed as a parking lot, both the castle itself and its generous gardens remained intact. Today, it housed the newspaper, the mayor's office, the museum, a small café, and several lovingly restored rooms that were open to the public. Working for a struggling weekly rag wasn't the glamorous career I'd envisioned at university, but it paid the bills—well, some of them—and I had the privilege of working within the castle walls four days a week.

I wasn't alone in my admiration for the fortification. It had earned a well-deserved place as one of Ireland's most popular tourist attractions. Even at low season, buses braved the steep incline and disgorged tour groups in front of the wooden drawbridge. At high season, as it was now, the stream of tour buses seemed endless.

One such bus spluttered its way up the road in front of me, moving at a painful pace. I swerved to overtake it and narrowly missed mowing down a man who was crossing the street. He leaped sideways to avoid me and landed in a puddle.

"Hey," he roared, glowering at me under bushy red

eyebrows, "watch where you're going."

"Sorry," I said on autopilot.

The word caught in my throat when I recognized the guy I'd almost rendered roadkill. Charles O'Rourke, better known as Mr. Chuckles, was a popular street performer whose clown routine delighted children and tourists alike. He was also the dude I'd kneed in the nuts last month. I doubted I'd make it onto his Christmas card list, but then, he wouldn't make it onto mine.

Ignoring Mr. Chuckles's squawks about my reckless driving and general tendency to harm his person, I zoomed into the parking lot and deposited Mavis in a free space. I pulled off my helmet and yanked up the hood of my jacket. The downpour was turning into a deluge, and the brief moment between removing my helmet and getting my hood in place was all it took to turn my hair into a sodden mess.

As I exited the parking lot, my phone vibrated with an incoming call. My hand went to my pocket on reflex, but I pulled it back and kept moving. It was wet out, and I was late. Whoever was calling me could wait.

Before I stepped onto the road, a second tour bus pulled up to the curb opposite. If I wanted to dodge a swarm of geriatrics, I needed to pick up my pace. I speed-walked across the road and then broke into a run. With a wave of greeting to the guard on duty, I bounded over the castle's wooden drawbridge and entered the courtyard. The cobblestoned ground was slick with rain, and puddles formed in patches where the stones needed to be replaced. Standing beside one such puddle was none other than my good pal, Mr. Chuckles. I swallowed a groan. He must've reached the courtyard just before me. Seriously, why couldn't I catch a break this morning? With my deadline imminent, the last thing I needed was an argument with the clown.

I surveyed my surroundings. A gaggle of elderly tourists huddled in front of the castle's main entrance, all wearing bright orange raincoats emblazoned with the name of their nursing home. If I zigzagged past them and ran the rest of the way, I'd be at my desk in five.

In spite of the slippery surface, I accelerated into a sprint. I'd almost reached the door when the clown stepped in front of me, forcing me to stagger to a standstill. He was dressed in full regalia: baggy polka-dotted pants, luminous green shirt, wide yellow sash, fire-engine red wig, and a shiny, red plastic nose. The addition of a leopard-print rain poncho completed the look. I tried to dodge the guy, but at that moment, the second influx of tourists trundled over the drawbridge and swarmed into the courtyard en masse, nixing the option for me to sidestep my adversary. Before I had time to react, Mr. Chuckles was up in my face, yelling and shaking a fist.

To the casual observer, we must've appeared a

comical pair. Last time I'd checked, the average Irish male stood five-feet-nine-inches tall. I barely missed the six-feet mark. I'd inherited my considerable height, sturdy build, and masses of blond hair from my father, an American with Swedish roots. The clown, in contrast, must've been descended from leprechauns.

The little man gesticulated wildly, jumping up and down to emphasize his points, none of which were flattering and several of which would've required a bleep censor.

"You came through the incident unscathed." My gaze dropped to his mud-strewn legs. "Apart from your pants."

He moved closer, still eye level with my chest. "I ought to call the cops on you, Flanagan. You're a menace, on and off the roads."

A hushed silence fell over the elderly tourists, and I sensed several pairs of eyes upon me. I ignored them and focused on the clown. "Calling the cops didn't work out so well for you the last time. As I recall, the encounter ended with you receiving a formal warning for sexual harassment."

A gasp of excitement rose from our audience, but the clown appeared to be oblivious to the onlookers. "That cop is your friend," he muttered. "She'd believe any pack of lies you fed her."

I rolled my eyes. "Dude, there was CCTV footage of you groping my butt *before* I kneed you in the groin. Sergeant Healey didn't have to take my word for it."

The clown moved closer, and my stomach roiled. Everything about this creep made my skin crawl. I took a step back to regain some semblance of personal space and sought an escape route. The old folks spilling over the drawbridge surged toward the main door. Unless I wanted to shove octogenarians out of my way, my best bet was to take a detour via the museum, where an upstairs corridor connected the building to the castle. First, I had to get the clown to back down and let me get to work.

"Look, I'm in a rush..." I tried to bypass him, but he blocked my attempt and jabbed me in the chest with a chubby finger.

"If Dunleagh had a proper cop in charge," he snarled, "you'd have been arrested for assault."

"If by 'proper' you mean 'male,' I doubt even the most chauvinistic man on the force could ignore the evidence on the tape." A churning panic warred with my rising anger, but the sneer that stretched his painted lips tipped the balance. I gritted my teeth and cast an exaggerated glance at my watch. "Fun though this has been, I gotta get to work. Unless you want a replay of last month's nut-crushing incident, you'd better let me past."

Red-hot rage flickered across his face, and the knuckles of his fists turned white. The misogynistic pig would love to hit me, but he didn't have the guts to do it in front of witnesses. What he did have the guts to do was to keep blocking my way.

I bit back an oath and thought fast. In a flash, I opened my backpack and extracted a small can, careful to conceal the logo. "Well now, would you look at that. Is this pepper spray lurking in my bag?"

My words had an instant effect. The clown's beady eyes widened. He leaped back, colliding with a group of tourists.

"Why don't you juggle a few balls for our visitors?" I winked at the open-mouthed seniors. "No pun intended." Giving the clown a look laced with contempt, I squeezed past. This time, he didn't try to stop me.

Courtesy of the spectacle Mr. Chuckles and I had provided, the old folks parted to let me through, sparing me the necessity of a detour via the museum. A few of the tourists even clapped. I reached the door to the main entrance in record time, executed a mock bow, and bounded into the castle.

Larry, a fellow member of the Historical Murders Club, was on the phone at reception. He nodded to me as I dashed past and mouthed, *Morning*. I gave him a thumbs-up and climbed three flights of stairs to the North Tower, home to the *Dunleagh Chronicle* for the last one hundred fifty years.

I burst through the modern glass door and tumbled into the newsroom, panting, sweating, and dripping with rain. Even in my out-of-breath state, it took me less than a millisecond to register that chaos ruled supreme. A workman kneeled by the printer, surrounded by power tools and pieces of machinery. Behind the wreckage, splatters of ink stained the wall, as though the staff of the *Chronicle* had engaged in a frenzied game of paintball during my absence.

"I don't know which circle of hell I've walked into," I announced to the room at large, "but I think I'll leave you guys to it."

"No, you won't." Marcus, the subeditor, emerged from behind the towering pile of papers on his desk. He was short and chubby and adorable. What was left of his brown hair stuck out in wild tufts from the sides of his shiny pate. His black-rimmed glasses were askew, and his tie looked as though it had survived a nuclear war. I was enormously fond of Marcus, in spite of his Grinch-like persona.

"You're in press day mode," I said, stating the obvious.

"And you're *late*." Marcus drew his bushy eyebrows together and tapped his watch. "I needed that story five minutes ago, Dee. Even your mother got her horoscopes in on time this week."

Well done, her. "Give me another ten and you'll have it in your inbox, complete with a photo of stampeding poultry to plaster across the front page."

His gloomy expression deepened. "It'd better be spectacular. We've got nothing else worth printing this week, let alone make our lead story. With our circulation numbers dwindling, we can't afford to have yet another filler story on the front page."

"Leave it to me," I said cheerily, faking a confidence I didn't feel. "Why don't you have a coffee while I type? You look exhausted."

Marcus grunted and scratched his shiny pate. "I might just do that."

With my subeditor appeased, at least temporarily, I covered the last couple of meters to my desk. Aido Lafferty, the *Chronicle*'s other junior reporter, sat at his side of our shared desk. His green-tipped hair, piercings, and psychedelic color choices contrasted with my black-and-white wardrobe. My one nod to color was my rocking red lipstick collection. Today, I was wearing my favorite brand of liquid lipstick in the shade Oxblood. I'd completed my look with black trousers and a plain white blouse. Not exactly fashion forward, but that was how I rolled.

I dumped my bag and helmet on the floor and struggled out of my wet jacket and waterproof pants. "My morning is a classic example of 'no good deed goes unpunished,'" I whispered as I slid onto my chair. "I should've let Cian's call go to voicemail and stayed in bed."

Aido twirled a pen between his fingers, and a slow grin spread over his handsome face. If I were five years younger, I'd have fallen for his charm and good looks, but I was pushing thirty. Bitter experience had taught me that guys like Aido were best kept in the friend zone.

"I take it the cockfight didn't go according to plan," he said, his grin widening.

"Seamie Dean got tipped off that the Guards were going to raid the place. By the time I arrived, everyone was scrambling to get away. I got a few shots of the stampede, and that was the extent of my coverage." I screwed up my nose. "Then when I got back to town, I almost mowed down Mr. Chuckles."

Aido laughed. "I'd love to have seen that."

"He threw an epic tantrum."

"He's not exactly your greatest fan," my friend said dryly.

"I'm not his, either. The guy's a creep. And he made me even later getting to the office." I opened my laptop and fired it up. "Fabulous. This piece of excrement is insisting on installing updates. Estimated time, ten minutes."

"Write what you can in the time you have," Aido advised. "If they get desperate, Cian said he'd run a piece by your mother. Something about chakras and crochet. Apparently, it's her most popular class."

I groaned. "I still have people asking me to explain that article she wrote on reincarnation and knitting."

His lips twitched. "I never did grasp the connection there, but then, I find her weekly horoscopes indecipherable."

"That's Bliss. She specializes in vagueness and empty promises." This attitude also extended to motherhood, an observation I kept to myself.

Aido's lips twitched. "I take it her prediction for your love life hasn't panned out?"

"The one about the dark-haired dude in uniform?" I rolled my eyes. "She's been saying that for years. I pay no attention."

"Larry at reception has dark hair," Aido said with a sly grin. "And he wears a uniform."

I arched an eyebrow. "Larry is thirty years my senior, not to mention the fact there's a Mrs. Larry in the picture." While my laptop laboriously installed its updates, I checked my phone. The missed call was from my sister, and she'd followed it up with three text messages.

The first read as follows:

Can you bring Nana to her hospital appointment? Cliona's throwing up and Jack's screaming the house down. The appointment's at eleven-thirty with Dr. Sanyal. Thanks! River xx

Sent five minutes later:

Yo, sis. Did you get my message about Nana?

And the most recent:

Dee????? I'm getting desperate here. Bliss isn't answering her phone. You're my last chance.

Acid burned in my stomach. Of course Bliss was incommunicado when she was needed. Our mother—a self-proclaimed New Age hippy—was too busy "finding herself" to bother with such banalities as looking after her elderly parent. She was currently away on a yoga retreat, a fact she'd obviously failed to mention to my sister.

I glanced at my watch. It was twenty past ten. *Yikes.* I'd barely have enough time to write my story and get to Nana's. I drummed an impatient rhythm on my desk with one hand and typed a response to my sister with the other.

"Problem?" Aido peered at my laptop. "Is the computer giving you trouble?"

"It's still updating." I grimaced. "Looks like I'm on taxi duty. Nana needs a lift to the hospital, River's bailed, and Bliss is away. I have to skedaddle once I get this story written."

"Smart move in any case." Aido jerked a thumb in the direction of our editor's office. "Cian wants you to read his play again."

I pretended to bang my head against my desk. "Just kill me now. I never thought I'd regret specializing in 1920s Irish history, but *A Fighting Man* might break me."

Cian's latest dramatic masterpiece was set during the Irish War of Independence, the topic of my doctoral thesis and the main focus of my history video channel. The War of Independence, or Anglo-Irish War, was fought from 1919 to 1921 between the Irish Republican Army (IRA) and the British forces. The British side included members of the Royal Irish Constabulary (the police force of the day), the British Army, and various paramilitary factions.

Cian's play allegedly focused on events leading up to the signing of the Anglo-Irish Treaty and the subsequent end of the war, but was in fact a tale of doomed love. The last thing I wanted to do was wade through his turgid script for a fourth time, especially as I'd be forced to sit through the opening night. In spite of being at least fifteen years too old for the role, my mother had bagged the main female part.

"Our beloved editor is a determined man with a ruthless streak," Aido continued. "He's counting on you being so grateful for your job that you'll agree."

This statement was an accurate summary of my predicament. Cian had given me a job when I'd been desperate to find work in Dunleagh. Although I'd run my history channel for the last few years, I had no formal training in journalism. I owed the guy, and we both knew it.

"He doesn't listen to my feedback," I grumbled. "Last time I read the play, I spotted the same historical inaccuracies I'd flagged during the first two readings."

"He enjoys having a historian vet his script," Aido said. "It makes him feel like a professional playwright."

"Dee won't be a professional anything if she doesn't get moving on her article," Marcus shouted across the room.

"Hold on to what's left of your hair, Marcus. I'm on it." I winked at Aido. "Duty calls. Thanks for the heads-up about Cian."

My friend waved a liberally ringed hand. "No problem."

I put on my headphones and spent the next half hour pounding out a four-hundred-word plea for an end to animal fights and harsher punishments for their organizers. It was heavy on the hyperbole, but it got the point across. I read it over one last time, nodded in satisfaction, and emailed my article to Marcus.

Once I'd hit send, I removed my earphones and leaned back in my chair. "Done and sent, complete with a horrendous photo of Seamie Dean's toothless grin. If you hear Marcus scream, you'll know why."

"It won't be the first time he's screamed this morning." Aido's smile was wry. "The exploding printer made him blow a gasket."

I pushed back my seat and pulled on my still-wet rain pants and jacket. "Sorry to love you and leave you, boys, but taxi duty calls."

Marcus looked up from his desk, and his eyebrows formed a hairy V. "Off so soon?"

"It's my free day. I told Cian I'd cover this story and that was it. Besides," I added, grateful for the excuse, "I have to take my grandmother to the hospital."

"All right," Marcus muttered. "See you tomorrow."

With a goodbye chorus ringing in my ears, I waved to my coworkers and headed back down the North Tower's winding staircase.

* * *

When I reached the ground floor, I paused by the empty reception desk to secure my hood. Larry's booming voice blasted out of the Great Hall. He was lecturing a group of tourists on the history of the castle. The thought of tourists triggered a memory of Mr. Chuckles's leering sneer. I shuddered. Hopefully, the creep had endured a thorough soaking while plying his trade in this morning's rain.

I slung on my backpack and opened the heavy oak door. Outside, rain pounded off the ground, and a strong breeze swept through the courtyard. Rain cascaded over me and the strong wind ensured I received the maximum impact from the elements. The farther away I moved from the main entrance, the worse the condition of the cobblestones. Water surged over the broken stones, forming determined streams and forcing me to perform an ungainly dance to avoid them.

I mentally cursed the mayor. The sorry state of the courtyard was his fault. In his determination to gut the top two floors of the castle and turn them into luxury apartments, Mayor Hyland had refused to sanction any repairs on the castle until after the town council voted on his renovation plans. I leaped across another rivulet of rainwater. My best bet to avoid wet feet was to take a detour across the courtyard to the south side of the castle. I swung to the left and picked up my pace.

A high wall divided the courtyard from the armory and soldiers' quarters, now home to the museum. The armory and barracks were a late-medieval addition to the castle. At the time of their construction, the castle wall had been extended to surround the new buildings. The original border wall was left intact, adding an extra layer of defense within the castle grounds. To form an access way between the two parts of the castle, a gate had been constructed in the center of the wall. Known as the Green Archway, this stone gate was a moss-covered edifice on which flowers bloomed in summer. It was the first point of note on a tour of the castle gardens, and it always drew my eye. Today was no exception. Which was unfortunate, as my lack of attention to the ground landed me in a puddle. Muttering, I shook water off my ankle boots and stepped through the archway.

Without warning, the sky darkened, draining the museum's courtyard of light. I glanced up and sucked in a breath. Instead of the black clouds I'd expected to see, the sky had turned a curious shade of deep plum, shot through with flecks of gold. The color was mesmerizing. Not taking my eyes off the sky, I slid my phone out of my jacket pocket. I was no pro photographer, but I'd do my best to capture this rare slice of beauty on a wet summer's morning.

Speaking of wet...

I held out a hand and frowned. Not a drop of the previous rain shower was in evidence. I blinked and checked the puddles for confirmation. No fresh raindrops splashed against their surface, and the water within stood unnaturally still. Ireland was renowned for its stop-start rain showers and strong winds, but I'd never known the weather to go from a blustery downpour to still and dry within a matter of seconds.

Whatever the cause, the sky was a wondrous sight. I opened the phone's camera app and snapped several shots. Perhaps this week's issue of the *Chronicle* would have a spectacular front-page picture after all. Once I was satisfied I had enough photos, I switched to video mode. If I brought back an awesome clip to feature on our website, it'd make my editor's day.

Suddenly, a mammoth gust of wind broke the stillness. The strength of the gale sent me staggering, and I bashed my head on the side of the archway. Pain sliced through me. Dazed and seeing stars, I slumped against the wall. I lost my grip on the phone, and it fell to the ground with a clatter. The sky shifted and shimmered before metamorphosing into a crackling plum-colored cyclone—a cyclone that was heading straight for me.

An icy sweat trickled down my spine. Fighting the force of the wind, I tried to stand, but I was too late. Purple wisps coiled around my wrists and ankles, holding me prisoner. The sound of my roaring blood rang in my ears. I screamed, but the wind whipped my words away. I might as well be shouting into a vacuum.

Breathing heavily, and well into panic mode, I tugged at my restraints. Every time I tried to yank free, the purple coils grew tighter. What was this stuff? Air didn't turn into shackles. And wind didn't crackle. Whatever I was experiencing, it couldn't be real.

I drew in a deep breath. Yes, that was it. None of this was real. I was having a nightmare. That third slice of Nana's apple pie last night hadn't been my smartest move. If I stayed calm, I'd soon wake up and this would all be over. I closed my eyes, wincing at the pain in my head, and sifted through my mind for the one and only meditation session I'd ever done.

A man's shout punctured my bubble of forced calm.

My eyes flew open. Still clad in his mud-splattered clown costume, Mr. Chuckles staggered through the Green Archway. Underneath his clown makeup, he wore an expression of abject terror. It took him a second to register my presence.

"Run," he rasped. "They've got guns."

My stomach leaped into my rib cage, and I struggled to break free. "Who's got guns? The old folks?" The question was ridiculous, but so was this entire situation. A gun-toting senior might well fit in with this wild tale.

Mr. Chuckles didn't reply. With a last terrified look over his shoulder, he lurched into forward motion. His awkward gait drew my attention to a red stain on his left leg.

"You're bleeding." My voice rose in panic. Had he been serious about the guns? I'd heard nothing. Or had I? Had the crackling sound I'd attributed to the wind been gunfire? I tried to stand, but the purple restraints held me down.

Before the clown had taken more than a few steps, the air around him shimmered and vibrated. Fragmented noises broke the silence: male shouts, heavy breathing, and the unmistakable pop of gunshots. The blow to my head and my shallow breathing had left me sore and light-headed, but even in my confused state, escape was paramount in my mind. I thrashed against my confines, feeling the purple cords bite into my skin. Frustration and fear swelled in my chest as I tried and failed to free myself. Hot tears burned a path down my cheeks. It was no good. I was a sitting duck for whoever, or whatever, was coming through that archway.

Another blast of purple wind raced by me with a deafening roar. Angry voices rose and fell, followed by several rapid reports. Blinded by the force of the wind, I curled myself into a protective ball and prayed for this madness to end.

I didn't have long to wait. A few minutes after the initial blast of wind, everything fell silent. The pressure around my wrists and ankles eased. I opened one tentative eye and flexed my hands and feet. My restraints were gone. I opened the other eye and looked up. The fabulous purple sky had disappeared, replaced by a mundane gray. The brisk breeze of earlier was back, as was the relentless rain. A scent of burning lingered in the air. Gunpowder? My gaze moved to the ground, and my breathing stopped. Less than a meter away, the clown lay face down, unmoving. His bright red wig floated in a puddle to his right. Scarlet liquid pooled beneath his prone form and mingled with rainwater. A wave of nausea bent me double. Was he *dead*? And where were the gunmen? Would they emerge from the other side of the archway and shoot me? My eyes darted around the courtyard. It was empty, save for the clown and me, but the Green Archway lay in my blind spot. I had no idea what waited on the other side.

"Mr. Chuckles?" I barely recognized my own voice. "Charles?"

No response.

My stomach cramped with fear. *Please, don't be dead.* With shaking hands, I groped across the ground until my fingers closed around my phone. The screen had cracked but the device still worked. I hit the button for emergency services and put the phone on speaker. The dial tone rang while I crawled toward Mr. Chuckles, clutching the phone between my unsteady fingers. I'd have reached the man faster if I'd stood and run to his side, but if Dunleagh Castle was turning into shoot-out central, I figured I was safer staying near to the ground.

I closed the space between the clown and me and checked him for a pulse. Nothing. I rolled him onto his side and recoiled at the sight of a gunshot wound to his chest. I tasted bile. I didn't need medical training to know the man was dead. Panic spiraled through me, making it hard to think. In my state of shock, it took me a moment to register the woman's voice on the phone, asking me to state my emergency.

"A man's been shot in the courtyard of Dunleagh Castle. I need an ambulance and the pol—"

An agonized groan arrested my attention. I jerked around, losing my tenuous grip on the phone. A dark-haired man in a black uniform stood framed in the archway, clutching his upper chest. Blood seeped between his fingers, and his blue eyes clouded with pain. A revolver dangled from his other hand.

I froze for an instant, and then the adrenaline kicked in. My heart pounding, I leaped to my feet. Before I had time to leg it, the man's grip on the revolver slackened. The handgun hit the ground with a clatter. The injured man took faltering steps in my direction, mouthing silent words. His arresting blue eyes pinned me in place with an urgency I couldn't ignore.

"Eliza?" He drew out each syllable of the name as though speaking cost him all his energy. "What are you doing here?"

The shock and blood loss must be giving him hallucinations. "I'm not—"

Before I could finish my sentence, the man lost his balance and careened into me, sending us both hurtling toward the dead clown.

TWO

Mr. Chuckles's body cushioned the impact of my fall. The respite was temporary. A millisecond later, the stranger landed on top of me. His weight pressed onto my chest and squeezed the air out of my lungs. A vision of my mother's tarot card prediction of a handsome man in uniform flashed before me. In spite of my predicament, a laugh gurgled up my throat and rapidly turned into a wheeze. Even my eccentric mother wouldn't foresee a bloodstained, gun-wielding stranger as her future son-in-law.

I struggled to get free. The lack of air made my head ache even more. I gasped for breath and defaulted to my go-to defense mechanism: humor. "This is a little up-close and personal for my taste. Do you mind moving?"

No answer. The guy was unconscious or worse, and no help in rectifying our situation. Was I sandwiched between two dead men? A shudder coursed through my body, wiping any further quips I might've made from my mental hard drive. I sagged against the clown, rallied my strength, and pushed the stranger's rock-hard chest. It took several attempts to roll the man off me, and a few more to scramble to my feet. Bombarded by the double whammy of pain and shock, I swayed before regaining my sense of balance. My hood was askew and water dripped down my collar, but the rain was the least of my worries. I sucked in air like it was going out of fashion and contemplated my situation.

Apart from the two men and me, the courtyard was deserted. There was no sign of the elusive gunmen. Not that I was complaining. My day had gone south long before the shoot-out, and I didn't fancy adding a bullet wound to my list of woes.

As none of my esteemed colleagues had seen fit to put in an appearance, I could only assume they were cowering behind their desks at the *Chronicle*. Well, the time for saving their own necks was over. I filled my aching lungs and screamed. With the weird wind gone, I had no trouble projecting, and I gave it my all.

Caterwauling like a banshee, I bent to retrieve my phone from a puddle. Neither the movement nor the screaming was good for my head. My ribs ached, probably from the man falling on top of me. The pain sent a wave of nausea cascading over me. I swallowed hard, took another deep breath, and reached into the puddle. My hand closed around a hard cylinder lying beside my phone. I removed it from the water, held out my palm, and examined my find. It was a cartridge, presumably from the shoot-out. Didn't cartridges fall directly from the gun when it was fired? If so, what was one doing here? I hadn't seen any shooting this side of the archway. A shiver snaked down my spine. I darted a glance around the courtyard, but we were still alone.

My mind switched back to the injured man. I shoved the cartridge into my pocket and rescued my phone. The second fall had added a fresh crack to its screen and ended my call to emergency services. I hit restart. If my yowling didn't summon help soon, I'd abandon the guys and run back to reception. For now, I'd have to play paramedic.

Out of breath and out of screams, I assessed the men. The clown was morgue bait. A laugh turned into a sob at this image. Okay, maybe I hadn't entirely wiped the humor drive clean. I wasn't sure if this was a good sign for my physical and mental health.

The guy in uniform lay on his side, next to his revolver. His cap had flown off during our tumble and landed in a puddle. I kicked the revolver out of my way and kneeled beside him. First, I checked his pulse. Present, if slow. Breathing, ditto. No need for CPR. Which was just as well, as the last time I'd performed CPR was ten years ago on a demonstration dummy.

I unbuttoned the man's jacket with fumbling fingers. Up close, it was dark green, not black, and had insignia pinned on either side of the high collar. The fabric was mostly dry to the touch, indicating he hadn't been outdoors for long. Weird. The courtyard offered nothing in the way of shelter, and the closest building to the Green Archway was the museum. If the man had come from there, he should have endured a thorough soaking in this downpour.

With uncertain fingers, I pulled open the jacket. The shirt underneath was drenched with blood. Sweat beaded on my upper lip. I was way out of my comfort zone, and even farther out of my area of expertise. Surely someone at the *Chronicle* had recent first aid experience? But until my coworkers got their cowardly rear ends out of the castle, the guy was stuck with me.

I ripped open the man's shirt, not bothering with the buttons, and carefully eased up his blood-soaked vest. In other circumstances, I'd have paused to admire his impressive six-pack, but right now, my eyes were riveted on his wound. The injury was to his upper chest on the right side. Even my rudimentary knowledge of human biology told me that the shot had missed his heart. Whatever else it might have hit remained a question mark. One thing was certain: he was losing blood fast.

In the recesses of my mind, a memory stirred. I'd read a book in which a woman had used a sanitary pad as a makeshift bandage. I unzipped my backpack and found a pad. I tore open the packaging and placed the pad over the man's wound, applying as much pressure as I dared.

Not having a clue what else to do, I opted for a rinse-repeat of my screaming efforts. This time, I yelled, "Fire!" over and over at the top of my hoarse voice. I'd recently researched an article on personal safety, and this had been recommended as the most effective method to get people's attention.

Within seconds, a scramble of feet echoed over the cobblestones. Richard Daley, the museum's director and a regular contributor to my history channel, raced down the path that led from the museum. His thick mop of curly gray hair formed a halo of corkscrew curls. Like the man in uniform, Richard had a penchant for eccentric clothing. Today's outfit consisted of an elaborate ruffled shirt and a pair of skintight leather pants. If the local amateur dramatics club ever turned to musicals, Richard would be a shoo-in for the lead in *The Pirates of Penzance*.

As Richard surveyed the situation, his face paled. "What on—?"

I cut him short. "Check on the clown. I'm pretty sure he's dead, but we should make sure."

Richard slow-blinked, shook himself, and lurched toward Mr. Chuckles. When he saw the gunshot wound, he recoiled. "These men were *shot*?"

"Dude, seriously?" I stared at him in exasperation. "Didn't you hear the shooting? We had a full-on O.K. Corral situation out here."

Richard gaped at me, wide-eyed and slack-jawed. "The first I heard was you yelling your head off just now."

I recalled the strange sky and the wind that had sucked my screams into oblivion. Had no one but me heard the shots? That was impossible. But then, so was the idea of a snake-like wind that turned into cords around wrists and ankles. Given the general craziness of the last half hour, I didn't dwell on these incongruities. After all, I'd taken a blow to the head. Maybe I was concussed.

In the distance, ambulance sirens blared. Relief flooded through me. I was doing my best for the man, but dealing with copious blood loss was way out of my comfort zone. Suddenly, the man's blue eyes flew open. He stared at me as though transfixed. Then he grabbed my wrist.

"Ouch," I squeaked. "Let go. I have to keep the pressure on your wound."

"Forget my wound. You have to get out of here." His voice was deep and gravelly and held a hint of a northern accent.

"Don't talk," I admonished, sounding like a middle-aged hospital matron. "The ambulance is on its way."

His intense gaze remained fixed on me. "Eliza, you have to run. They'll kill you if they find you."

"Who'll kill me?" Truth be told, I was more interested in who this Eliza chick was, but I reluctantly conceded that the identity of the shooters was the more pertinent question.

The man's eyes clouded in confusion. "You know who."

"If you say their names, I promise I'll leave." I might not be a pro reporter, but I knew a story when I smelled one. If this guy could name the gunmen, I'd score my first front-page feature.

A look of exhausted resignation settled over his handsome features. "Ma. Hell. Gut."

"I can't understand you. Can you repeat it?"

"Ma—"

Before he could finish, pandemonium broke out around us. The ambulance roared into the outer courtyard, lights flashing. The archway was too narrow for it to drive through, and the driver brought it to a screeching halt just outside. The ambulance's arrival coordinated with a flurry of activity. The guard on the gate, presumably alarmed by the sight of the ambulance, barreled through the archway, leaping back when he saw the men on the ground. At the same moment, the side door next to the museum burst open, disgorging a motley crew, including the staff of the *Chronicle*.

Having youth on his side, Aido reached us first. The sight of his familiar face brought a sob to my throat. He skidded to a stop a few centimeters shy of the revolver. "Dee, are you okay? Wait...is that a *gun*?"

"Yes to both questions."

Aido stared at me in open incredulity. Before he could pepper me with more questions, three paramedics ran through the archway. As if by silent agreement, two ran over to Richard and the clown, and the other made a beeline for us.

The injured man's grip on my wrist tightened, his voice low and urgent. "Take my revolver and hide before they come back."

"You haven't finished telling me who *they* are," I reminded him gently, but my hope of scoring a front-page story was dwindling. The guy was talking like we were characters in a play. Maybe he'd hit his head when we'd fallen. Or the blood loss had addled his mind.

One of the paramedics dropped to her knees beside the man, effectively nixing my front-page feature. "What happened?"

"Gunshot," I said. "I'm applying pressure, but I don't know what else to do to stop the bleeding."

The woman gave me an assessing once-over and indicated the blood on my jacket. "Are you hurt?"

"The blood's his. I hit my head, but I think I'm okay." Now that the shock was subsiding, so was the pain.

"One of us will have a look at you once we've treated the men." The paramedic removed various implements from her bag. I hovered next to her, not sure what to do next. She glanced up at me, her expression firmly in the detached professional zone.

"I'll take it from here. Go and sit down, and one of us will be with you shortly."

I opened my mouth to object, but Aido put a hand on my shoulder. "Let's leave it to the pros."

I looked down at my erstwhile patient. His grip on my wrist slackened.

"Go," he whispered, a faint smile on his bloodless lips. "I'll be grand."

"Grand" seemed an unlikely description for his immediate future, but I didn't argue the point. "I'll visit you in the hospital."

The man's eyes closed and he didn't answer. I wasn't sure he could.

"I'll take Dee to the castle's café," Aido said to the paramedic. "She'll wait for you there."

The woman nodded, keeping her focus on the injured man.

To me, he added, "A cup of hot, sugary tea is what you need. And you can use their dishcloths to dry your hair."

I murmured my assent, but my gaze was still fixed on the stranger. Would he make it? Had my fumbling attempts to help made any difference to his outcome?

"Come on." Aido picked up my helmet and my backpack. "If the castle isn't on fire, then there's no harm in us going back inside. Want to join us, Richard?"

The museum director stood beside the clown, watching a paramedic pull a plastic sheet over the body. At Aido's question, he turned to stare at us with vacant eyes. "I'm going home. I need a shower." In his haste to reach me, Richard had forgotten to put on a coat, and his soaked ruffled shirt now clung to his lean body.

"Go," I said. "Get warm. And have a shot of whiskey."

The man nodded, still visibly in a state of shock. With a last look at the body, he turned and retraced his steps back to the museum.

"At least he lives on site," Aido said, steering me through the archway and into the front courtyard. "Not far for him to go for that shower."

"When it works. I don't like the mayor's plans to gut the castle, but the place needs renovating. Richard's apartment is a dump. A tidy dump, but a dump nonetheless."

"True that."

I regarded the members of the *Dunleagh Chronicle*'s meager staff, now huddled under an awning by the castle's main entrance, trapped by a sea of senior citizens. I hadn't noticed them file past the crime scene, but then my focus had returned to the injured man as soon as the paramedics had arrived. "Why did you guys take so long to react? There was a full-on gunfight in the courtyard, and I was screaming my head off. Are you all hard of hearing?"

I addressed Aido with less belligerence than when I'd confronted Richard with the same questions. I knew what he was going to say, but I needed to hear it. Was I the only one who'd heard the gunfire?

My friend's baffled expression provided the answer. "First I heard was you screaming about a fire. We legged it right away."

"I'd yelled for help before that, but no one responded. I figured the prospect of saving your own skins might get you moving."

Aido's forehead creased, drawing his pierced eyebrows closer together. "I'm sorry, Dee. I don't understand why we didn't hear the shots. It's not like the castle has decent windows, and the ones in the North Tower fall under the definition of sucktastic. They barely keep out the cold, never mind noise."

That thought had occurred to me too. I had to wear noise-canceling headphones to get work done in the *Chronicle*'s main office. Ideas whizzed through my mind in a confused jumble of facts, what-ifs, and wild speculation. The situation was surreal, but maybe my confusion was due to my sore head.

More people spilled out of the castle, forming a mass of impatient energy in the courtyard. Larry and the guard from the gate were making ineffectual attempts to keep the nursing home tour group back from the ambulance and the archway. The fact that the ambulance partially blocked their view appeared to have made the seniors all the more eager to get an unimpeded gawk at the crime scene.

An elderly lady tried to break through Larry's

provisional barricade of fold-down plastic chairs. Following her lead, a sea of orange-coated geriatrics surged forward, straining to get a better look at the injured men, batting off their competitors with their canes. As soon as they spotted me, I was treated to a barrage of questions.

I ignored them, preoccupied with scanning the throng for the face I'd expected to see holding court. "Where's the mayor?"

Larry rolled his eyes. "Hyland legged it at the first sign of trouble. But don't worry, he'll be back as soon as the inevitable TV crew arrives."

"With his spray tan refreshed," I said acidly.

"And wearing his best suit," Aido added.

An old lady knocked over one of the chairs, forcing Larry to grab hold of her. "You'd better go to the museum," he gasped, struggling to maintain his grasp on the wriggling woman. "We're still evacuating the castle."

"Okay," Aido replied. "Maybe Richard will give Dee a shot of whiskey to settle her nerves."

The very thought of whiskey turned my stomach. "I'll stick with tea, thanks."

Before we'd had a chance to retrace our steps, a succession of horns blared, followed by a chorus of outraged screams and expletives from the crowd. Two mobility scooters roared into the melee, forcing the old folks to hurl themselves to safety. As they threw themselves to the sides, a proliferation of canes, walking frames, and handbags clattered onto the cobblestones. The security guard scrambled onto a bench by the castle entrance and avoided the crush, but Larry was knocked over in the stampede.

The man fell as if in slow motion, his pudgy hands grasping at the air. The guard's safe position proved to be temporary. A moment later, he was whacked in the face by a flying handbag, and then obliterated from view when four elderly ladies threw themselves onto the bench to avoid being mown down by the scooters.

Seemingly oblivious to the mayhem they'd caused, the mobility scooters bulldozed their way through Larry's makeshift barricade, creating a domino effect on the chairs. Having ensured maximum destruction, they screeched to a halt in front of Aido and me. The drivers of the offending vehicles wore the same bright orange raincoats as their peers. One had her hood pulled close, obscuring much of her face. The other wore a pair of swimming goggles over her hood, giving her the appearance of a crazed beetle.

The beetle pushed up her goggles, revealing a pair of deep-set green eyes. A riot of purple curls framed her wrinkled visage, and her hot-pink lipstick clashed violently with the orange raincoat. She addressed me in a voice louder than a sonic boom. "Hey, Dee. I hear Mr. Chuckles got clipped."

My shoulders drooped in resignation. "Hello, Nana."

THREE

My grandmother beamed at Aido and me. "Isn't it fantastic? We haven't had this much excitement in Dunleagh since Barney Black got busted for selling stolen laxatives."

"I can think of several descriptors for today's events," I said dryly. "'Fantastic' isn't one of them."

Aido looked from her to me. "Stolen laxatives? What the—?"

I shook my head. "Trust me, you don't want to know. Why are you here, Nana? I was on my way to collect you."

Ignoring me, Nana squinted and peered around the courtyard. "Where's the corpse? We need to get a look at him before the fuzz arrive."

The driver of the second mobility scooter pushed back her hood. Dottie Carty, Nana's neighbor and partner in crime, regarded me with an expression of abject horror. "Is that *blood* on your jacket?"

"Never mind the body. Forget about the blood." I pointed at the carnage they'd left in their wake. "What's with the dramatic entrance? You two could've killed someone. Poor Larry got squashed in the stampede."

Nana made a dismissive gesture. "Larry will be fine. He's well padded."

In the background, Larry struggled to his feet, swayed, and righted himself with the aid of an abandoned walker.

Aido lost the struggle against laughter. "I'd better go help. I don't think Larry's in a fit state to deal with the golden oldies. Can you handle these two delinquents on your own?"

I snorted. "I doubt anyone can handle Nana and Dottie."

"Take them to the museum," Aido advised, handing me my backpack. "The Guards will arrive any second, and those mobility scooters were moving mighty fast to be legit."

He had a point. I scrutinized the scooters. At first glance, they looked fine, but knowing Nana, anything was possible. "Aren't they supposed to travel at a maximum of ten kilometers an hour?"

"How am I supposed to get anywhere at that speed?" Nana demanded. "I'm old, not dead. I've got places to be."

"My Gary fixed them for us," Dottie supplied in a conspiratorial tone. "We'd never have made it up to the castle before the Guards if he hadn't."

I suppressed a groan. Gary Carty, Dottie's grandson, had his beefy paws involved in most of the petty crimes that occurred in Dunleagh. Given Gary's loose interpretation of the law, I doubted his method of "fixing" the mobility scooters was legal.

I shifted my gaze from the scooters to my grandmother. "You told me you'd spend a quiet morning knitting at Dottie's house before going to your cardiologist appointment. Even if Dottie's grandson doctored your scooters to go faster, you can't have gotten here from her place in the time since I raised the alarm."

"Change of venue." Nana dropped her voice to a stage whisper. "Gary needed to burgle the joint."

"My last electricity bill was outrageous," Dottie supplied before I'd had a chance to realign my jaw. "My grandson was kind enough to stage a break-in and nick my TV. The insurance payout will be enough to cover the bill."

"Looks like Gary wasn't the only one to steal something this morning." I eyed the orange raincoats. "Last I heard, you two weren't residents of Glencool Nursing Home."

"Oh, we didn't steal these," Dottie protested. "A bus driver gave them to us."

Nana jerked a thumb at the nursing home

residents, the fittest of whom were wading through the proliferation of canes and other walking aids to assist their fallen comrades. "Sure, half that lot can't remember their own names. We knocked on the door of one of the buses outside and told the driver we'd lost our raincoats. He believed us."

"Hmm." I eyed them with suspicion. "What happened to your raincoats?"

"We left ours at *Elaine's*," Dottie said. "It's only a short run up the hill from there. We weren't expecting a traffic jam in the courtyard."

"So *that's* where you were," I said, shaking my head. "Knitting indeed. Instead of taking it easy and looking after your bad heart, you went tearing off to the smoky hellhole that is Elaine's back room."

Elaine's was a café beloved by Dunleagh's senior citizens. It served bad coffee, strong tea, and an all-day full Irish breakfast fondly known as the Coronary Classic. The place had a permanent smell of grease, booze, and cigarettes, even though it had no official liquor license, and in spite of Ireland's strict no-smoking laws. The café proper was divided from Elaine's private residence by a thick beaded curtain. As Nana was wont to say, what happened behind the beaded curtain stayed behind the beaded curtain.

"We did knit, didn't we, Dottie?"

Nana's companion nodded vigorously. "We can play poker and speed knit at the same time. Eda won a tenner off Big Jim."

Nana grinned. "So you see, we were just down the road from the castle when the mayor burst into the café, ranting about being under attack and needing to preserve the government of Dunleagh."

I rolled my eyes. "Typical. Why did Hyland pick *Elaine's* as his refuge?"

"He'd heard she has a secret room from back in the days of the War of Independence. He demanded access." A sly grin suffused Nana's face. "Elaine was only too happy to oblige. With any luck, she'll leave him locked in there until the end of his term in office."

"We can hope." I frowned. "Did Hyland say he'd been shot at? I didn't see any sign of him during the shooting." Not that I'd seen much through the purple haze, including the gunmen. For all I knew, Henry Hyland was the intended victim, and the clown and the other guy had been collateral damage.

Nana considered my question before answering. "Not exactly. He babbled about 'them' being after him. Allegedly, he's received several threatening anonymous letters. I didn't lend his words much credence, to be honest. Melodrama is the man's middle name. I only got interested when he mentioned you."

My lip curled, and anger bubbled in my veins. "He must have seen me in the courtyard when he was fleeing for his life. And the two injured men I was struggling to help." A siren wailed in the distance, becoming louder every second. "Let's head to the museum," I said, eyeing the scooters with distaste. "We can't afford to bail you out of jail. Then I'll figure out a way to get you to your appointment."

Pretending she didn't hear me, Nana wiped rainwater off her goggles and adjusted them to her satisfaction. "Much better. I left my glasses at Big Jim's house last night, but at least these have prescription lenses. Now, where's that corpse?"

Before I could stop her, she'd restarted her mobility scooter and zoomed over to the Green Archway, stopping in front of the ambulance. The paramedics were in the process of bundling the stranger into the ambulance. His eyes were closed and he wore an oxygen mask over his pale face. A sensation of dread crept over my body. Would he make it? My efforts to help him had been fumbling at best.

Nana leaned forward to get a good look at the man on the stretcher. "I didn't know a second fellow had been shot. He's a handsome lad, isn't he?" She addressed the female paramedic. "Will he live?"

The paramedic ignored her and turned to me. "We have no room to take you in this ambulance, but I'll stay behind and check you out."

"There's no need," I insisted. "My head is already feeling a bit better. My grandmother has an appointment at Dunleagh General this morning. I'll accompany her and get checked out then."

The woman looked dubious. Her gaze moved from me to the waiting ambulance, indecision written across her face. Her fellow paramedics had loaded their patient into the vehicle and slammed the doors. She eyed me hard. "Are you sure?"

"I'm positive. I'll be fine." In truth, my head felt a lot better than it had a few minutes ago, and the nausea was gone.

The paramedic shrugged. "Okay, then. Just make sure you get a doctor to look you over, and sooner rather than later."

"I promise."

With a curt nod, she hopped into the ambulance's passenger seat. A moment later, the vehicle roared to life and forced us and the old folks to clear a path for its exit.

Nana's gaze sharpened. "What's all this about your head?"

"It's nothing, Nana. I banged it earlier and I still have a bit of a headache. Like I told the paramedic, I can get it checked out when you go to the hospital."

"Too late," Nana replied with blithe unconcern. "My appointment was fifteen minutes ago."

My gaze flew to my watch face. She was right. "If you insist on riding these scooters, you should've gone to the hospital instead of haring up to the castle." I sighed. "I'll call and see if they can squeeze you in this afternoon."

"Are you sure your head isn't too bad?" she demanded.

"Yeah, it's fine. I'll get it checked by a doctor, but

I'm pretty sure they'll give me pain relief and send me home."

A broad grin stretched across my grandmother's face. "In that case…"

Before I could stop her, she'd restarted her mobility scooter and zoomed through the Green Archway, Dottie in rapid pursuit. Unlike the ambulance, the mobility scooters had no issues driving through. My grandmother and her friend made straight for the clown. Nana grabbed her walking stick from its holder at the back of her scooter and used it to nudge back the plastic sheet.

"Nana, no," I squeaked, running through the archway to join them. "This is a crime scene. You can't touch anything."

Nana pushed the sheet further back, giving her an unimpeded view of the body. "I like his poncho," she said to Dottie. "Do you think I'd look good in leopard print?"

At that moment, a squad car crunched over the cobblestones and screeched to a halt in front of the archway. My friend, Sergeant Louise Healey, sat in the driver's seat. Beside her, Garda Eoin Duffy shoveled the end of a sandwich into his mouth. When she spotted Nana and Dottie violating the crime scene, Lou mimed banging her head against the steering wheel. Eoin started to laugh.

Lou leaped out of the car and advanced on the scooters with a menacing gait. "There's not enough coffee in the world to deal with you this morning, Eda. Back away from the corpse."

My friend's authoritative police sergeant voice was at odds with her appearance. At barely five-feet-two-inches, Lou was a diminutive figure with elfin features and tousled short black hair. Her partner, Eoin, was a huge, lumbering man and was usually mistaken for the one in charge. This impression changed the instant Lou opened her mouth.

Dottie scooted back a meter.

Nana reined in her cane. "I was only taking a peek," she said defiantly. "After all, it might've been my Dee lying there. She was involved in the shoot-out, you know."

"I wasn't," I assured Lou before she could ask. "Not really. I heard the shots and gave first aid to one of the victims."

After a momentary look of alarm, relief passed over Lou's face, only to be replaced by confusion. "*One* of the victims? The caller to emergency services mentioned a single gunshot casualty."

"At the point I hit the number for emergency services, I was aware of only one victim. The second man staggered onto the scene as I was making the call. He was the patient in the ambulance that just left. The other guy's Mr. Chuckles." I pointed to the still form under the sheet and swallowed past the lump in my throat. "He's dead."

Lou regarded the dead man for a long moment

before turning back to me. "If you're a witness, you'll have to stick around. We'll need to take your statement and go through the usual routine."

She didn't need to elaborate. I'd read enough crime fiction to know the score. They'd need to test me for gunshot residue, take my fingerprints, and keep my blood-spattered clothes as potential evidence.

"She can't," Nana interjected. "She wasn't shot, but she banged her head. We were about to call the hospital when you two rolled up."

"To get *you* a cardiology appointment," I pointed out. "I'll tag along. Is it okay if we go to the museum, Lou? I'll change the appointment and then order a taxi to take Nana and me to the hospital and drop Dottie home."

"Yeah, okay. The statement can wait, but I'm going to have to test you for gunshot residue right now." Lou grimaced. "Sorry, but we have to do everything by the book."

"I understand."

While Eoin set up markers around the crime scene, Lou got a portable forensics kit from the back of the squad car. After she'd disinfected her hands and put on gloves to avoid cross-contamination, she went through the process of testing me for gunshot residue using a series of adhesive-coated discs on each hand. The chance to witness a cop at work provided a momentary distraction for my CSI-obsessed grandmother.

"Do you have a spare kit of those disc thingies?"

Nana asked, edging toward the police car's open boot. "I could test Big Jim at bingo tonight. He'd love that."

Lou shot her a warning glance. "Stay away from my car, Eda. This is an official GSR testing kit. They don't come cheap." After she'd placed the used discs in a container and sealed it, the police sergeant put the container into a box in the back of the car and closed the boot. As she came back through the Green Archway, Lou regarded the ground with a frown. "I was told there were two victims, both male. You said you gave one of them first aid?"

I nodded. "The guy who was just taken off in the ambulance."

"So he's still alive," Lou murmured. "Was he conscious when you treated him?"

"Yeah, but fairly out of it."

"I wonder if that man is single," Nana mused. "He'd do nicely for you, Dee."

"He would," Dottie piped up. "Even shot, he was hot."

"Seriously?" I exclaimed in exasperation. "Now isn't the moment for matchmaking."

Lou's lips twitched briefly, but her expression soon returned to its former gravity. "Did the man say anything to you, Dee? His name? The name of the person who shot him?"

"He didn't say anything that made sense. He mistook me for someone called Eliza. When I asked who'd shot him, his response was garbled. It sounded like 'Ma-hell-gut,' which makes no sense."

Lou considered this new information for a moment. "Before we take your statement, I'd like you to think over what happened. If anything occurs to you, no matter how insignificant, I want to know."

My cheeks grew warm. How could I tell her a crazy story about being held captive by purple wind? She'd decide I had a concussion and had imagined it all. Maybe she'd be right. Even the photos I'd snapped with my phone wouldn't show more than the pretty sky. "Sure. I'll make a note of anything that I remember."

"Before you go..." Lou jogged back toward the car and returned a moment later carrying a folded plastic bag. "Any chance you have a change of clothes at the castle? I'll need to take your jacket and pants. Process of elimination and all that."

"I'm fully dressed under my rain gear," I said, taking the proffered bag. "I assume you don't need all of my clothes?"

"No. Just the outer layer."

"In that case, I have everything I need except a jacket, and I might have a spare in the gym bag I keep at the *Chronicle*."

"You can have my new raincoat," Nana said. "The orange will clash nicely with your red lipstick."

I exchanged an amused look with Lou. "Most people don't think clashing colors are a positive, Nana."

"Nonsense. A splash of bright color will do you good."

"I can ask Richard to lend me a coat. He lives on site." I held up the folded evidence bag. "I'll drop this back to you before we head to the hospital."

Nana's cane inched closer to the remains of Mr. Chuckles.

"Don't even think about it, Eda." Lou fixed Nana with a hard stare. "I'm going to have the higher-ups breathing down my neck over this case. The last thing I need is you and Dottie causing havoc."

Eoin placed the final marker on the ground. He stood, stretched, and surveyed the wreckage of the chairs and the now-limping Larry. "Looks like they've already caused havoc." He turned to Nana and Dottie. "That was you, right?"

Dottie had the good grace to appear sheepish. My grandmother had no such compunction. "When I heard Dee was involved in a shoot-out, I had to get here to make sure she wasn't hurt."

I laughed. "You knew I wasn't hurt, Nana. If you'd thought I'd been injured, you'd have asked me how I was the moment you arrived instead of hunting Mr. Chuckles."

"Now that you've assured yourself she's fit and well, you can leave us to do our jobs." Lou placed her hands on her hips. "Get them out of here, Dee, or I'll arrest them for obstruction."

"Come on," I said, placing a steadying hand on

Nana's rebellious cane. "Let's go to the museum. I'll make us all tea while we're waiting for our taxi."

Muttering under her breath, Nana allowed me to confiscate her cane. With a martyred sigh, she started her scooter and she and Dottie drove at a sedate pace down the path that led to the museum. I cast a last look at the clown. The form under the sheet was unnaturally still. I shivered and had to resist the urge to wrap my arms around myself. I hadn't liked the dude, but I didn't wish him dead.

Still carrying my gear and Nana's cane, I stepped away from the crime scene, leaving Lou and Eoin to do their thing. Now that my dizziness had passed, I was able to regard my surroundings with a critical eye rather than the dazed haze of earlier. Apart from the dead man, there was no evidence of a shoot-out. Well, no evidence of the shoot-out that had occurred this morning. During its long history, Dunleagh Castle had seen plenty of violence, and the walls and buildings bore the scars. I inspected the stonework for fresh damage. The archway, in particular, showed evidence of several skirmishes that had been fought in the castle grounds, the most recent of which had occurred in the early 1920s, during Ireland's struggle for independence. I ran my fingertips over the familiar nicks, including the bullet that was still lodged between two of the archway's stones. No changes from the last time I'd guided museum visitors through the archway. At least, none that I could see. Maybe the police would have more luck.

A cobblestoned path wound its way from the archway to the museum buildings, bordered on either side by a neat stretch of lawn. The grass showed no signs of trampling. During the wild windstorm, I hadn't been able to see much, but I'd had the impression that the shooters hadn't strayed through the archway and into this inner courtyard. My cursory and unprofessional assessment of my surroundings cemented this belief.

I cast my mind back to when Aido and I had walked through the outer courtyard, right before Nana and Dottie had rolled in and caused mayhem. Had I noticed any signs of the shoot-out? Admittedly, I'd still been dazed, but I couldn't recall seeing stray bullets or spent cartridges on the ground. If the gunmen had concentrated their efforts in the outer courtyard, it was logical to assume they'd used the main exit to escape. If so, why hadn't the security guard on the gate reacted? And why hadn't he noticed them entering the castle? As far as I was aware, the only entry and exit point to the castle was through the main gate and over the drawbridge. There'd once been a system of escape tunnels running under the castle, but they'd been filled in years ago.

Frowning, I made my way slowly toward the museum, sweeping Nana's cane over the stone pathway as I walked. I doubted I'd find anything of interest this side of the archway, but it was worth a try. By the time I was a few meters from the museum's door, I hadn't discovered anything more sinister than a discarded cigarette butt. Not a single shell or cartridge was in evidence.

The back of my neck prickled.

Save for the one in my pocket…

FOUR

My hand moved instinctively to the bulge in the left pocket of my rain pants. I'd forgotten all about my find. I cast a look over my shoulder. Lou was on the phone, her expression grave. Eoin was taking photographs of the scene. When I gave the police my clothes, I'd hand over the cartridge. For now, my priority was making sure Nana and Dottie were safely installed in the museum and out of trouble.

Footsteps echoed over the cobblestones. Aido jogged down the path and fell into step with me, out of breath and dripping with rain. "How did you persuade Eda and Dottie to leave the body alone?"

I cocked an eyebrow at him and grinned. "I didn't. Lou threatened to arrest them for screwing up her crime scene. That got them moving."

Aido chuckled. "Good on Lou. She terrifies me."

"When she's in uniform, she terrifies everyone."

She had no choice. The Guards weren't exactly known for gender equality among the ranks.

"We didn't cause any damage," Nana piped up from outside the entrance. "All we wanted was a peek at the dead guy. What's the harm in that? Sure, wouldn't we be seeing him at his wake anyway?"

A vision of the clown's chest wound loomed large in my memory, sending icy prickles down my spine. "I don't want to see him again, Nana." To Aido, I whispered, "We'd better help them climb the steps before they decide to drive their scooters inside. I wouldn't put anything past my grandmother."

Aido grinned. "She's a riot."

I cast him a martyred look. "You don't have to live with her. Between Nana and my mother, it's like herding goats."

After we assisted the ladies off their scooters and up the short flight of steps that led to the museum's staff entrance, Aido opened the door and ushered us inside. We walked through the narrow corridor and into the museum's entry area. Stepping into the familiar space, I'd never felt so grateful to inhale the crisp, musty air.

There was little left of the original interior. In the early part of the twentieth century, this part of the castle had housed the police force of the day, the Royal Irish Constabulary. Two exhibition rooms harked back to this period, but the rest had undergone a thorough renovation during the Seventies. The museum was closed to the public this morning to allow Richard to prepare for a special exhibition he was co-hosting with the library. In contrast to the usual Thursday morning bustle, the reception desk and exhibition rooms were deserted.

I motioned Nana and Dottie into Exhibition Room One and over to the two battered leather chairs that represented the museum's only public seating. I eyed them sternly. "Sit tight while I go to the *Chronicle* to check my gym bag for a spare coat. Once I'm back, I'll fix tea and call the hospital to rearrange Nana's appointment."

"I can reschedule the appointment myself," Nana said, bristling with indignation. "Why does everyone think old people are incapable?"

"You're well able to reschedule it, but you won't," I pointed out. "You believe there's nothing wrong with your heart."

"How would you like being lectured to by a man barely out of nappies? If I stopped having fun, I might as well cock up my toes here and now."

Dottie's vigorous nod indicated her hearty endorsement of Nana's views on medical advice. "My doctor is the same. They're all about getting us to live longer with no regard to our quality of life."

It was an argument we'd had many times, and I didn't have the energy for it today.

"Why don't I deal with the gym bag and call the hospital?" Aido suggested.

It would certainly save time and leave me free to keep an eye on Nana. "Are you sure?"

"Yeah, no problem. I left my phone at the office and I wanted to get it in any case." He grinned. "I'll schmooze the hospital's receptionist."

I suppressed a smile. Unlike me, Aido had the gift of the gab. With minimal effort, he could schmooze even the grumpiest person into doing his bidding. "Thank you. That'd be great. Barry's Gold Blend all round?"

"Yes, please," Nana replied. "And don't stint on the sugar."

Leaving the ladies to their gossip, and Aido to deal with the gym bag and the appointment, I headed for the tiny staff kitchen and pulled off my rain gear. I stuffed them into the plastic evidence bag Lou had given me. Once I'd dealt with my clothes, I grabbed a small sandwich pouch from one of the kitchen cupboards and dropped in the cartridge. Presumably, the Guards would want it kept separate from my personal effects. In case I lost it, I slipped the sandwich pouch into the pocket of my trousers.

My civic duty done, I grabbed my personal stash of tea bags and biscuits from a shelf and filled the kettle. While I waited for the water to boil, I glanced at this week's staff roster and skimmed the names. Mine was among them, scheduled for my usual Monday and Saturday morning slots. I volunteered at the museum twice a week, mostly behind the scenes. My current task was the photographing and cataloging of material that was gathering dust in storage. The museum boasted an extensive collection for such a small museum, but it had lost two of its exhibition rooms last year. When the current mayor took office, he'd repurposed the space into conference rooms. The inevitable result was that part of the museum's collection was boxed for storage and eventual sale.

With a violent burst of steam, the kettle's automatic switch clicked into the off position. I poured hot water into four teacups and placed them on a tray, along with an assortment of mismatched saucers, a jug of milk, a sugar bowl, and the biscuits. Picking up the tray, I maneuvered my way out of the kitchen and back toward the first exhibition room.

My entrance with the tea coincided with Aido's return. A corridor on the top floor connected the museum building with the main castle and provided an alternative route to reach the North Tower. All the same, Aido must've run most of the way to have gotten back so quickly. He slipped his phone back into his pocket, his smile verging on smug. "Mandy was on reception at the cardiology department. Dr. Sanyal will see your grandmother in an hour."

I bit back a laugh. Mandy was one of Aido's many past conquests and still harbored a major crush on him. "Thanks to your phenomenal ability to sweet-talk the ladies."

"Much as I'd like to take the credit, this favor was

in spite of me being the caller." He lowered his voice. "Mandy and I hooked up again a couple of weeks ago, and I've been dodging her calls."

"A true gentleman," I said dryly. "So how did you persuade her to squeeze in Nana on short notice?"

"Apparently, your grandmother gave her a herbal salve that's worked miracles on her eczema."

I raised an eyebrow. "'Gave' is generous. I'd imagine Nana charged Mandy a tidy sum, citing her healing gifts and vast knowledge of herbal medicine."

"People swear by her remedies, though. She must know what she's doing, with or without the woo-woo component."

I gave a noncommittal shrug. The women in my family were reputed to have special gifts. Earlier generations had even claimed to be witches. Personally, I thought it was all bunkum. If Nana's teas and lotions worked, it was solely due to their ingredients. If my mother's so-called spiritual handicrafts and fortune-telling produced results, it was a combination of placebo effect and coincidence. Even my down-to-earth sister claimed she could tell exactly what was troubling her students merely by putting her hand on theirs. I was more inclined to believe that River's innate empathy and sharp intuition helped her to read the kids' emotions. Whatever the truth behind my relatives' claims, the Flanagan woo-woo gene had definitely skipped me.

"Thanks for your help with the appointment," I

said to Aido. "As soon as I've served the tea, I'll book a taxi."

My friend shook his head. "Not necessary. I met Cian on my way back. I told him I had to drive you to the hospital. I'll swing by Dottie's place after I've dropped you off."

"Thank you," I said, truly grateful. Until payday, my purse was light on cash.

"Mr. Chuckles looked good and dead," Nana roared to Dottie as we approached their chairs. "Do you think they'll bury him in a clown costume?"

I groaned. "Why won't Nana wear her hearing aid? She insists she doesn't need it and then proceeds to deafen the rest of the world."

"She's great fun," Aido said. "I wish my gran was as sprightly."

"I don't think 'sprightly' wholly encompasses the whirlwind that is my grandmother."

I deposited the tray on the small side table next to my grandmother. Before I'd begun to unload the tray's contents, Marcus burst through the museum door.

"Dee?" He bounded across the room and enveloped me in a bear hug—if being rib-crushed by a man half my size qualified for the description. "Are you okay?"

"I'm fine, but your shirt won't be after this hug. My hair's soaking."

"A little water never hurt anyone." He stepped back and examined me. "One of the ladies in the crowd said you were covered in blood. Are you okay?"

"I'm fine," I said for what felt like the twelfth time that day. "My white rain gear made it look more dramatic than it really was. The blood was from one of the men who got shot. He fell on me."

And I'd fallen on Mr. Chuckles. I shivered at the grim reminder of the dead clown.

"You'd better get a towel for your hair," Aido said, helping me to unload the contents of the tea tray. "You're channeling 'drowned rat.'"

"Gee, thanks, oh King of the Compliments," I rejoined with a laugh. All the same, I grabbed a couple of towels from the kitchen while Marcus and Aido fetched chairs from Richard's office. They wouldn't help against the inevitable frizz, but they'd at least absorb some of the wet.

"I can't stay," Marcus said when I took a seat. "I have to go back and help Cian cover this story. We just wanted to make sure you were all right."

"I'm fine. Really." I was. Mostly.

"Cian says to tell you to take tomorrow off work," Marcus added. "He'd like you to write an eyewitness report on the shootings, but it can wait."

My chest swelled and I blinked back tears. Our editor was usually dogged in his pursuit of a story, and Marcus was even worse. For them to suggest I rest instead of write meant they were genuinely concerned for my welfare. "Thanks, guys, but I should be fine by this evening. I'd like to get my thoughts down while they're still fresh."

Marcus squeezed my arm. "All the same. Take it easy and have a sleep-in tomorrow."

After Marcus left, Aido and I served tea. We'd just sat down in the seats when Richard stepped through the door that divided the museum from his private quarters. He'd changed out of his wet clothes, but his skin was still ashen. He took in the scene, and the strain on his face eased. "I thought I heard voices down here. Can I offer anyone a shot of whiskey?"

Nana beamed at him. "I'll take one in my tea."

"Me too," Dottie added.

"Not for me, thanks," Aido said, "but Dee should have one. She's still cold and in shock."

"I don't like the taste of whiskey," I protested.

"Doesn't matter," Nana said, adhering to the belief beloved by the Irish that a shot of whiskey could cure any number of ailments. "A drop of the hard stuff will do you good."

Richard nodded in satisfaction. "I'll bring down the bottle."

"I wonder what'll become of the clown's wig collection?" Nana asked when Richard reappeared a minute later, clutching a bottle of Jameson. "He had a nice green one he wore every year to the Saint Patrick's Day parade. I think I'll pay a call on his mother. Show my respects."

"No, Nana," I interjected. "You are not to call Mr.

Chuckles's mother and ask to raid his wardrobe. The guy's only just headed to the morgue. Besides, his mother hates me."

Aido grinned. "Well, yeah. You reported her son for harassment."

"He did harass me," I retorted indignantly.

"I believe you, but she never will."

Richard poured a generous helping of whiskey into Nana's and Dottie's cups.

"Just a small drop for me," I said. "I know my limitations. More than a hint of whiskey knocks me on my rear end."

While Aido fetched another chair for Richard, I got an extra cup from the kitchen. Once we were all seated, my mind returned to my musings. Nana and Dottie chattered loudly about the events of the morning, bombarding Richard with questions about the clown. I was barely aware of their words. What was it the injured man had said when I'd asked him the names of the shooters? Ma-hell-gut? That couldn't be right. And who was the person he'd mistaken me for?

"Anyone know someone called Eliza?" My question cut through the conversation. Several pairs of eyes regarded me with surprise.

"I don't know any Elizas." Nana turned to Dottie. "You?"

Dottie shook her head. "It's an old-fashioned name."

"Or posh," Aido said. "Why are you asking?"

"The guy I helped mistook me for an Eliza."

"Wife, girlfriend, or sister," Richard suggested. "The man thought he was on death's door. It makes sense that he'd look for her."

"Right." I frowned. If the man wasn't local, Eliza mightn't be from Dunleagh.

The intensity of the man's stare lingered in my memory. His hard-fought words had been for my—well, for Eliza's—safety. He'd known the shooters' identities and that they were after him. Which meant Mr. Chuckles hadn't been the intended target, nor the mayor.

My hands shook when I lifted my cup to my lips, and I ended up with most of the tea in the saucer.

"You're cold and in shock," Richard said gently. "Come up to my apartment and take a hot bath."

I shook my head. "Thanks, but I can't."

"Will you at least go for a lie down?" he asked. "You look wrecked."

"I have to escort Nana to the hospital. I'm fine, honestly." My teeth chattered as I spoke.

"Give her a warm jumper to wear over her blouse, Richard," Nana said, "and a second shot of whiskey."

"It's June," I said. "I shouldn't be cold this time of year."

"Shock makes people cold, and your hair is wet," Aido pointed out. "And we're not exactly enjoying a warm summer so far."

"Okay. I'll take the sweater, and a spare raincoat if

you have one, but no more whiskey for me. I don't want the doctor thinking I have a concussion when I start slurring my words."

Richard caught my eye, and a silent understanding passed between us. "No problem. I have a selection of jumpers you can borrow, and I'm sure I can rustle up a spare coat. Why don't we go upstairs while your grandmother finishes her tea?"

"Okay." I replaced my cup and saucer on the side table and stood. "I'll be back in a sec, Nana."

She nodded and waved a hand. "Go and get warm, love. Dottie and I are fine here." She winked at Aido. "We have a handsome man to entertain us."

I grinned at my spiky-haired friend. "Just don't let Nana convince you to play cards with her. She cheats."

With my grandmother's squawks of outrage ringing in my ears, I followed Richard into the corridor. A winding flight of metal stairs to our right led to the passage that connected the museum to the castle towers. A second flight of stairs to our left led up to Richard's apartment, a dubious perk to his position as museum director. The apartment was in desperate need of renovations. In spite of its shabbiness, Richard kept his home impeccably clean and tidy, right down to two perfectly aligned stacks of magazines on the living room's coffee table.

I looked around the small living room and at its floor-to-ceiling bookshelves, all arranged according to the subject matter. "You terrify me. I'm afraid to breathe in here."

Richard gave a rueful smile. "I can't relax in an untidy environment." He pointed to the sofa. "Take a seat. I'll need a minute to select suitable clothes."

While he disappeared into his bedroom to look for clothes, I sat on his lumpy sofa and thumbed through an old magazine. There were several pages torn out. Given Richard's insistence on neatness and order, the ripped magazines seemed out of character. He must have inherited them from one of the hair salons in town, as my grandmother did hers.

A moment later, Richard threw open his bedroom door. "Want to see what I've found?"

I followed him into the bedroom. He'd selected several sweaters and draped them across his bed.

"I don't have many jumpers in your size," he said with an air of apology. "These are the best I could come up with. Take whichever fits you best."

"Thanks, Richard."

After he stepped out of the bedroom, I turned my attention to the clothes. Either his sweaters were less outlandish than the rest of his wardrobe, or he'd selected the tamest of the bunch for me. I chose an oversized gray sweater and pulled it over my shirt. As I was straightening the shoulders, a shaft of sunlight broke through the gray clouds and bathed the room in a soft golden glow. I slipped a hand into my pocket and withdrew the bag containing the cartridge.

Holding it up to the light, I examined it from every angle. What was it about the round that bothered me? I had the sense I was missing something that should be obvious.

"What have you got there?" Richard stood in the doorframe, staring at the cartridge with open curiosity.

"See for yourself." I handed him the bag. "I found this on the museum's side of the Green Archway. Something about it bugs me, but I can't figure out what."

Richard peered at the cartridge and emitted a low whistle. "No wonder it struck you as odd. This is an old Mauser round."

"Is this supposed to mean something to me? All I know is that Mauser is a German arms manufacturer."

"Is and *was*. They've been making weapons since the early 1800s." He held the cartridge through the plastic, rotating it between his thumb and forefinger. "This little beauty is at least one hundred years old."

I sucked in a breath. My mind raced, sifting through a moving kaleidoscope of shifting images. "That's not possible. I found it in the courtyard today. It can't have been lying around unnoticed all these years."

"I doubt it has. It's in excellent condition. If I didn't know better, I'd say it was new." Richard's voice brimmed with excitement. "I'll need to compare it with the examples in the museum, but my first guess is that it came from a C96. You might know it as a Peter the

Painter from your research into weapons used during the Irish War of Independence."

Shock hit me in the solar plexus. "The uniform..." I whispered, my voice trailing off.

With Richard's inevitable, "What uniform?" ringing in my ears, I raced out of the apartment and back down the stairs to the museum. My heart pounded as I ran by Aido and the old ladies, ignoring their surprised exclamations at my abrupt reappearance. I sprinted through the first two exhibition rooms, past artifacts pertaining to the history of Dunleagh Castle up to the turn of the twentieth century. I barreled into the third room, which was devoted to the castle's role during the War of Independence.

I slid to a stop in front of a glass display in the center of the room. Behind the glass frame, a mannequin wore a uniform so dark green that it almost appeared black. Insignia were pinned to either side of the jacket's collar—a harp beneath a crown. A metal emblem on the cap boasted the same symbol, plus the words Royal Irish Constabulary in embossed capital letters.

I sucked in a breath. The man I'd helped in the courtyard had been wearing a one-hundred-year-old police uniform.

FIVE

The doctor shone his light into my left eye, and then into my right. "Any nausea?"

"Not anymore." I shifted position on the uncomfortable examination table and avoided looking at my grandmother. Instead of remaining in the waiting area—or better still, heading upstairs to the cardiology department—Nana had insisted on accompanying me. She was now perched on the only chair in the cubicle, surveying the doctor with open curiosity.

The doctor, an earnest Sri Lankan called Weerasinghe, squirmed under her gaze and consulted his clipboard. "Do you have a headache?"

"Only slight." I glanced at the pale green curtain that separated me from freedom. Impatience hummed through my veins. How much longer was his examination going to last? My willingness to accompany my grandmother to the hospital had increased the instant I'd seen the uniform in the museum. I had to get another look at the one the injured man had been wearing before the Guards whisked it away as evidence.

"Dee fainted," Nana barked, banging her cane on the ground for emphasis. "Keep her in for observation."

Dr. Weerasinghe took a cautious step out of Nana's reach. Ever since she'd regained control over the cane in Aido's car, she'd been wielding it like a weapon and playing the senior card with shameless aplomb. Thanks to her shenanigans at the registration desk, I'd been seen almost immediately after our arrival at the emergency department. A win, to be sure, but the examination couldn't end fast enough for my liking. I had snooping to do.

"I didn't faint," I corrected, focusing on Dr. Weerasinghe. "I *felt* faint. There's a difference."

Even this modified version of events was an exaggeration. The sight of the uniform had shocked me, but I'd been in no danger of collapsing onto the floor. First, I'd never fainted in my life, and second, I'd had one bump on the head today already and I wasn't keen to add another to the list. My headache had faded to a dull ache, and I was sure that seeing the doctor was a waste of time. Unfortunately, Nana hadn't been prepared to let me get away with sneaking off the instant we'd arrived at the hospital.

The doctor scribbled something illegible on my chart. "Do you have pain medication at home?"

"I have Panadol in my bathroom cabinet."

"Which type?" His clipped English was perfect and delivered with a pleasant lilt.

I had no clue, but prevarication was my middle name. "ActiFast," I said, the distinctive green packaging present in my mind after a recent trip to Boots.

"Soluble or solid?"

"Soluble." We did have a pack of something in the bathroom cabinet, but I couldn't recall what.

He nodded in satisfaction. "That'll do. Dissolve two tablets a maximum of four times a day."

"Will do." I eyed the curtain. "Can I go now?"

"Yes, but if you experience anything beyond mild nausea, or if the pain gets worse, come straight back to the hospital."

"She will," Nana said firmly, "although I still think you should keep her overnight."

The doctor ignored Nana and shook my hand. "I'll put a note on your chart that you're to be seen at once if you return."

I returned the firm handshake. "Thanks." After the doctor left, I slid off the examination table and put on my boots. "What was all that about me fainting? You know I didn't."

"You don't take a hint, do you?" An amused smile tugged at Nana's mouth. "I was trying to give you an excuse to stay longer."

I schooled my features into a neutral expression. "Why would I need an excuse?"

"Because you're up to something. You shot down the stairs from Richard's apartment like you had a hot poker up your bum, and you practically hurled yourself into Aido's car."

"I work for a newspaper," I countered. "I'm merely doing a little investigating."

"I knew it." She preened with satisfaction. "What can I do to help?"

Alarm bells clanged in my head. "Oh, no. You've caused enough havoc for one day."

"I'm hurt," she said, adding an unconvincing pout to illustrate her feelings. "All I wanted was to make sure my granddaughter was safe."

I raised an eyebrow. "And get a look at the body."

"Of course." Her eyes twinkled. "Come on, Dee. All good sleuths have a sidekick. Let me be yours."

"Absolutely not. Even if you had time to tag along, I wouldn't let you." I pointed to my watch. "You need to go to the cardiology department. Your appointment is in ten minutes."

She waved a hand in a dismissive gesture. "I consider it my civic duty to find out what happened to the clown and the hottie."

"The cops don't want you sniffing around their investigation. At least I have a semblance of an excuse." I helped my grandmother to her feet and handed Nana her bag. "I'm serious. Go to your appointment. Only your wonder salve persuaded Mandy Dillon to rearrange your appointment for this afternoon."

Nana chuckled. "I bet the mention I'd been delayed due to the shoot-out at the castle sealed the deal. Mandy's nosy. The instant I approach the desk at cardiology, she'll want every detail."

"All the same, you're lucky to be seen at short notice."

"How are you going to get into the morgue without me creating a distraction?" Nana demanded.

I stared at her, mouth opened. "How did you guess I was heading there?"

Nana tapped the side of her head. "Logic, love. That fella you saved is still in surgery, meaning you can't quiz him. That leaves the morgue as the only place of interest. What do you need to do down there? Question Lev?"

Lev, my brother-in-law, was a junior doctor specializing in pathology, and an occasional source of information for a story. "Yes, but I doubt they'll have started the autopsy on Mr. Chuckles yet."

Actually, my primary interest in infiltrating the pathology department was locating the stranger's clothes, but sharing that info with Nana would lead to questions I didn't want to answer. On previous visits to pester Lev for information for news stories, I'd learned that a storage unit next to the autopsy rooms acted as a temporary holding bay for clothing and personal effects collected from patients who were connected to criminal investigations. By now, the medical staff would've bagged the injured man's clothes and personal effects for the Guards to collect, and there was a good chance they'd already sent them downstairs. As I had no legitimate excuse to barge into an operating theater, the morgue was my best bet to get a look at the uniform.

After I'd retrieved my bag and Richard's spare coat from a chair, I pulled the flimsy green curtain aside, and we exited the emergency room, dodging hurrying nurses and irate patients. Although Dunleagh boasted a population of no more than twenty-five thousand inhabitants, including its environs, Dunleagh General was large for a regional hospital. It served as the primary hospital for the county. Patients with complex cases or rare diseases were sent to one of the university hospitals in Cork, Galway, or Dublin. For everyone else, Dunleagh General was their first port of call, and the hospital was teeming with activity.

Nana leaned on her cane but kept a brisk pace, neatly navigating a path through the throng. Out in the corridor, we swung left and made a beeline for the elevators. I hit the up arrow for one and the down arrow for another. When the doors for the ascending elevator slid open, I gestured for Nana to enter. "You don't want to miss your appointment."

She made no move to enter the lift. "I won't miss my appointment. It doesn't take long for me to create a fuss. Lev's such an innocent he'll believe me when I tell him I picked the wrong floor. I'll have him so frazzled that dealing with your questions will seem a relief."

"You're incorrigible," I said, but when the doors to my elevator slid open, I made no move to block her entrance.

Seconds later, we reached the basement. To the left of the elevators lay the labs. To the right, staff offices, autopsy rooms, and the morgue. Nana and I turned right. In contrast to the disinfectant smell that pervaded the upper floors, the basement's air was tinged with damp.

Nana wrinkled her nose. "This place stinks. When I end up down here, promise you'll spray me head to foot with Chanel No.5."

I laughed. "Keep your cardiology appointment, and it's a deal."

"I'll make it on time. Don't you worry about that." She tapped her cane against the peeling linoleum flooring. "What do you need Lev to do? Answer questions? Or do you need me to keep him occupied while you snoop?"

Nana was sharp as a tack. She must've noticed my momentary hesitation when she'd asked me if I wanted to quiz Lev. "You're assuming he'll be alone."

She chuckled. "I'll create a hullabaloo that'll have his entire department hopping."

A smile tugged at the corners of my mouth. "All

right. Seeing as you've insisted on tagging along, do your best to buy me a few minutes of snooping time."

Quizzing Lev was on my to-do list, but not until he'd performed the autopsy on the clown and could answer my questions about the age of the lethal weapon. We passed a door emblazoned with the words Post-Mortem Examinations and stopped outside its unlabeled neighbor. This was where Lev and his colleagues had their offices. Nana attacked the door with her cane. Seconds later, Orla Tierney, one of the doctors training with Lev, threw open the door and leaped back at the sight of my grandmother.

"Where's my useless grandson-in-law?" Nana demanded in her most menacing voice, still brandishing the cane. "I want a word with him."

Poor Lev. Insofar as she tolerated anyone of the opposite sex, Nana was rather fond of him.

Orla opened and shut her mouth, but no words came out. I knew Orla from the Historical Murders Club. She was the sort of timid creature Nana could walk all over.

Lev emerged from one of the offices, looking flustered. His brown hair stood in wild tufts and the dark circles under his eyes screamed sleep deprivation. With a newborn and a sick toddler in the house, this was hardly surprising.

"What sort of circus are you running?" Nana demanded. "There's no reception desk, no water cooler, and no free chocolates."

Lev slow-blinked. "It's a morgue, Eda, not a hotel."

The cane inched closer, forcing Lev to perform a rapid sideways shuffle. "I expect better hospitality when you toe-tag me." Nana jabbed her cane into his chest. "And a professional makeover."

Sweat beaded on Lev's upper lip, and he tugged at his collar. "That's a job for the undertaker. Dunleagh General doesn't offer mortuary services."

By now, three people had gathered behind Lev, including Orla, a ginger-haired nurse, and a dour-looking man of fortyish. I presumed the latter was the consultant in charge of that shift. I glanced at the whiteboard at the side of the entrance. Four staff names, including Lev's, were listed under the current time slot. Nana had succeeded in flushing all of them out, but how would she get them from the department's entrance room to the corridor? I couldn't waltz into the storage room with an audience.

"And I want a decent blow-dry," Nana continued in deafening tones, "from Sally at Darnelle's salon."

"I'm not the person to talk to about this," Lev said, his eyes darting from side to side, seeking an escape route. "And you're not dead."

"Don't speak too soon," Nana said, beaming. "I'm having a cardiac moment."

With these words, she smashed her cane against the fire alarm, breaking the glass and setting loose a deafening cacophony. Then she clutched her chest, gave a dramatic grimace, and sank onto the floor in a swoon, neatly landing on the corridor floor.

My grandmother's playacting was too over the top for me to worry she was genuinely ill, but the unexpected shock of the noise from the fire alarm froze me in place. As Nana had intended, the combo of her fake heart attack and the alarm ensured pandemonium. Workers spilled out of the labs, security guards came running, and a stretcher was procured as if by magic. While Lev and his coworkers treated Nana, I gathered my wits and slipped through the door of the pathology department. I made a beeline for a small storage room to the left of Lev's office. With a quick glance at the main door, I switched on the light and stepped inside.

Medical supplies occupied the majority of the space, except for one narrow shelf. I extracted a pair of disposable gloves from a container on a supply shelf and put them on. I had no idea if fingerprints showed up on clothing. Even if they did, I'd given the man first aid and had a rational explanation for why mine would be on his clothes. All the same, I didn't want to destroy genuine evidence.

It didn't take me long to find the injured man's effects—Dunleagh wasn't exactly a hotbed of crime. I grabbed a pre-cut sheet of exam table paper from a box and used it to cover the floor. Then I removed the injured man's possessions from the plastic evidence bag and examined each item in turn. At the top of the pile lay his cap. The emblem on front was identical to the one in the museum: a crowned harp with the words Royal Irish Constabulary carved into the metal.

My pulse quickened as I checked the other items. The bloodstained white shirt and underclothes were old-fashioned and had the stiffness I associated with heavy-duty bleach. The sight of the blood triggered a wave of nausea. I inhaled deeply and willed it away. I had no time to waste on emotion. I had to stay focused and finish examining the uniform.

I spread the jacket, and then the pants, across the papered floor. The crowned harp insignia was repeated on the metal studs on either side of the jacket's collar, as well as on each of the jacket's buttons. Medal ribbons were pinned over the left breast pocket of the jacket, indicating the wearer had extensive military experience. On the arm of the jacket, three embroidered stars proclaimed the rank of District Inspector 2nd Class, the equivalent of an army captain. I fingered the material. Even through the rubber gloves, it felt coarse to the touch but finely made. I checked all the pockets, but no incriminating letters or other handy clues leaped out at me.

The only other item of interest was an old-fashioned wristwatch. I picked it up and examined it carefully. The numerals glowed bright, even in the poor lighting. The words S. Smith & Son were written on the watch face in small black letters. At first glance, it looked like a well-preserved museum piece. I wasn't a vintage-watch expert, but one of the contributors to my video blog had submitted a piece about First World War wristwatches. I'd look it up later—Nana's theatrics wouldn't occupy Lev and the rest of the staff for long. I turned the watch over. My pulse quickened. On the back, the following words were engraved:

To M.S.:

All my love, now and forever.

E.R.

Slipping my phone out of my pocket, I snapped several photos of the cap, the buttons, the medal ribbons, and other details. I finished my photographing frenzy with close-up shots of the watch, both back and front. Slipping my phone back into my pocket, I returned the injured man's belongings to the evidence bag, but my fingers lingered on the watch.

On impulse, I switched off the light in the storage room. The numerals on the watch dial continued to glow. Not an antique in that case. Trench watches—the wristwatches worn by soldiers during the First World War—were coated with radium paint to make them glow in the dark. The idea was to eliminate the necessity of lighting a match to tell the time at night, and thus alerting an enemy sniper to a soldier's position. While the radioactivity of such a watch would endure for more than a millennium, the luminous effect only lasted for an estimated three years. This watch, like the uniform, must be a finely made replica.

I dropped the watch in with the rest of the

evidence and replaced the bag on the shelf. As there was no rubbish bin in the room, I shoved the used exam table paper into my backpack. I slipped out of the storage room in the nick of time.

Lev burst through the door, a harassed expression on his lean face. "That woman," he muttered, "is a human wrecking ball."

"Did Nana make it on time for her cardiology appointment?" I asked, feigning innocence.

"Knowing her, she's up there barking orders and demanding a five-course meal." Lev eyed me with suspicion. "Meanwhile, you're in an area that's out of bounds to the public. You've got to get out of here. Moriarty's talking to a lab tech, but he'll be back any second."

"Is Moriarty the dude who looks like he doused his breakfast cereal with hydrochloric acid?"

Lev grinned. "The very guy." He grabbed my elbow and dragged me into the hallway.

Dr. Moriarty approached from the opposite direction. He gave me a disapproving once-over and opened his mouth as though to speak.

Lev got in first. "Dr. Moriarty, this is my sister-in-law. She's upset about her grandmother falling ill. I'll escort her to cardiology and be right back."

Moriarty's eyes narrowed. "You're in that silly club with Orla and my wife." He said it in an accusatory fashion that set my teeth on edge.

"You make belonging to the Historical Murders

Club sound like an offense," I said lightly, ignoring Lev's warning squeeze.

The man pressed his lips together to form a tight line. "I'm surprised Mary wastes her time on such nonsense."

Mary... He must be referring to Mary Yates, Dunleagh's head librarian and the secretary of the Historical Murders Club. In addition to these duties, Mary acted as a castle guide twice a week during high tourist season.

"And I'm surprised Mary's married," I shot back. The words "to you" remained unspoken, but he got my meaning.

The older man grunted, shot me a look that could curdle milk, and stomped down the hallway.

"A true gentleman," I drawled when Lev and I were out of earshot. "Did he fail his bedside manner test?"

Lev's lips twitched. "Not much call for it down here."

The lift arrived, and we stepped inside, along with a woman clutching a clipboard. She exited on the ground floor, leaving Lev and me alone.

"Did Eda's theatrics have anything to do with the dead clown?" he demanded the instant the doors closed.

"I saw him die." I didn't have to fake the quaver in my voice.

His stern expression softened. "I heard. How are you bearing up?"

"Trying to keep busy. I'm writing an eyewitness account for the *Chronicle*."

"And you want me to spill the details of the post-mortem." Lev sighed. "No can do, Dee. I hear the mayor thinks he was the intended target of a professional hit. That means the case won't stay with the Dunleagh cops for long. Lou might tolerate me slipping you a few slivers for your article, but I'm not messing with the NBCI."

The National Bureau of Criminal Investigation, or NBCI for short, was the main criminal investigative branch of *An Garda Síochána*, Ireland's National Police Service. Officially, they assisted and advised local police to investigate serious crimes. Unofficially, they swept in with their fancy equipment and took over the case.

"I might be able to help you impress Dr. Grumpy."

Lev looked skeptical. "How?"

The elevator arrived at our floor, and the doors slid open. We stepped out, and I navigated my way past the waiting patients and staff. I paused in front of the floor-to-ceiling windows until the elevator had left with its fresh cargo.

I removed my phone from my bag. A few swipes later, I handed it to Lev.

He squinted at the photo of the cartridge. I'd given the original to Lou, along with the bag containing my clothes. "How's this supposed to help me? We know the clown was shot."

"Ah, but you don't know what gun killed him. Are the bullets still in the body?"

"I've only had a chance to glance at it so far, but yeah. There's at least one."

I reached for my phone and slid it back into my bag. "I'm betting the bullets you pull out of Mr. Chuckles will be from a historical firearm, most probably a Mauser C96."

"Seriously?" Lev's eyebrows went skyward. "How do you know that?"

"With a little help from Richard. When you remove the bullets from the body, you'll want to make a show and dance about consulting the museum. Throw around terms such as 'Mauser C96' and 'Webley RIC,' and get permission to show it to Richard."

Lev's expression was doubtful. "Okay. I can try." He checked his watch. "Sorry, Dee. I've got to get back to work. Moriarty's been a bear all day. I don't want him throwing a fit and deciding I can't assist on the clown's post-mortem."

"Go," I said. "I'll be in touch."

He regarded me with amusement. "Try to stay out of trouble."

"I'll do my best." Trouble, it seemed, had a tendency to find me.

Lev opted for the stairs, taking them two at a time in his rush to appease his taciturn boss. When he'd disappeared from sight, I turned back to the window and stared through the glass, unseeing.

Why had the injured man been wearing a historical uniform? Cian's play was set during the early Twenties. Was the man an actor in the play? The time period fit. If so, Cian's budget was higher than I'd thought—a replica uniform that detailed didn't come cheap. And what about the guy's revolver? A Mauser C96 was a pistol and not generally used by the Royal Irish Constabulary. In other words, the cartridge I'd found on the ground couldn't have come from the injured man's weapon. Was I certain the firearm he'd dropped had been a revolver? It would fit with the standard-issue RIC firearm of the time.

I cast my mind back to the scene in the courtyard. The man's weapon had impinged on my consciousness twice: first, when he'd staggered through the archway, still carrying his old-fashioned gun, and second, when I'd kicked the weapon out of my way before I'd given him first aid. I was no expert on firearms, modern or historical, but I'd swear that gun had a cylinder.

I glanced at my watch. Just after two o'clock. By now, Lou would've retrieved the revolver from wherever I'd kicked it and placed it in an evidence bag. Could I persuade her to let me take a look at it before the NBCI crowd arrived? I had to find out if it was a genuine vintage firearm or a replica. And what were the implications if it was the real deal? Why were a bunch of guys taking potshots at one another with hundred-year-old weapons? A reenactment that had turned fatal? Or was it something more sinister?

The memory of the purple sky stirred, sending an icy shudder through my body.

"I don't believe in ghosts," I said aloud. "And I am absolutely normal."

I'd inherited none of my family's so-called gifts. There was no reason to assume I'd had some sort of vision, or an out-of-body experience. Personally, I'd always suspected my mother's ephemeral qualities were due to recreational drugs. As for Nana's herbal remedies, I tolerated her teas but I wouldn't touch the rest. Besides, the bullets fired into Mr. Chuckles and the stranger were real, regardless of the age of the weapons they'd been fired from, and the blood definitely wasn't fake.

I wrapped my arms around my chest to ward off a sudden chill. There'd be a rational explanation for all of this morning's oddities. Of course there would. The photos I'd taken with my phone would show the existence of the purple sky, if not the strange wind. And hadn't I switched my phone onto the video setting at one point? Yeah, a clip of the sky would prove I wasn't crazy. Once I got Nana home, I'd find Lou and ask about the revolver. Whatever was going on, I needed to know I wasn't losing my mind.

SIX

After Nana's appointment had finished, we made our way down to the main entrance and scored a taxi that had just pulled into the taxi rank. It was five past three in the afternoon, but it felt like midnight. The two lousy coffees I'd downed while waiting for my grandmother had failed to do their job. Only visions of the warm bubble bath I intended to have this evening were keeping me going. Stifling a yawn, I helped my grandmother to secure her seat belt.

"I'm not a child," she grumbled. "I never wear seat belts in taxis."

"I don't know why people don't. It's not like a taxi is any safer than a private car." Once I'd handed Nana her handbag and cane, I closed the door and scooted around to the other side of the vehicle. I had one leg in the taxi when a police car pulled into the visitor's parking lot. Lou sat behind the wheel, her expression tense. My pulse quickened. If I wanted to corner her about the revolver, now was an excellent time to do so. "Are you okay to go home alone, Nana? Lou's just arrived, and I still need to give her my statement."

And quiz her about a vintage firearm, but I didn't mention that to my overly curious grandmother.

Nana settled back in her seat. "I'll be grand, love. Go and talk to your pal. Can you see about getting the mobility scooters home later? I'll need mine tomorrow."

I'd happily erased the mobility scooters from my mind. "I'll see if Aido will help me ride them home." This would mean an extra trip back to the castle to collect Mavis, my Vespa, but I'd already accepted that today was destined to be a royal pain.

Nana jerked her head in the direction of the hospital entrance. "You'll have to run if you want to catch up with Lou."

I pulled my purse out of my backpack and extracted a twenty-euro note. "That should cover the fare."

"No need." My grandmother patted her handbag. "I have the cash I won off Big Jim this morning. That'll get me home."

"All right. Just promise me you'll take it easy for the rest of the day. No more gallivanting."

"I'll be a model patient," Nana said with a wholly unconvincing look of innocence on her lined face.

I closed the door and waved her off. By the time I jogged back to the main entrance and slipped through the sliding doors, Lou was at reception, in earnest conversation with a woman in a nurse's uniform. My heart skipped a beat. Had she received bad news about the stranger? I speed-walked across the lobby.

Lou spotted me before I reached the reception desk. "Hey, Dee. How's your head?"

"A little sore, but I don't have a concussion." I nodded to the nurse. "Any news on the patient?"

"He's not out of surgery yet," Lou said, sparing the nurse the necessity of telling me I was neither a relative nor a member of the police force. "Want to walk and talk? I need to collect the man's things from the basement."

I adopted my best poker face. "Sure."

Lou shot me a knowing glance. "I didn't think you'd turn down the opportunity to eavesdrop."

"I am a reporter," I said with a grin.

I fell into step with her and was unsurprised when the police sergeant bypassed the elevator in favor of the stairs. In spite of Lou's tough stance, she had an aversion to small enclosed spaces.

"Here's the deal," she said when we were halfway down. "If there's stuff I need to keep quiet until we're further into the investigation, you cooperate. Everything else is fair game."

"Deal. And thanks. I appreciate the opportunity."

She grunted. "Enjoy it while it lasts. The NBCI

crowd will arrive at any moment. I doubt they'll be as accommodating to the local press."

We reached the bottom of the stairs and headed right, back in the direction of the post-mortem rooms and the storage room where the man's belongings were waiting for the Guards to collect.

"Have you discovered the guy's name yet?" I asked.

Lou shook her head. "Nurse Brennan tells me they found no ID among his belongings. We'll have to hope he's in a position to identify himself once he's out of surgery."

"And if he's not? Will you check his fingerprints and DNA?" I failed to keep the excitement out of my tone. While I didn't share Nana's obsession with crime scene investigation shows, I wasn't immune to the intrigue of a real-life shoot-out.

"Fingerprints, yes. DNA as a last resort." Her mouth quirked in amusement at my crestfallen expression. "Even the NBCI isn't immune to budget cuts, Dee. Those tests are expensive. We'll only go the DNA route if an appeal to the public doesn't provide concrete proof of his identity."

We stopped in front of the door Nana had attacked an hour earlier. Lou's knock summoned Orla Tierney, the junior doctor who'd had the misfortune to encounter my grandmother. She recoiled at the sight of me, her eyes darting around the corridor, searching for a crazy lady with a cane.

Lou held up her ID. "Sergeant Healey. I'm here to collect evidence from the shoot-out at Dunleagh Castle."

Orla shoved a stray strand of limp brown hair behind her ear and shot me a curious glance. "Come in. I signed for the evidence bag a couple of hours ago."

"I take it the post-mortem on the clown is still in progress?" Lou looked pointedly at the closed door straight ahead of us, through which muffled voices could be heard.

The doctor inclined her head. "Dr. Moriarty just started."

Lou removed a card from the breast pocket of her uniform jacket. "Get him to call me the instant he's done."

The implication was clear to me, if not to the other woman. Lou wanted a personal heads-up on the post-mortem results, even if the NBCI had arrived and taken charge of the case.

The doctor put the card in her pocket. "I'll give this to him when he's finished."

The phone in Lou's pocket vibrated. She glanced at the display and her lip curled. Ignoring the call, she focused her attention on the closed door of the storage room. "I'll take that evidence bag, please."

"Sure," the doctor said. "The door's unlocked. Go on in."

The police officer's eyes shifted to the doctor.

"Unlocked? Surely you don't leave it unlocked all the time?"

The doctor flushed. "We're a small team, Sergeant Healey. Hardly anyone comes in here but us."

"You're storing material that's part of an ongoing investigation." Lou's voice had developed a sharp edge that hadn't been there before. "I expect such material to be kept secure."

The other woman's shoulders stiffened. "We rarely get material for the police. This is only a makeshift arrangement, after all."

"All the same, I expect you to tighten security."

The doctor developed a sudden fascination for her shoes. "I'm sorry, Sergeant Healey. I don't run this department. I just do what I'm told."

Lou's mouth formed a hard line. "I'll have a word with Dr. Moriarty about security. This is unacceptable."

The police officer swept into the storage room and angled the door so that the evidence shelf was blocked from view. A few seconds later, she emerged, her expression thunderous. "Are you sure the trauma surgery staff sent down his stuff?" she demanded. "The evidence shelf is empty."

My heart skipped a beat. I'd put everything back exactly where I'd found it.

The junior pathologist paled. "It's definitely there," she stammered. "I signed for the bag myself and I put it in storage."

"Well, it's not there now. Look for yourself." Lou gestured for the doctor to enter the storage room.

Orla obeyed, emerging a moment later with a green tinge to her pale face. "It doesn't make sense," she said, wringing her fingers in a classic gesture of distress. "I know I put the bag on the evidence shelf."

I stared at the empty shelf in the storage room, my mind racing. "Did another police officer collect it?" I asked. "Maybe someone from the National Bureau of Criminal Investigation?"

The doctor jerked her neck from side to side. "Before you two showed up, the last person to knock on the door was your grandmother."

Lou's gaze swiveled toward me, her eyes narrowing. My cheeks grew warm under the intensity of her stare. "Eda was in here?" she demanded. "Why?"

"She wanted to talk to Lev," I prevaricated, "but she wasn't anywhere near the storage room." I'd have to admit I'd been in there, but it could wait until we didn't have an audience.

Lou folded her arms across her chest. "Are you sure about that? Eda had no compunction about poking Mr. Chuckles's mortal remains. It would be just like her to snoop on the injured man's stuff."

"No," the doctor interjected. "Mrs. Flanagan yelled at Lev, set off the fire alarm, and then claimed she was having a heart attack. All the action went down in the corridor, not in here."

The police sergeant's gaze bore into me. "Indeed. And where was Dee while all this was going on?"

My stomach sank. Lou didn't miss a trick. Thankfully for me, Orla wasn't as sharp. "She was in the corridor too." A pause. "At least, I think she was."

"Is that so?" My friend's voice was laced with sarcasm. "No quick dash in here to take a peek at the evidence, Dee? Evidence that's now missing?"

From behind us, a man cleared his throat. "Good afternoon, ladies. I'm Detective Inspector Bradley of the NBCI. I believe you've been expecting me."

At the sound of the masculine voice, the three of us whirled around. DI Bradley stood in the doorframe, regarding us with a lazy stare. He was fiftyish and of average height and build with dark hair shot through with silver. The only notable aspect of his appearance was a pair of piercing green eyes. At this moment, those eyes were fixed on Lou. "What missing evidence?"

Lou, Orla, and I exchanged desperate glances. After an uncomfortable pause, Lou stepped forward and extended a hand to the newcomer. "Sergeant Louise Healey of Dunleagh Garda Station."

The man's mouth curled, but he shook the proffered hand. "Not your usual sort of case, eh? The last small town I went to, the Guards spent most of their time looking for lost sheep."

Lou's stance stiffened, and I could sense her

struggle not to yank her hand away. "We do a little more than hunt for sheep, sir."

"Yes," he said placidly. "Losing evidence is also part of your repertoire, or so I'm given to understand."

This dude was starting to annoy me. "Lou didn't lose evidence. Whatever happened to that bag, it wasn't her fault."

The man raised a sardonic eyebrow. "And you are?"

"Dee Flanagan. I helped one of the shooting victims."

"She's also a reporter for the *Dunleagh Chronicle*," a familiar voice from behind me said, "as well as a member of a rather dubious club that interests itself in murder."

Swallowing a groan, I turned to face Lev and Orla's boss, Dr. Moriarty. He stood by the open post-mortem room, his attention fixed on Orla.

At the appearance of her boss, the young doctor dissolved into sobs. "I'm so sorry. No one told me to lock the door."

Dr. Moriarty stepped forward and laid a fatherly hand on her shoulder. "You did nothing wrong, Orla."

She clung to him, her sobs growing louder. Dr. Moriarty rubbed her back comfortingly. I reassessed the situation. Was this a caring boss offering comfort to a young underling, or was there more to Orla and Dr. Moriarty's relationship?

As if sensing my thoughts, Dr. Moriarty glared at me before focusing his attention on DI Bradley. "Dee and her grandmother were down here earlier, snooping."

The detective turned his piercing green eyes back to me. In spite of my best efforts, I squirmed under the intensity of his stare. "Did you remove the evidence bag from the storage room?"

"No," I replied, feeling Lou's questioning gaze on the back of my neck.

The detective inspector's stare didn't let up. "Did you touch the evidence bag?"

I shifted my weight from one leg to the other. "Okay, yes, but I didn't take it out of the storage room, and I certainly didn't steal it."

"Can you recall what was in the bag?" Lou demanded. Her tone held a harshness that hadn't been there before. She was annoyed with me, and rightly so. I should have 'fessed up to looking at the bag the moment we'd realized it was missing.

"A vintage uniform from an officer of the Royal Irish Constabulary," I said, enjoying the look of astonishment that crossed the DI's face. "Either an excellent replica or the real deal."

DI Bradley recovered his composure. "And you know this how?"

"The subject of my PhD was the War of Independence. This uniform was the sort worn by RIC officers from the time of the First World War until their disbandment. The evidence bag also contained an old wristwatch, also of a similar vintage." I smiled, relishing the effect my next words would have. "The engraving on the back was to an M.S. from an E.R. Perhaps the initials will help you identify the injured man, although I doubt it was his originally."

A muscle in DI Bradley's cheek flexed. He looked at Lou and then at me. "Are you quite sure you didn't take that bag, Ms. Flanagan? It sounds like its contents are valuable. Did you want to show them off to this murder club the doctor says you're a member of?"

"The Historical Murders Club isn't interested in contemporary crimes, as Dr. Moriarty should know—his wife is also a member." *Take that, Doctor Death.* "As for the value of the items in the evidence bag, you're assuming they're genuine and not replicas."

"Something you might have wanted to check for yourself," Bradley pointed out.

"I put everything back in the bag before I returned it to the shelf," I insisted. "If you want to play the blame game, why don't you ask Dr. Moriarty why he doesn't see fit to lock the storage room?" Moriarty emitted a blast of protest, but I ignored him and pulled my phone out of my pocket. "If it's any help to you, I photographed each of the items in the bag. Take a look."

DI Bradley took my phone and frowned at the

screen. "Why would you take pictures of the evidence?"

I rolled my eyes. "Isn't it obvious? I'm a reporter and a historian. As well as general curiosity, I wanted to be sure I was correct about my identification of the uniform wearer's rank. I intend to check it when I get home."

Lou cleared her throat. "Dee discovered an unusual cartridge at the scene of the crime. It appears to come from an old sidearm."

Bradley's eyebrows rose. "Was this also in the missing evidence bag?"

Lou shook her head. "No. Dee gave it to me while we were still at Dunleagh Castle. The cartridge is currently at the museum."

"Why?" Bradley demanded. "The cartridge should be examined by our forensics team."

"And it will be. I left it in the care of Richard Daley, the museum's director and a noted expert on nineteenth- and early-twentieth-century weapons. It's in an evidence bag, and I instructed him not to remove it from the bag without my permission. All he's doing is comparing the cartridge to historical cartridges in the museum's collection."

The Dublin detective pursed his lips and drew his own phone from his pocket. "I want Ms. Flanagan to transfer those photos from her phone to mine and then delete them from her phone's hard drive."

I took both phones with a sigh. "Fine."

"And from your cloud storage," he added, not missing a beat. "Unless you want me to confiscate your phone for the duration of this investigation, you'll cooperate."

"I'm not an idiot, Detective Inspector. You can't confiscate my phone without a warrant."

His slick smile made my skin crawl. "Given that you rifled through evidence that is now missing, getting a warrant won't prove to be a problem. Now do as I say and get out of my sight."

Five minutes later, my phone was an evidence-free zone, as was my iCloud account. Glaring at the man, I handed DI Bradley his phone. "Can I go now?"

The man nodded. "I'll let Sergeant Healey escort you off the hospital grounds. I don't want you sneaking upstairs to try to interrogate the nursing staff."

That had been precisely my intention, but I wasn't about to admit this to the detective.

"Come on, Dee," Lou said in a low voice, propelling me out into the corridor. "I'll walk you out."

We took the stairs up to the entrance level in silence. When we were outside, I turned to my friend. "I'm sorry. I should've mentioned I'd looked in the evidence bag."

Lou folded her arms across her chest. "Yeah, you should've."

I took a deep breath. "And I probably should've mentioned that I have a second cloud storage account."

The police officer unfolded her arms, indecision

flickering across her features. After a beat, she exhaled a sigh. "I'm taking a page out of your grandmother's book and opting for selective deafness. On one condition."

"What's the condition?"

"Whatever you find out about the man's uniform and belongings, I want to know. Maybe he's part of a reenactor group."

"That possibility occurred to me."

"If you find out anything, I want to be the first person you call. Not your editor. Me. Got it?"

I nodded, my mind already whirling with possible research avenues. "It's a deal. Can I tell Cian about the evidence bag?"

Lou shoved a hand through her hair and a frown line appeared between her brows. "You can tell him about the contents, but please don't mention that the bag is missing. I'd like to keep that information under wraps for the time being. I'm hoping the bag will turn up before we have to inform the public. And I want you both to sit on the uniform story for the next twenty-four hours. In return, I'll give the *Chronicle* an exclusive on whatever we can share. Deal?"

It was a better offer than I'd expected and I'd be a fool not to accept. "Deal. Thanks, Lou."

She motioned for me to follow her, and we walked in the direction of the parking lot. "I'm still mad about you poking around the evidence bag. What possessed you?"

"The uniform freaked me out. I only realized what the man was wearing when I escorted Nana to the museum and saw one of the displays. I wanted to take another look at the guy's outfit to be sure I wasn't losing my marbles. I was about to tell you when DI Bradley showed up."

My friend nodded. "Okay. I believe you. You handed in the cartridge, after all."

"Exactly. I don't want to steal evidence, especially not anything that can help you catch the killers, but this shoot-out has me spooked."

"You're still in shock," Lou said gently, "even if you don't feel it."

"It's not just because I was in the courtyard when it happened. Something's not right. We have old-fashioned guns and cartridges and uniforms and a dude no one can identify."

"Not yet, at any rate," Lou corrected. "I'm sure we'll figure out who he is." When we drew near her police car, Lou unlocked the doors. "Hop in. I'll take your statement at the station and then drive you home."

"Don't you need to get back to Detective Inspector Charm?"

My friend laughed. "He asked me to escort you off the hospital grounds. He never told me to return to the pathology department. If he wants to throw his weight around, he's more than welcome to hunt down the missing evidence bag." She slid behind the wheel, and I got in the passenger side.

"At least you still have the cartridge," I said, fastening my belt, "and the revolver."

Lou stalled the engine and stared at me. "What revolver?"

SEVEN

In spite of spending an hour in my much-anticipated bubble bath, I tossed and turned all night. After Lou had realized that a vital piece of evidence had disappeared from the crime scene, apparently from right under her nose, she'd raced back to the castle, leaving me in front of the castle's parking lot. By the time I'd driven Mavis home, I'd had zero motivation to arrange for the collection of the two mobility scooters. Instead, I'd updated my history channel and then focused on writing my eyewitness account for the *Chronicle*.

It had been after eight o'clock when Lou'd shown up at Nana's house to take my statement, tense as an elastic band pulled to its full extent. I was bone-tired and pretty sure my statement made no sense. I suspected the report I'd penned for the *Chronicle* could also be filed under the category of Hot Mess.

After hours spent trying to sleep, I'd resorted to drinking one of my grandmother's herbal teas and had conked out soon after.

I was deep asleep when my phone buzzed to the tune of Chopin's funeral march. I opened one eye and winced at the sunlight streaming in through my thin curtains. Whatever Nana had put in her herbal sleep tea must've been designed for an eighteen-hour, uninterrupted stretch. I rolled over and buried my face into my pillow. If it was important, the caller could leave a message.

Five seconds of soothing silence later, the funeral march resumed. By this point, I was awake enough to remember to whom I'd assigned that particular ring tone, and I wasn't in a position to ignore him. With a sigh, I groped for my phone. "Hey, Cian." My voice sounded like that of a sixty-a-day smoker.

My editor chuckled. "Morning, Dee. Your accent sounds more mid-Atlantic than ever."

"It's called not being awake." I glanced at my bedside clock. It was almost eleven. "What's up? Is there a problem with my report?"

"No. Your eyewitness account of the shooting was excellent."

"Really?" I wasn't fishing for compliments. I genuinely had no idea if what I'd written made sense. When I'd sat down in front of my laptop yesterday evening, the words had tumbled out of me.

"Yeah. It arrived in the nick of time and I was able to put it on the front page."

"That's awesome." In spite of the circumstances of me scoring my first front-page feature, I couldn't help smiling. "Speaking of the shooting, there's something I didn't mention in my report because Lou asked me to sit on it for twenty-four hours."

"Oh?" His editor's journalistic nose for a story sharpened his tone. I could practically see him reach for a pen and notepad.

"The second man who was shot—the guy I helped —was wearing a replica of a Royal Irish Constabulary uniform. Could he be an actor in your play?"

"Ronan O'Gara? Paddy Patel? Was one of them shot?"

"They're too old to be the man I treated. I'd put him in his early to mid-thirties. Definitely no more than thirty-five. And he had a northern accent. Donegal, maybe."

"Ronan and Paddy's characters are the only RIC officers in my play," Cian said, "and they've got Kerry accents thick enough to cut."

"Then I'm at a loss to know why he was dressed up as a member of the RIC."

"Are you sure you have the correct uniform? When you read my play, didn't you tell me the emblem was essentially the same as the one the Royal Ulster Constabulary continued to use until...when was it?"

"Until 2001," I answered on autopilot. "You're

correct about the emblem, but the man's cap clearly said Royal Irish Constabulary. The cap was the style worn by RIC officers in the years right before they were disbanded in 1922."

"How bizarre," Cian said. "The time period fits with my play. Why didn't you mention the uniform to me when you emailed your report?"

I didn't have a concrete answer to this question, but I suspected it was connected to the reason I'd failed to mention finding the vintage cartridge. The old-fashioned uniform and firearms disturbed me almost as much as my experience with the purple wind. I'd also wanted to see if the missing items would reappear, thus allaying my suspicions that they'd been deliberately stolen. It wasn't like me to sit on a story, but everything about this case made me twitchy.

"I forgot," I prevaricated. "It was late when I wrote my account, and I was exhausted."

"Fair enough." Cian appeared to accept this explanation. "Maybe Richard can tell you why the man was wearing a historical uniform. His exhibition also concerns the War of Independence."

"Perhaps, although he didn't mention hiring actors. I'll ask him later." I stretched my stiff neck from side to side. "What are you calling me about? I thought I had the day off."

"I know, but I need your help," my editor said without hesitation. "Seamie Dean is up to his old tricks again."

"Another cockfight after yesterday's debacle? You have to admire the man's resilience." I stifled a yawn. "Can't someone else cover the story?"

"Someone else *is* covering the story," Cian said. "Aido's out at Dean's farm now. I need you to collect him."

I rolled my eyes. "Let me guess—the Alfa Romeo is in for repairs again." Aido had an inexplicable attachment to his ancient Alfa Romeo. Unfortunately for Aido, the loyalty was one-sided.

"A reporter without transport is the last thing I need," Cian muttered. "Today of all days."

"Why? What's going on?" The words slipped out before I could stop them. My editor thrived on drama. He managed to create a crisis out of a stubbed toe. In the five months I'd worked for him, I'd learned that engaging with his Drama Du Jour was dangerous territory.

"Paula and Declan are still sick," Cian replied in a mournful tone, "and Marcus is at the circuit court in Tralee. I had to give Aido a lift out to Seamie Dean's place to cover the cockfight story, but I'm tied up for the next couple of hours. I need Aido back at the office to field calls, and I'm relying on you to get him here."

Mmm-hmm...relying on me to be so grateful for my job that I'd play the role of an unpaid taxi driver. So not happening. "I'm not the *Chronicle*'s chauffeur. What's so vitally important that *you* can't collect Aido?"

"I'm interviewing Mayor Hyland about his plans to gut part of the castle. He's been giving me the runaround for weeks, but I managed to pin him down for an appointment this morning."

"Dude's slippier than an eel," I said. "Ten to one he'll find an excuse to bail on you again."

"Maybe, but if his claim that he was the intended target of yesterday's shooting is true, I want to know why. It might be connected to his dodgy business dealings."

"Of which we have no proof," I reminded him. "Marcus's exposé on Bart Adams resulted in the paper getting sued. We can't afford a rinse and repeat."

"But Bart Adams is one of Hyland's secret-handshake pals. There's got to be dirt we can use as leverage to stop the mayor from wrecking the castle."

"Leverage sounds an awful lot like blackmail. Are you sure you want to go down that road?"

"I'll do whatever it takes to protect the castle."

I blinked at the vehemence in Cian's tone. My editor was relentless in his pursuit of a story, but I'd never known him to stray into ruthless territory.

"Can I rely on you to be in the Great Hall later?" Cian asked. "I'd appreciate your feedback."

The sudden change of topic confused me. I searched my fuzzy brain for clues but came up blank. "Huh? Why do I need to be in the Great Hall?"

"For the dress rehearsal, of course."

Ugh. The play. I'd blocked it from my mind.

"Once you drop Aido to the castle, you can stick around and work in the archives. That way, you'll be on site for the performance."

"The dress rehearsal doesn't start until six," I pointed out, "and I wasn't planning to attend." With my mother in a starring role, I had no choice but to attend the opening night of Cian's latest theatrical extravaganza, but no way was I sitting through it twice. He'd pump me for last-minute feedback I didn't want to give.

"Please, Dee." A hint of desperation had crept into my editor's voice. "I'm nervous about this production. I'd appreciate your input. A theater critic from Dublin will be at the premiere. This could be my big chance."

Having read the script of *A Fighting Man* more times than I cared to count, I doubted Cian was destined for stardom. On the other hand, squeezing in a couple of hours for the archival project I was working on for the paper wasn't a bad idea. I'd been busy over the last two weeks, and I'd neglected my task to sort back issues of the *Chronicle* for digitalization.

"Okay, I'll collect Aido," I said finally, "but I'm adding the time it takes to my overtime sheet at time and a half." Yeah, I owed Cian for my job, but I wasn't a complete pushover.

"Now, come on," my editor squawked. "Surely—"

I cut short his protest. "At the pathetic rate you pay us, it'll work out cheaper for you than paying Karl's Kabs for a sixty-minute round trip. If you want me to play taxi after sacrificing my day off yesterday, that's the deal."

"Fine," he muttered. "Just make sure the pair of you take plenty of photos of the cockfight before the Guards arrive."

I grinned. "Tipped off by you, no doubt."

"Hey, it pays to keep on the right side of the Guards," my editor replied without a hint of remorse. "We need them to give us the full scoop on the shootings."

Still clutching my phone, I staggered over to my wardrobe and rifled through my clothes. "Can I interview the man I helped yesterday? He knows me, after all." This was assuming the poor guy survived his injuries. I'd swing by the hospital later and weasel an update out of Lev or one of my friends from the Historical Murders Club.

"Yeah, sure," Cian said. "Seeing as you helped him, he's likely to give you an exclusive. Can you be at the farm in thirty minutes?"

I selected a pair of black slacks and a clean white shirt. "Make it forty-five," I said, adding underwear to my pile of clothes. "I have to shower."

"It's a deal." A long pause. "Please come to the rehearsal, Dee. I'll pay you time and a half if you sit through it."

"Pay me double and include the time it takes me to give you feedback."

Cian's drawn-out sigh emphasized his sense of

martyrdom. "You'll bankrupt me, but I suppose I have no choice."

"Not if you want me to cooperate," I said cheerfully. "See you later."

After I'd disconnected, I replaced my mobile phone on my nightstand and padded out of the room, clutching my clothes. I headed for the bathroom. Hopefully, a blast of cold water would wake me up. As I neared the top of the stairs, a blinding vision in canary yellow and hot-pink rooted me to the spot. I slow-blinked. "Nana?"

My grandmother sat in her unmoving stair chair, stuck halfway up the stairs. She held a pen in one hand and her newspaper open at the crossword in the other. Today's outfit consisted of a canary-yellow dress, and green-and-white-striped tights. In combination with her fuchsia lipstick and purple hair, Nana was a kaleidoscope of color.

I tossed my bundle of clothes onto the floor and took the steps two at a time until I'd reached her stair chair. "What happened? Did that ridiculous contraption break down again?"

Nana peered at me over the rims of her horn-rimmed spectacles. "A series of unfortunate malfunctions. The chair gave up the ghost halfway up the stairs, and my safety strap is stuck. I'll get Barney to come over and do a repair job."

I trusted Barney Black to fix a problem about as much as I'd trust my mother to change a plug. Which was to say, not unless I wanted to be electrocuted. "That crook? It's his fault you're in this predicament."

"He prefers to call himself a purveyor of black-market goods," Nana said dryly.

"I don't care what he likes to call himself. He probably stole your stair chair from the factory's reject pile."

"Very likely, but he got me a great deal on my mobility scooter. All the Dunleagh seniors love Barney."

"Why didn't you shout for help?"

She chuckled. "I did. I guess I overdosed you on sleep tea."

"I zonked out the instant my head hit the pillow," I admitted. "I'm sorry you had to wait."

"Don't worry about it. I figured you'd wake up eventually. At least I had the crossword to keep me occupied." My grandmother leaned forward, eager interest on her lined face. "Who were you talking to just now? Was there another shoot-out?"

"No shoot-outs. Cian called. Aido's car broke down again and he needs a lift." I unstrapped the stair chair's safety belt and helped my grandmother to her feet. "How long were you sitting here?"

"Long enough to give my incontinence pants a workout."

I held up a hand. "Whoa with the TMI."

"Just stating a fact," she said cheerfully. "You'll learn all about it when you get to be my age."

"I'm kind of hoping I never get trapped in a stair chair and obliged to put incontinence pants to the test."

Nana laughed until she wheezed. "I intend to send Barney a detailed review. Maybe he'll give me a discount on my next order."

My jaw descended. "Barney sells incontinence pants?"

"After constipation cures, they're his bestselling wares."

"Ugh. Why did I ask? I need mind bleach."

Nana leaned on me until we'd reached the top of the stairs. I handed her the cane she kept on the landing and guided her in the direction of the bathroom. "Bridget will be home later. Maybe we can all have dinner together."

I gave a noncommittal grunt. I was still steaming over my mother's failure to answer any of our calls yesterday. Breaking bread with her wasn't high on my list of priorities. Still, if she rolled up, at least Nana would have someone to help her. "When's Bliss due back?" I asked, using my mother's chosen moniker rather than her legal name.

"She said she'd be home before lunch," Nana replied, "but you know what she's like."

I did know. My jaw tightened, and a wave of resentment rolled over me. My mother was the reason I'd cut short my postdoctoral studies and moved back to Dunleagh to look after Nana. Bliss was fun and carefree, but also feckless and irresponsible. When

Nana had had her first heart attack, my mother had cheerfully volunteered to move in and look after her. I didn't trust Bliss to look after a flea. My sister lived in Dunleagh, but she had two small kids. In contrast, I was newly single, and my only ties were to my studies. The day I'd gotten the news that Nana was in the hospital, I'd given notice on my Dublin apartment and bought a one-way train ticket to Dunleagh.

I steered Nana into the one functioning bathroom. "I'll help you wash and put on fresh clothes," I said. "Then I'll hop under the shower. Will you be okay on your own this morning?"

Nana waved a hand. "I'll be fine. You go off and rescue your friend."

I eyed her with suspicion. "Do you promise not to get into mischief while I'm gone?"

My grandmother looked the picture of innocence. "Dottie and I don't have our mobility scooters. They're still at the castle, remember? Where can we go without them?"

"Hmm... Knowing you, far. As for the mobility scooters, I'll figure out a solution to get them home." Better still, I'd dump the task on Bliss. After a week of wrapping herself into pretzel-like shapes, the least she could do was sort out the scooter mess.

"Perhaps you can get that lovely boy with the green hair to ride mine home and stay for dinner," Nana mused. "Now he's a looker."

"No more matchmaking, Nana. I'm still recovering from the time you set me up with Dottie's grandson."

"That was years ago," she protested. "And you two went on more than one date. Doesn't that count as a success?"

"Of a dubious kind. Most grandmothers wouldn't want to set up their granddaughter with a guy who's probably on the Guards' Usual Suspects list."

Nana's eyes widened. "Picking locks is a life skill, dear. What if you lose your house key? With a guy like Gary, that'd never be a problem."

"Apart from the inconvenient periods when he was behind bars," I said dryly. "What about safe-cracking? Or disabling alarms?"

"Valuable talents. I forget my PIN codes all the time."

I threw my arms in the air. "I give up. You're impossible."

Fifteen minutes later, Nana was clean and freshly clothed, and I was showered and dressed. I didn't have time to apply full makeup, but I selected one of my favorite lipsticks in a cheerful shade of orange-red and applied it to my lips. I blasted my hair with the dryer for a few minutes before abandoning the effort. It'd have to stay wild today. I'd tie it back and hope for the best.

After I'd helped Nana downstairs and installed her in her favorite armchair, I checked my bag. Thanks to the confusion yesterday, I still hadn't had a chance to look at the photos and video I'd taken of the sky. On impulse, I opened my photo app and swiped through the pictures. There it was, in all its weird glory. I hadn't imagined the unusual color. An icy dread spread through me. If the sky hadn't been a hallucination, then what about the wind that had held me prisoner?

"What have you got there?" Nana demanded, trying to get a glimpse of my screen.

"I don't know," I said honestly. "Right before I heard the shooting, the sky turned a strange shade and the air seemed to change." The latter description hardly did credit to a wild wind that had turned into shackles, but I couldn't bring myself to say the words.

"Can I have a look?"

I handed my phone to Nana.

She adjusted her glasses and peered at the screen. "That is an unusual color. What did you say about the wind?"

I shrugged, reluctant to voice what was sure to sound like the delusions of a mad woman. "It seemed to crackle," I said finally. "Maybe the sound had something to do with the gunshots that followed. I'm not familiar with firearms."

My grandmother handed back my phone and reached for her knitting basket. "You should take it easy today, love. Yesterday was quite a shock for you."

"It's all good. Cian's paying extra for my work today, and we can use that to pay Rachel." Nana's private nurse was wonderful, but the few hours she visited a week cost more than we could comfortably afford.

Nana clucked in disapproval. "You're always on the move. We have to find a solution so you're not under so much pressure."

"I'm fine. Honestly." I glanced at my watch. "Will you be okay until Bliss gets home? Do you need me to do anything else before I leave?"

"I'm fine, love." She held up her phone. "I have this if I need to call someone. This time, I'm not moving without it."

Her words jogged a memory. "Wasn't the plumber supposed to be here last Friday? Today's Wednesday."

Nana gave a derisive harrumph. "He said he'd be here on Friday, but the rat didn't specify *which* Friday."

I swallowed a sigh. "Give me his number. I'll track him down."

"Don't worry about old Frank. I left him a blistering message on his voice mail earlier this morning. If I follow it up with a graphic description of my time trapped in the stair chair and the inevitable consequences, I expect he'll slink over before long."

Normally I'd feel sorry for anyone on the brunt of Nana's ire, but Frank could suck it. She needed a functioning downstairs toilet, and he needed to make it happen. Once I got the money together, we'd extend the downstairs bathroom and add a shower, but it was beyond my means at the moment. "Should I get you a cup of tea before I go?"

"Definitely," she quipped, "as long as you don't make it."

I gave a hoot of laughter. "Smart woman. I'll boil the water and leave you to do the rest."

After I'd filled the kettle and set it to boil, I rummaged through the fridge for a yogurt. I needed to eat a proper meal, but there was no time. Once the water was ready, I poured it into a teapot and put it on a tray alongside a cup, a saucer, and a jar of Nana's homemade herbal tea.

Sunlight streaked through the bay window where Nana was sitting, glinting off the bowl of citrine crystals on the sill. Mellie, Nana's black cat, stretched out on a blanket beneath the window, basking in the warmth. In the bright light, Nana's garish lipstick and blush couldn't disguise the gray pallor of her cheeks, and the lines around her eyes appeared deeper than usual.

As I placed the tray on the table beside her, cold fear seeped through my limbs. "Are you feeling okay?"

She raised an eyebrow in defiance and forced a smile that did nothing to ease my concern. "I'm not about to keel over. I'm just a little tired." I opened my mouth to argue the point, but she cut me off. "I know what you're going to say, so I'll say it for you. Gallivanting with Dottie yesterday wasn't a smart move, but it was fun. There's no point in being alive without having a bit of fun now and again."

I glanced at the clock. "When Bliss gets back, tell her to sort out the mobility scooter problem."

"What mobility scooter problem?" The melodious tones rang through the room and instantly set my teeth on edge. In one fluid movement, my mother drifted into the room, deposited her small carrier bag on the coffee table, and sank onto the sofa. In her floaty dress and vegan open-toed sandals, she was a living, breathing caricature of a New Age hippy. Her petite frame and long, dark hair contrasted with my tall, sturdy build and wild mane of blond curls. As my mother loved to point out, we looked nothing alike.

"Can't you make a little noise when you arrive?" I groused, my heart still thumping after her unexpected appearance.

"Sorry, darling. I'll be sure to bash the wind chimes the next time I arrive." Bliss crossed her ankles and leaned against the back of the sofa with the lithe grace of a ballet dancer. "What's this about your mobility scooter, Mum? Have you been up to mischief?"

"Dottie and I had to leave our scooters up at the castle after yesterday's shenanigans," Nana said. "Wholly unnecessary in my opinion, but I was overruled."

"Shenanigans?" Bliss's green eyes brimmed with curiosity. "That sounds ominous. What happened?"

I crossed my arms over my chest and glowered at her. "Don't you read the news?"

My mother's lips twitched. "Not when I can help it, and never when I'm on a retreat. I make a point of leaving my phone at home."

"That would explain your failure to answer our umpteen calls," I said acidly.

"Darling, don't be grumpy. The planets are out of alignment. Everyone's feeling odd. What you need is a nice Reiki session, followed by an aromatherapy massage. I can fit you in this afternoon if you have time."

"I don't think a Reiki session can erase the memory of seeing a man shot to death in front of me," I snapped, "but thanks for the thought."

My mother's exquisitely shaped eyebrows formed two perfect arches. "Murder? How thrilling. Sit down and tell me everything I've missed."

"If your digital detox is at an end, go online and look it up. I've got to go to work."

"I'll do that," my mother said, apparently oblivious to my anger, "but be careful today, darling. This sort of planetary aberration always spells trouble, both for nature and mankind. Be wary of any changes to the elements."

I didn't disguise my disdain. "Save your predictions for the *Dunleagh Chronicle*'s most gullible readers, Bliss. I'm not interested."

"You're such a skeptic, darling. If you'd only open

your mind to the universe, you'd be so much happier." A feline smile curled her lips. "You might even find a man."

"Leave the poor girl alone, Bridget, and pour yourself a cup of tea." Nana sent me a warning look. "You don't want to be late for your friend. See you later, love."

I took the hint. "Bye, ladies."

With the soothing click of Nana's knitting needles ringing in my ears, I stuffed my second set of rain gear and a spare pair of shoes into my backpack, grabbed my helmet, and slipped out the front door.

EIGHT

Almost an hour after my conversation with Cian, I rode Mavis, my trusty red Vespa, up the bumpy drive of Seamie Dean's property. Underneath my helmet, my hair was still damp from the shower, and I was pretty sure I'd put on my underpants backward. My stomach growled in protest at the painkillers I'd swallowed before leaving the house. I still felt lousy, but the combo of the shower, the fresh air, and the meds had taken the edge off my headache. Besides, it was hard to stay grumpy on such a gorgeous day. The temperature was balmy, the sky a cloudless blue, and the breeze pleasant. The first sunny day we'd had this month. Once I'd escaped from this evening's dress rehearsal, I'd take a stroll by the sea, maybe treat myself to ice cream at my friend Amy's café.

Encouraged by the thought of a chocolate-peppermint sundae in my very near future, I surveyed my surroundings with a cheerful disinterest. The Dean farm consisted of several buildings in various states of disrepair and several acres of neglected land. The main house was a dirty white that hadn't seen a lick of fresh paint this side of the millennium. Having met its owner, the property was exactly as one would expect. A part-time farmer and a full-time crook, Seamie Dean specialized in illegal gambling. He arranged everything from backroom poker games to cockfights, and was a frequent guest of the Irish prison system.

As I neared the farmhouse, raucous laughter floated through the air, occasionally punctuated by squawks. I couldn't see the spectators or the animals they'd come to watch, but they had to be close.

Before I could find the cockfight, there was a crunch of car tires behind me. I slowed my bike and looked over my shoulder. A squad car bounced over the uneven track. The blue lights flashed, but the sirens remained silent. I braked and allowed the vehicle to draw up beside me. Lou and Eoin grinned at me through the windscreen.

Lou lowered the driver's side window. A sardonic smile tugged at the corners of her rosebud mouth. "Hey, Dee. Cian said you'd be here."

"Merely as Aido's taxi service." I flipped up the visor on my helmet and smiled at my friend and her partner. "Are you two taking a break from the murder inquiry?"

Eoin guffawed, and Lou's expression darkened.

"Cian's tip-off gave us a welcome excuse to ditch the paperwork DI Bradley dumped on us this morning," she said. "The man seems to think all we're good for is making tea and sorting files."

"Any news on the injured man's identity? Or the missing evidence?"

"Nothing so far. His fingerprints aren't in the system. If we haven't identified him by this evening, we'll issue an appeal to the public. As for the evidence —" Lou's nose wrinkled with distaste, "—Bradley blames me."

"I'm sorry. With a bit of luck, he'll wrap up the case soon and be out of your hair."

Lou forced a smile. "Here's hoping."

"When can the *Chronicle* mention the uniform? Journalists from the nationals are already here. I don't want anyone stealing my scoop."

"I'll call you this evening. Until then, please don't spread it around."

"Cian and Richard know," I reminded her. "Richard won't tell, but Cian's chomping at the bit to put it on our website."

She pulled a face. "I bet he is. Just remember our deal. Play fair with me, and I'll play fair with you."

Eoin leaned forward in the passenger seat. "Speaking of scoops, the *Chronicle* must be desperate if Seamie and his pals are considered newsworthy."

"We live in desperate times," I replied cheerfully, grateful for the opportunity to jolt Lou out of her mood slump. "Can I persuade you two to charge in wearing full riot gear? Now that would make an excellent photo op."

Eoin patted his burgeoning beer belly. "It's been a while since I've worn my riot gear. Not sure I'd fit into it anymore."

"If you're not going to provide me with drama, can you at least give me a head start?" I flashed an ingratiating smile at Lou and dangled the carrot I knew she'd grab. "I'll get Bliss to give you a free card reading."

The offer of my mother's fortune-telling services elicited a peal of laughter from Eoin, but Lou's elfin face perked up. "Seriously? That would be awesome. I've been wanting to book an appointment, but her rates are way out of my league."

I rolled my eyes. "Her rates are outrageous, but her clients love her."

"Not a fan of the occult?" Eoin asked, an eyebrow raised. "I thought your whole family was known for being on the witchy side. My wife swears by Eda's herbal remedies."

"I leave the woo-woo stuff to the others. My only special gift is my ability to sniff out the best pizza joint in any town." I grinned and shifted my attention back to Lou. "A five-minute head start will give me a chance to snap a few shots before you two swoop in to restore law and order. In return, Bliss will predict your love life. Deal?"

Lou pulled a face. "If my future love life is anything like my past, that's not something to look forward to. Okay, I'll give you two minutes, and not a second more."

I grinned and revved my engine. "You're an angel." With a backward wave, I shot forward in the direction of the noise.

It didn't take me long to find the cockfight. Seamie had dug a half-hearted pit in the scraggly field that backed onto his house, and a rope cordon separated a makeshift parking lot from the action. I zoomed into a spot next to a sleek black Porsche that had an expensive-looking golf kit stuffed into the back.

Although it was dry today, yesterday's heavy rain had turned the field into a muddy quagmire. I'd anticipated such an eventuality and I'd come prepared. I pulled my spare pair of rain pants from my backpack —the other pair was still with the police—and shook them out. In a maneuver I'd practiced many times, I drew my rain pants over my boots and work pants before sliding off the bike. The rain pants were a horrendous shade of mustard yellow and definitely not a color I would have chosen. My grandmother had found them in a bargain bin and foisted them upon me. I hated to admit it, but they'd come in handy more than once.

I removed my helmet and surveyed my surroundings. A crowd surrounded the pit, waving fists and cheering. In addition to the prerequisite elderly farmers in tweed caps, the spectators included well-to-do college kids in designer casual wear, a couple of men in business suits, a group from the traveling community, and several of Seamie's drinking buddies from the Quack and Quail pub. My goal was to find Aido and skedaddle. With a bit of luck, we'd be on the road in five minutes. Whistling a tune off-key, I strode toward the action.

I scanned the crowd for Aido's spiky green hair and spotted him instantly. He stood apart from the throng, leaning against a dilapidated shed. He was deep in conversation with a tall man in a pinstriped shirt who had his back to me. A third man hulked behind Aido's companion.

When I approached, Aido's eyes met mine. A lazy grin spread across his face. "Yo, Dee. Come to spirit me back to the castle?"

"Yeah." I gestured toward my bike. "I'm your knight on a red Vespa."

"Not as cool as riding off on a white stallion, but it'll do." He took in my mustard yellow rain pants and laughed. "That's some fashion statement you're making."

"Hey, don't knock them. They'll keep the mud off my clothes better than your jeans."

The man in the pinstriped suit turned to face me, and I started at the sight of his familiar features. "Mr. Hyland? I didn't expect to see you at the cockfight. I thought you were still cowering in Elaine's safe room."

My gaze moved to the mayor's burly companion. "I see you wasted no time in hiring a bodyguard."

A dull flush stained the mayor's cheeks. "It's smart to take precautions."

"Mr. Hyland doesn't want the *Chronicle* to cover the fight," Aido explained in a sardonic tone. "Stories like this will damage Dunleagh's reputation."

"I'd have thought our coverage of yesterday's shoot-out would be more detrimental to your plans," I said. "Potential investors don't tend to like murder."

Hyland's jaw tensed. "My point exactly. After yesterday's unfortunate incident, the last thing Dunleagh needs is more bad publicity. It's embarrassing enough that we've made nationwide news."

"How inconsiderate of the murderers," I quipped. "At least you can take comfort in the fact you weren't shot."

The mayor paled beneath his fake tan. "Don't make light of it, Ms. Flanagan."

"Why are you convinced you were the intended victim? You've made enemies during your time in office, sure, but from what I could tell, yesterday's shoot-out involved some sort of gang." I could tell no such thing, but winding up the mayor was one of my favorite pastimes. I leaned closer. "Do you have gangland connections, Mayor Hyland?"

Hyland's sculpted features turned a mottled shade of purple. "I have nothing further to say to you. I was just about to leave. I have several important meetings today."

"Don't let us stop you." I gestured toward the parking lot. "Our editor is waiting to talk to you. And after that, I'm sure you have a vital appointment at the golf course, no?"

Hyland's lips moved, but no sound came out. With a nod to Aido and a glare at me, the mayor scurried off to his Porsche, followed by his bodyguard.

"What's got the mayor worked up about Seamie Dean's antics all of a sudden?" I asked Aido. "It's not like this is the first illegal fight Seamie's hosted. If Hyland wanted to stop it, he'd have sent one of his minions."

My friend shrugged. "Beats me. I tried to pump him about his decision to slash the museum's budget, and he acted like he was dancing on hot coals."

"Dude's gaining enemies left, right, and center," I mused, "but who'd have the resources to hire a gang of hit men?"

"An inept gang of hit men," Aido added. "If the mayor was the target, why shoot Mr. Chuckles? Hyland doesn't prance about in a clown costume."

"Nor does he wear replica RIC uniforms," I murmured.

"What was that?" Aido asked, curious.

"Never mind. I'll fill you in later." Once Lou gave me the go ahead and I'd had time to examine the photographs in detail. The watch, in particular, intrigued me. Maybe Richard knew where I could find one. It was worth asking.

"Oy." Aido's attention was fixed over my shoulder. "The law's arrived."

I followed the direction of Aido's gaze. Sure enough, Lou marched toward the spectators, wearing a determined expression. Eoin brought up the rear, adding muscle to Lou's authoritative stance. "You'd better snap a few shots and we'll get out of here," I said.

He nodded and pulled his phone out of his bag. "Can you help me? It'd get us on the road quicker."

"Sure." I slipped my phone from my pocket and opened the camera app.

By silent agreement, Aido headed left, and I shimmied to the right, deftly avoiding a collision with the Guards. I raised my phone and took photos of the crowd.

This close to the pit, the smell of the cockerels mingled with the stench of unwashed bodies. I pushed my way closer. I loathed situations that involved injured animals, but I had a job to do. If I did my job well, maybe I'd rouse enough outrage from the *Chronicle*'s small readership to persuade them to protest against Seamie's lenient treatment by the justice system.

At the edge of the trench, caged past and future contestants watched their comrades peck it out in the mud. The pit was a lazy attempt at a circular arena, measuring roughly two meters in depth. Its uneven sides crumbled in places, and the dirt that had been removed to form the pit had been unceremoniously dumped behind the caged birds.

Down in the makeshift arena, two cockerels strutted their stuff, circling one another in a menacing fashion. One was bleeding, and both were missing a quantity of feathers. My stomach roiled and I tasted bile. I hauled in a breath and snapped a few dutiful pictures of the combatants before returning my attention to the spectators.

I photographed as many people as possible in my quest for that one perfect shot. While I took photos, I matched faces to names, mainly to take my mind off the bleeding cockerel. The cast and crew of Cian's play were well represented, as were the regulars from the Quack and Quail. I spotted several of my grandmother's bingo pals, all of her vintage or older.

The mayor's son, Rob, lounged by a stile, observing a scuffle between two of his preppy friends with bland indifference. I focused on this group for a while, capturing the moment Lou and Eoin intervened to break up the fight. It was an awesome shot. Pity that Cian would never use it. He loathed the mayor as much as I did, but he was reluctant to attract his ire. Publishing photographs of Hyland's son's friends being hauled apart by police officers was unlikely to please him, and the struggling *Chronicle* couldn't afford to upset the mayor. I grimaced. So much for journalistic independence.

I inched nearer to the edge and concentrated on the spectators on the other side, snapping photos and matching faces to names. A man who looked vaguely familiar was in hushed conference with a tall guy with a neck tattoo. I turned my phone to the right, snapping more photos. A flash of canary yellow caught my eye. My brow puckered. No way could Nana be here. My pulse quickened, and I flicked my fingers across my screen to zoom in. I'd barely had a chance to focus the camera app when a palm pressed against my upper back and shoved me hard.

With an audible gasp, I pitched forward, arms flailing in a futile effort to break my fall. While the ground rushed up to meet me, the cockerels made a last-second dash for safety. I hit the dirt hard. The air left my lungs in a *whoosh,* and a sharp pain shot up my right arm where I'd tried to cushion the impact. Shock held me immobile for a moment, but I was blasted back to reality by angry squawks and sharp beaks pecking at my arms. Thank goodness I'd kept on my biker jacket. I shook off the cockerels and pushed myself onto my knees. Suddenly, I was surrounded by people. Seamie Dean grabbed one of my attackers, and Aido grabbed the other.

Still dazed, I stared at my filthy hands. "If I'd known I'd be rolling around in the dirt, I'd have brought gloves."

"Are you okay?" Aido asked, struggling to avoid

being pecked by his captive. "Did you get too close to the edge?"

"No." My jaw hardened. "I was pushed."

Aido reeled back, narrowly avoiding falling over a cockerel cage. "Deliberately?"

"That's what I'd like to know." I jutted my chin and addressed the crowd that had gathered at the edge of the pit. "Did any of you see who pushed me?"

A sea of faces stared back at me, wearing expressions ranging from shocked to bemused.

"Pushed or slipped, you've had a nasty shock." The lines on Seamie Dean's craggy forehead deepened. "Are you okay? You came down hard."

"Not hard enough to have imagined the hand between my shoulder blades." My voice rose in anger, and a red-hot rage burned in my chest. "I'm telling you, I was pushed."

"The ground around the edge of the pit's uneven," the man countered. "It'd be easy to slip."

"But I didn't slip," I said through gritted teeth. "I was shoved. I don't know if the person who pushed me wanted me to fall in or just planned to make me move out of their way."

"Can we leave?" Aido had a greenish tinge to his tanned complexion. "The smell of bird is making me gag."

I allowed him to steer me in the direction of the ladder. I'd barely had a chance to mount the first rung when the vision in canary yellow that I'd spotted earlier swam into sight.

I narrowed my eyes. "So I didn't imagine seeing you earlier. What happened to your plan to spend a quiet morning? And where's Bliss?"

From the edge of the pit, my grandmother leaned on her walking frame and peered down at me. "I'm here for the sex toys. What's your excuse?"

NINE

After almost a year of living with my grandmother, I should've been unfazed by Nana's eccentricities, but this utterance left me slack-jawed. Judging by Aido's strangled intake of breath, I wasn't the only one.

"Sex toys?" he spluttered after we'd both scrambled out of the pit. "Did I miss something about today's event?"

Dottie shuffled into view behind Nana. Next to Nana's wild colors, Dottie's beige dress appeared drab. Her personality was anything but bland. "Barney said he was getting a delivery of adult toys," she explained to us with a beatific smile. "I guess Eda and I got the day wrong."

"We didn't get the day wrong. Barney said Friday morning at Seamie's place." Nana cast an accusatory look in Seamie's direction. "How were we to know you were staging one of your bird fights instead of catering to the sexual needs of the elderly?"

Huffing with the effort of hauling his out-of-shape body, plus a struggling bird, up the ladder, Seamie staggered onto firm ground. "Shush about Barney's merchandise. This place is crawling with Guards."

"Lou and Eoin didn't mention Barney's latest enterprise when I spoke to them," I pointed out. "They're probably in happy ignorance about his plans to supply Dunleagh's seniors with stolen sex toys."

"I wish I was," Aido quipped, earning him a haughty harrumph from my grandmother.

"Whatever the reason, this is the second day in a row you've snuck out of the house," I said to Nana. "Why didn't you tell me you were heading here?"

"I'm an adult. I don't need to sneak out of my own home, and I don't have to tell you everything I do." Nana jutted her chin. "After all, you said you were collecting Aido, but you didn't tell me you were heading here. How was I to know we'd run into each other?"

I closed my eyes for a moment and drew in a deep, cleansing breath. "Where's my mother? Why isn't she with you?"

"I left while Bridget was unpacking." Nana, clearly bored by my interrogation, shifted her attention to our host. "You're taking a police raid in your stride, Seamie. Last I saw, Lou and Eoin were busy breaking up a fight between Rob Hyland's college friends. I bet a chat with *you* is next on their list."

"I'm always on their list." Seamie grinned. "What would they have to do all day if I didn't provide some action? Especially now that those fancy cops from Dublin have swept in and taken over the murder investigation. Lou should be thanking me, not locking me up."

"I see you're making a great effort to evade capture," I said dryly.

"Ah, sure, I'll take off now in a sec and let Eoin chase me." He rocked back on his heels and patted his bulging stomach. "We're both doing a diet program at the community center. We need to get in our daily step count."

"Don't talk to me about steps." Nana glared at Seamie. "Dottie and I had to limp out to the main road to hitch a lift. That's not easy for two women with dodgy hips. And after we went to all that effort, Barney's not even here."

I sighed. "You're unbelievable. You know what the doctor said—"

"The doctor is an eejit," my grandmother retorted. "He seems to think that a seventy-six-year-old with bad hips and a weak heart should sit at home and wait to die. If a ride on a tractor with Dottie kills me, then so be it. At least I'll go out having fun with a friend."

"A tractor ride?" I groaned. "This story goes from bad to worse."

"And after a trying morning," Nana continued, pointing an accusatory finger at Seamie, "I find you rolling around in the dirt with my granddaughter."

"Ew." I shuddered. "Trust me, there was no recreational rolling around happening."

"I'm sorry your granddaughter fell," Seamie said in a soothing tone that had no effect on my grandmother's stony expression, "but it's not my fault if Barney's goods are late. He canceled the sale a couple of days ago. Didn't you get his message?"

"If I had," Nana snapped, "I wouldn't be here. That's no way to conduct business."

Seamie shrugged. "Barney'll be in touch when the goods arrive. He's never one to miss a potential sale."

On the far side of the crowd, Lou appeared to have the belligerent college students under control, and Eoin was barreling toward Seamie.

"Now looks like a good time to get in those steps," I said to him.

The man shoved the cockerel he was carrying at me. "Take care of the bird, will ya? Gotta make a run for it." He took off with more speed than I'd expected him to be capable of and performed a noteworthy leap over a cage of cockerels. Huffing and puffing, Eoin followed suit.

"While those two eejits are giving themselves heart attacks," Nana said, "Dottie and I need to hitch a ride back to town."

Lou ran an exasperated hand through her short hair. "If it'll keep the pair of you out of trouble, I'll drive you. I'm going to have to escort Seamie to the station once Eoin catches him, and I can swing by your place on the way."

I regarded the sight of the two out-of-shape men hurtling across a muddy field. "Seamie's gonna smell even worse than usual after that race. And speaking of bad smells—" I held the squirming, stinking bird away from my chest, "—will someone please open a cage for me before I gag?"

Aido grabbed the cage Seamie had just jumped over and unlatched the opening. "Give him here. I'll make sure the birds are fed and watered before we leave."

"Please do, but bring them back when you're done," Lou said. "They're coming with us to the station. I'll have animal rescue collect them later."

I handed over the bird, and my friend carefully helped him into the cage. He relocked the latch and hauled the cage in the direction of the farmhouse.

"Are you sure about giving Nana and Dottie a lift?" I asked Lou once Aido had headed toward the farmhouse. "How will you fit the birdcage into the car?"

"It can sit on top of Seamie," she said firmly. "He's wide enough."

At that moment, Eoin made a grab for Seamie's

trousers. The older man's pants fell down, revealing underpants that looked like they had survived a nuclear war. The pants pooled around Seamie's ankles, tripping him up. In turn, Seamie's fall made Eoin lose his balance. Both men pitched forward and landed in the mud.

"I guess Seamie doesn't go in for tighty-whities," Nana observed, deadpan. "Dottie and I will hitch a lift back to Dunleagh with someone else, Sergeant Healey. Between the mud, the birds, and our proposed traveling companion, we'll pass on your kind offer."

"I'll call my Gary," Dottie said. "He'll drive us home."

Lou, who was well acquainted with Dottie's ne'er-do-well grandson, shot me an amused glance. "Okay, but promise me you'll stay out of trouble. I've enough chaos to deal with at the station without having to arrest you two."

"We'll be on our best behavior." Nana leaned on her cane and took a step forward. "Will we use the facilities before we leave, Dottie?"

Dottie shuddered. "I don't think I can face the porta-potties."

"No need," Nana said cheerfully. "Seamie always leaves his front door unlocked."

I raised an eyebrow. "With the crowd he attracts to these events? Brave man."

"It's called honor among thieves, love," Nana called over her shoulder.

"Probably means Seamie keeps anything worth stealing elsewhere," I said.

The older ladies shuffled off to the farmhouse, leaving Lou and me to contemplate the wreckage wrought by today's gathering.

"Does it look worse than it did before?" Lou asked, squinting at the mess. "It's hard to tell."

I regarded my mud-splattered clothes. "Seamie's farm might look no different, but I sure do. I didn't have a mud bath in mind when I agreed to collect Aido."

In the distance, my fellow junior reporter trundled back, lugging the cage.

"He doesn't look much better than you do," Lou remarked.

I checked out the cage. Its inhabitants appeared less restless than before their meal. "DI Bradley won't be pleased to find the police station invaded by poultry."

A sly grin lit up her face. "Why do you think I'm keen to take the cockerels with us rather than get animal rescue to collect them here?"

I laughed. "Remind me to never get on your bad side."

The police officer lowered her voice. "To be frank, I'm not exactly in a rush to get back to the station. DI Bradley is making me pay for the missing evidence bag with a mountain of paperwork."

"It's not your fault it went missing."

"Until the moment he arrived, I was the officer in charge of the case. Preventing potential evidence from going walkabout was my responsibility." She grimaced. "Bradley went ballistic when I told him about the revolver also being AWOL. Until I got Aido to confirm that he'd seen it too, Bradley was inclined to believe you'd made it up to deflect suspicion that you'd stolen the evidence bag."

Anger burned through me. "That man's a fool. I had no reason to steal the bag. I'd already taken photos."

"To be fair, I know you and he doesn't," Lou said. "A limited number of people saw the evidence bag, and you were one."

I blew out my cheeks and turned my thoughts to the missing firearm. "The same can be said for the revolver. I saw it, as did Aido."

"Saw what?" A sheen of sweat glistened on Aido's forehead. He eased the cage to the ground.

Judging by the warning look Lou aimed at me, she'd failed to tell Aido the revolver had pulled a Houdini. "We were talking about the revolver the injured man was carrying."

"Oh, right." Aido patted the cage of cockerels. "They're a nice bunch. I hope they'll find a good home."

"Are you volunteering?" I asked with a grin. "I don't see your sister taking kindly to a bunch of smelly birds as housemates." Aido's twin sister and I didn't see eye to eye at the best of times. If he showed up at home with a cage full of live animals, she'd probably blame me.

His headshake was vehement. "No way. Naido doesn't do birds."

As far as I could tell, Naido didn't do people.

Lou glanced at her watch. "We'd better make a move. I can't avoid DI Bradley indefinitely."

"I'll help you get the cage into the car," Aido said, reaching for the handle.

"Thanks. I'll catch up with you in a moment." When Aido was out of earshot, Lou turned to me. "I'll need to check with everyone who went near the crime scene yesterday, including your grandmother and her friend. I didn't bring it up just now because I didn't want Eda bellowing about the missing gun in front of a crowd."

I laughed. "Wise move. Nana's going to the dress rehearsal of Cian's play later. You can catch her there."

"Thanks. I'll do that."

Lou ran after Aido and they loaded the cage into the squad car. In the meantime, Eoin handcuffed Seamie and dragged him over to the car to join his erstwhile contestants. Eoin shoved Seamie onto the backseat and shut the door. "No amount of air freshener will get the smell out of the car," he muttered, pinching his nose.

Lou patted him on the back. "I'll take the car to the garage this evening and get it properly cleaned."

"Will Seamie be charged this time?" I asked. "You can't let him keep putting birds in danger."

"Given that we caught him bird-handed," Lou replied with a sardonic drawl, "he'll definitely face a judge over today's fight. I doubt we'll persuade him to give up all his dubious methods of earning money, but I'll do my best to dissuade him from animal abuse."

A moment later, the police car tore a path through the mud, leaving Aido and me to contemplate our situation. I examined his punk T-shirt and ripped jeans, both liberally decorated with dirt. "I hope you have a change of clothes back at the office. Or will we need to make a detour to your place on our way to the castle?"

"I was planning on hitting the gym after work. My sports bag is under my desk. I can clean up in the bathroom." He nodded at my mustard yellow pants and biker jacket, both covered in mud. "You're lucky you wore those."

"Yeah, but I don't want to see the state of my face. I can still taste mud in my mouth."

"You'll get it off quick enough in a sink."

We headed for my bike. While Aido was putting on my spare helmet, I reached into my coat pocket for my phone and came up empty. I swore beneath my breath. "My phone's missing. I must've dropped it when I fell."

"Are you sure?" His voice beneath the helmet was muffled.

"I'm certain. I was holding it when I was pushed." I sighed. "I can't believe I didn't think of it sooner. I'll have to go back to the pit. It probably fell in when I did."

"I don't remember seeing a phone lying on the ground," my friend said, removing the helmet, "but I was preoccupied trying to get to you and avoid the birds."

We retraced our steps back to the pit, keeping our eyes on the ground and dodging exiting spectators. Now that the excitement of the fight, my tumble, and the police chase was over, the crowd was dispersing. The area where I'd been standing when I'd fallen was deserted. I surveyed the mud-trampled grass. "I don't see the phone anywhere. It would've landed either here or in the pit."

Aido leaned over the edge. "No sign of it in the pit, but I'll climb in to be sure."

"No, let me go. My outfit is more mudproof than yours." I clambered down the ladder and hit the ground of the pit for the second time that day, this time with a lot less impact. At first glance, the phone was nowhere in evidence, but the surface of the pit was uneven. It might be under a mound of dirt. "See if you can find me a shovel, Aido."

"Will do." He disappeared from view and reappeared a few minutes later, carrying two shovels.

He slid into the pit to join me. "I'm already filthy. More mud won't make much difference."

For the next ten minutes, we thoroughly searched the pit, uncovering feathers, bird poop, and a few unidentifiable objects. There was no sign of my phone.

"This makes no sense," I said. "My phone's not the oldest model on the market, but it's by no means the newest. Who'd want to nick it?"

"Some people are light-fingered. They'll take anything. And maybe it wasn't stolen. Perhaps someone in the crowd found it and mistook it for theirs. With a bit of luck, they'll soon notice their mistake and give it to Seamie. Or even hand it in at the police station."

I stared gloomily at the mound of dirt I'd just unearthed. "I've got to hope. I can't afford to replace it."

We climbed out of the pit and returned the shovels to the shed where Aido had found them. Back at Mavis, Aido checked his watch. "Cian will be having kittens by now."

I grimaced. "Sorry to make you late."

"Not your fault. Look, it's almost time for my lunch break. Why don't you drop me at my place and I'll meet you at the castle later?" He indicated his dirt-streaked arms. "At this stage, we both need a shower."

"Sounds like a plan." I threw my leg over the bike, and Aido perched behind me.

"Say, Dee," he said before I started the engine.

"Were you serious about someone shoving you into the pit?"

I hesitated before answering. Was I sure? The longer ago it had happened, the more absurd the idea seemed. "I didn't slip," I said finally. "I'm sure someone pushed me, but I don't understand why."

"Might've been someone having a laugh, or someone who wanted a better view of the fight. Seamie's fights attract a lot of louts. They probably didn't mean for you to fall."

"Maybe." I wasn't convinced.

I started the engine, and we took off down the rough track that led to the road. During the ride back into town, the noise of the engine and the rushing wind precluded conversation and gave me time to think. Someone *had* pushed me. I hadn't imagined a hand exerting pressure on my back. If the shove had been meant as a joke, surely they'd have pushed me to the side rather than forward. I'd been standing right on the edge. With that shove between the shoulder blades, they'd have known I'd fall into the pit.

And that brought me to the question of *who*. A random thug with a grudge against women? Had my attempts to take photos blocked another spectator's view? Or had someone objected to me taking pictures in the first place?

I sucked in a breath. *The pictures...* Had I been pushed so I'd stop taking photos of the crowd? Or had someone wanted to look at the photos I'd taken of the injured man's personal effects? I overtook a tractor that was moving at a snail's pace and turned these questions over in my mind. Neither option made sense. While the crowd around the pit had been a more varied bunch than I'd anticipated, I couldn't see any of them having such a strong aversion to being photographed at the event that they'd attack me and steal my phone. As for the photos of the injured man's belongings, only Lou knew I still had access to those pictures. If she'd wanted me to delete them from my backup storage system, she'd have made me do it while we'd been in her car.

Yesterday's events were making me paranoid. People dropped their phones all the time, right? And these days, just about everyone used a cloud storage system to back up their files. Anyone wanting to delete my photos should know that stealing my phone wouldn't erase all trace of the pictures. Even if someone had pushed me—and I was convinced someone had—maybe they'd wanted a better view of the fight. My taking a tumble probably hadn't been their intention, but if they'd been drinking, maybe they didn't care.

In spite of my best efforts to seek logical explanations for what had happened, I couldn't shake the cold fear at the pit of my stomach. My eyewitness report had appeared in today's issue of the *Dunleagh Chronicle*. If anyone in town hadn't already known I'd been in the castle courtyard at the time of the shootings, they did now. Had the gunmen been present at Seamie's cockfight? If so, did they think I'd lied in my report about not seeing them? And if they thought I had seen them, to what lengths would they go to keep me silent?

TEN

In the end, I dropped Aido off at the castle, where he intended to throw himself at Richard's mercy and ask to shower at his apartment. Meanwhile, I zoomed back to Nana's house to wash and change my clothes. My mother was conspicuously absent, and my grandmother hadn't yet returned from Seamie's farm. The house was still empty by the time I was clean and ready to leave. For a brief moment, I considered staying at home and crawling back under my covers, but the lure of the extra money motivated me out the door and onto Mavis.

When I jogged over the drawbridge twenty minutes later, a blond TV reporter I recognized from an Irish news channel posed by the crime scene tape. She spoke into a massive microphone, while her film crew captured the scene. I expected the mayor to materialize at any second and throw himself in front of the camera.

Inside the castle, Mary Yates sat behind the reception desk. Mary was a woman for whom the term "mousy" might've been invented, both in terms of her appearance and her personality. Her age could have been anywhere between late thirties and fifty, and her thin features and dishwater-blond hair didn't allow for a more specific estimate. She was gentle and kind but not great at standing up for herself, as I'd witnessed more than once at meetings of the Historical Murders Club.

Mary glanced up when she heard the door click shut behind me, and a look of concern creased her wan face. "Hello, Dee. How are you?"

I didn't pretend not to know she was referring to yesterday's drama. "Much better, thanks."

"The Guards are crawling all over the castle." She shivered and pulled her voluminous cardigan tight around her slight frame.

They were hard to miss. When I'd crossed the drawbridge and walked through the gate tower, I'd deliberately avoided looking in the direction of the Green Archway. In spite of my best efforts to block yesterday's events from my mind, it was impossible to oversee the police presence, both uniformed and plain-clothed.

"Are you standing in for Larry?" I asked, happy to deflect Mary's attention from the shootings.

"Yes. He's bruised after yesterday, and his wife insisted he go to the doctor. I need to talk to Richard about the exhibition we're co-hosting, so it wasn't a problem for me to come by the castle for a couple of hours." An awkward silence descended. Mary fiddled with her fingernails, which were bitten to the quick. "I hope my husband wasn't too unpleasant to you. He's under a lot of pressure at work, and he's taken on too many extra commitments. He has a role in your editor's play, you know. When he's stressed, Charles can be...abrupt."

"Abrupt" wasn't the term I'd use to describe Dr. Moriarty, nor could I imagine any role in Cian's play that would suit his dour personality. I forced a reassuring smile. "It's fine. He probably had an awkward exchange with the Guards after I left."

"He mentioned they weren't pleased about an unlocked storage room."

She didn't elaborate, but her expression spoke volumes. So Mary was another person who knew about the missing evidence bag.

"Will I see you at tomorrow's meeting?" As Mary never missed a meeting of the Historical Murders Club, I posed the question to steer the conversation away from the shootings and into more pleasant territory.

Relief flooded her face. "Yes. I'm looking forward to it. It'll be fun to meet for breakfast instead of in the evening."

The club attracted a diverse demographic of history fans and true crime buffs. We met once a month in the castle's Great Hall to discuss long-forgotten murders, and I'd managed to recruit several members as regular contributors to my history blog. The club typically met once a month on a Friday evening, but Cian's play had forced us to make changes to our schedule and venue. The dress rehearsal for *A Fighting Man* would occur in the Great Hall, our usual meeting place. And with so many club members involved with the play, it made sense to change the date and time.

"I love having our discussions here in the castle, but I agree that a change will be nice." I lowered my voice to a conspiratorial whisper. "I'm also relieved that the suggestion to hold the meeting in the castle café was rejected. The Coffee Bean is a million times better."

Mary laughed and held up a takeaway coffee cup bearing The Coffee Bean's logo. "I agree. See you tomorrow."

I headed for the stairs, relieved to make my escape. I liked Mary but I needed time to think before I reached the North Tower and the staff of the *Chronicle*. I'd given Lou my word that I'd keep silent about the missing evidence bag until she gave me the go ahead. It was a promise I regretted making. If Dr. Moriarty had told Mary the evidence bag was missing, presumed stolen, the other doctors had probably divulged the information to their family members. In other words, it was entirely likely that half of Dunleagh knew by now. The *Chronicle* had the exclusive on the RIC uniform, another fact we'd agreed not to publish immediately, but the missing evidence was the real news. If another news outlet scooped the story before we'd had a chance to publish it, Cian would be livid.

I reached the entrance to the North Tower and climbed the steep winding staircase that led to the *Chronicle*. In contrast to yesterday's buzz of activity, the newsroom was empty, except for a freshly washed Aido. The door to our editor's office was closed, but raised muffled voices were audible through the wood.

I shrugged off my jacket and plunked myself onto my chair. "I need to grab a fresh notebook and pen and I'm out of here."

"You working in the archives today?"

"Yeah."

Aido wrinkled his nose in distaste. "Rather you than me. The dungeons give me the creeps."

"I rather like the quiet." I nodded toward our editor's closed door, through which the argument I'd overheard earlier had developed into a shouting match. "Speaking of quiet, or lack thereof, is Cian still talking to the mayor?"

Before Aido had a chance to answer, the door to the newsroom swung open, and a red-faced Marcus staggered in and collapsed at his desk. "I need to get fit. Those stairs are killing me."

"Eoin Duffy and Seamie Dean are doing some fitness class at the community center," I said, deadpan. "Maybe you can join them."

Marcus gave a crack of laughter. "Now that's a name combination I never expected to hear in any context that didn't involve Seamie breaking the law and Eoin upholding it."

"I didn't expect to see you here today," Aido remarked. "I thought you were at court all day."

"That was the plan. One of the lawyers in the case I was following had a medical emergency, and we were all sent home." Marcus tugged at his shirt collar, popping open the top two buttons. "Who's Cian yelling at?"

"Dee just asked the same question when you walked in." Aido grinned. "He's interviewing the mayor. I guess it isn't going well."

At that moment, our editor stomped out of his office, his freckled cheeks stained red and his green eyes blazing. Cian was a gangly forty-something with a penchant for baggy jeans and vintage rock T-shirts. Today's T-shirt, a homage to AC/DC, sported a rip across the abdomen. Cian either hadn't noticed or didn't care.

A second man stepped out of the office, a suave and controlled foil to our editor's informality. I took in the slicked-back hair, sculpted features, and designer suit of our mayor and wrinkled my nose. Henry Hyland stood for everything I loathed. In the few months since he'd taken office, he'd slashed funding to almost all of Dunleagh's cultural institutions. His smug satisfaction next to Cian's palpable anger didn't bode well.

Oozing self-satisfaction, Hyland bestowed a benevolent nod upon the newsroom, avoiding eye contact with either Aido or me, and turned back to our editor. "Once you've had a chance to calm down, I'm sure you'll realize this is the best solution."

Cian's face went from red to purple. He tugged on the end of his ginger ponytail, a sure sign he was stressed. "The best solution for whom? For you and your property developer cronies?"

The mayor shook his head as if admonishing a small child. "You're letting a sentimental attachment cloud your judgment. What difference does it make if you run the paper from the castle or another building? Isn't it the end product that counts?"

I sucked in a breath. Was the mayor planning to extend his castle renovations to the North Tower? Surely he wouldn't gut the interior of the entire castle?

"Of course it makes a difference where I run the paper," Cian spluttered. "The *Dunleagh Chronicle* has been part of the castle since its first issue. You want to erase one hundred fifty years of history and downsize us at the same time."

Downsize? An arctic freeze crept over my limbs. As the most junior employee, I'd be the first for the chop.

I met Aido's panicked eyes. Judging by the

horrified expression on my coworker's face, I wasn't the only one worried about losing my job. The paper paid us a pittance, but we couldn't afford to lose our paychecks. For different reasons, we both needed work that was close to home.

The mayor's smug smile stretched across his complacent face. "I never mentioned downsizing. That's merely your interpretation. You should save the drama for your plays."

"I'm not a politician," Cian snapped. "I call a spade a spade. The *Chronicle* is run on a shoestring budget. If you evict us, we won't be able to afford to rent a space as large as this. Covering the rent for whatever hovel I can afford will force me to reduce my staff's hours."

Henry Hyland flicked an invisible piece of lint from the lapel of his impeccable suit jacket. "The town council should never have permitted the *Chronicle* to set up shop in the castle rent-free, and the situation certainly shouldn't have been allowed to continue into this century. In these times of austerity, it simply isn't sustainable."

"We pay rent," Cian said through gritted teeth, "and we've done so for decades."

"A rent so low it barely covers your utilities," Hyland countered in a mild tone. "The rest is covered by the town's taxpayers."

"That's the whole point of the *Chronicle*," Cian insisted. "A paper for the people, by the people, and owned by the people. Housing the paper within the castle ensures Dunleagh has proper news coverage, even in troubled times. We've provided affordable news through two world wars, rebellions, and the Irish War of Independence."

"I'm not disputing the *Chronicle*'s contribution to Dunleagh's history," Hyland said, "but times have changed. As mayor, it's my responsibility to ensure that the town remains solvent. The renovation project will bring in millions."

My jaw tightened. "How many of those millions will end up in your pockets?" I demanded. "The proposed renovation plans were put forward by your brother-in-law's company, were they not?"

For the first time since our encounter at Seamie Dean's farm, Henry Hyland's eyes met mine. While his smile didn't falter, his steely gaze betrayed his annoyance at my interruption. "That's a nasty accusation, Ms. Flanagan. There are laws against slander."

"There are also laws against nepotism." I folded my arms across my chest and stared him down. "Are you denying that Kylemore Properties belongs to your wife's brother?"

An angry flush crept over the mayor's spray-tanned cheekbones. "The town council received proposals from various developers, and his happened to be the best."

I rolled my eyes. "The council is stuffed with your

business pals. No one else in Dunleagh wants the castle turned into an apartment complex."

"I certainly don't," Aido added. "The apartments will wreck the castle."

"Turfing us out to make room for fancy weekend apartments isn't the answer to Dunleagh's financial problems," Marcus said, glowering at the mayor.

"I didn't know you were an expert on town planning and finances, Mr. Wren." Henry Hyland's tone held a hint of acid. "I thought you specialized in writing articles that got you sued."

This swipe at Marcus's recent legal defeat over a story he'd written about corruption in a neighboring town brought a flush to the subeditor's cheeks. "Every word I wrote was true," he blustered. "And there's more I could've written but held back."

"Indeed?" Hyland's voice dripped sarcasm. "I don't suppose you've turned your efforts to anonymous letters? I've received a few recently. I wondered if you were behind them."

"Absolutely not." Marcus's bald head turned pink to match his cheeks. "I'm a journalist. I write exposés for a living. Why would I hide behind anonymous letters?"

"For fear of being sued again?" Hyland pointedly turned his back on Marcus and addressed the rest of us. "I'd appreciate the cooperation of the *Chronicle* as we introduce these changes. In spite of what your editor says, I don't want to see the paper close. However, the town needs money, and the castle needs repairs. The apartment project will give us a much-needed influx of cash and help us attract a certain caliber of resident."

Unlike many townspeople, I wasn't opposed to new blood in Dunleagh, but the mayor's blatant snobbery rubbed me the wrong way. "As opposed to the people who've lived here for generations?" I inquired, arching an eyebrow.

Hyland smirked. "Listening to your accent, no one has any doubt which of us *isn't* from Dunleagh."

My mid-Atlantic accent was the product of a childhood split between my Irish mother and my American father, and it confused people on both sides of the pond. I was proud of my heritage and I wasn't prepared to let a cocky politician use it against me. "Only the Irish think I sound American," I said, not missing a beat. "Not sure how I'd describe your accent, though. Posh boarding school, perhaps? I'd say neither of us has an accent typical for Dunleagh."

"Unlike you, I grew up in this town. No one is more loyal to Dunleagh and the people who live here. All I want is to attract the right sort of newcomer."

"Can I quote you on that?" I asked in a saccharine tone.

Hyland eyed me with blatant distaste. "If you'd like to feature a piece on the new apartments, I'd be happy to arrange an interview for you with Mr. Kylemore."

"You do that. I'd love to hear what your B-I-L has to say about where the profits for the venture will go."

A muscle in the mayor's cheek flexed, and his hands tightened around his briefcase. "I don't like your attitude."

"I'm not too fond of yours," I shot back.

"Need I remind you that your mother's woo-woo shop is in a building I own? I'm surprised you'd seek a fight with her landlord."

"Bliss and her woo-woo business pay you rent."

The man's tiger-like smile made my skin crawl. "Is that what she tells you? Naughty Bliss."

Was he implying my mother didn't pay rent? Or was he simply trying to provoke me? Frankly, either scenario was plausible, but I had zero desire to prolong this little interlude.

"Are you threatening to evict Bliss unless I play nice?" I tapped my chin. "Now that would make an excellent front-page exposé."

"Go ahead and print your exposé. Your grandmother's 'medicinal teas'—" he made air quotes, "—have addled your mind. Who's going to believe anything you write? You come from a family of certifiable nutcases."

I didn't disagree with his skepticism. Their mystical beliefs had caused me to roll my eyes many times over the years. However, I wasn't about to let a slick son of a gun insult my family. "They're entitled to their beliefs. Your threats and efforts to distract me make me wonder what you're hiding. Care to share, Mr. Mayor?"

Henry Hyland gave Cian a withering look. "If Ms. Flanagan is an example of your staff's professionalism, you should embrace the opportunity to downsize." With this parting shot, the mayor swept out of the newsroom.

After the door had slammed behind him, I cocked a hand to my ear. "I hear cloven hooves clipping down the hallway. Do you think we should get the joint exorcised?"

Cian leaned against an empty desk and scowled. "What we need is to get rid of him. The question is, how?"

"Bar unearthing a major scandal, I don't see it happening," Marcus said morosely. "How can you bear to have that man involved with your play? If it were me, I'd refuse to have anything to do with him outside of work."

Our editor's taciturn expression darkened. "Hyland didn't give me a choice. The instant I put out a call for auditions, he waltzed into my office and demanded a role, making it clear he'd deny me the use of the Great Hall if I refused. There's nowhere else I can afford to hire."

In addition to providing a spectacular atmosphere, the castle's Great Hall featured an original dais, or medieval raised platform, that was ideal for a stage. The council allowed the hall to be used for select gatherings for a nominal fee. Unfortunately for Cian, the ultimate decision as to who was allowed to hire the Great Hall lay in the mayor's purview.

I scrunched up my forehead. "Why does Hyland want to be in the play? I'd have thought a role in an amateur production would be beneath his dignity."

"He fancies himself an *actor*." Aido lay sarcastic emphasis on the word. "I remember him starring in a musical years ago, way before he became mayor."

Cian nodded. "True. There's also the mounting criticism over his decision to slash funds for cultural projects and institutions. Hyland thinks people will see him as a fan of the arts if he appears in my play."

"The man's a pompous idiot," Marcus muttered, "and a corrupt one. I'd bet my salary on it."

"I agree, but we need proof," I said. "How'd he get elected in the first place? The dude's more concerned with his next tanning session than anything related to Dunleagh's history and culture."

Cian's smile was wry. "Friends in high places, and promises he had no intention of fulfilling."

"That's what got him into office," Aido mused, "but it won't keep him there."

"I wouldn't be so sure about that." Cian beat a restless rhythm on the desk. "Hyland will keep the promises he made to his wealthy business associates if not to the rest of the town, and they wield influence over voters."

"Even if he doesn't get reelected, he'll have made

bank during his tenure." I frowned at my computer screen. "I'm going to take him up on the offer to interview James Kylemore. I doubt the interview will yield any useful info, but it'll rattle Hyland's cage."

"It's worth a try," Cian said. "I'm not prepared to sit back and let Henry Hyland bulldoze this paper's legacy."

"So what's the immediate plan?" I asked, looking around the room. "This week's issue is already published."

A sly smirk crept over our editor's face. "Yes, but we can do a special edition for our digital subscribers and add the highlights to our website. With the murder literally on our doorstep, it makes sense for us to write a few extra articles in any case."

The news of the missing evidence bag was on the tip of my tongue. I resisted the urge to blurt it all out. I'd given Lou my word, however much I regretted doing so.

"Extra articles?" Aido's alarmed expression matched my feelings exactly. "I don't know that I have time to write many extra words this week," he said. "My schedule's crazy."

"Same," I added. "I'm way behind on the digitalization project."

Cian flicked a hand in a dismissive gesture. "Forget the archives. If we don't act fast to get the support of the town, Hyland will crush us."

Aido opened his mouth as if to protest but caught

my warning glance. I wasn't thrilled about adding more work to my already insane schedule, but I was even less enthusiastic about losing my job. Whatever it took to keep the paper at the castle, we had to cooperate.

"Okay," I said to our editor. "What do you need me to do?"

"You could swing by the library this afternoon and cover a story for me." Cian dangled a carrot he knew I couldn't resist. "I'll let you use the good camera."

Marcus made a squawk of protest but held his tongue after a quelling glance from Cian. The "good camera" was the *Chronicle*'s only camera, and reserved for the senior members of staff. As the juniors of the team, Aido and I were expected to make do with our phones, much to my chagrin.

"Am I still on time and a half?"

A smile fractured my editor's grave demeanor. "You'll bleed me dry, Dee. All right. Same deal as this morning. Enjoy it while it lasts. If Hyland gets his way, it won't."

I leaped to my feet and grabbed my jacket. "What do you need me to do?"

"A task that's right up your alley," Cian said. "You know the library and the museum are co-hosting an exhibition of old photographs, right?"

"The ones from the War of Independence?" I nodded. "I helped Richard curate the photos."

"The exhibition won't formally open until Sunday, but it's already good to go. I'd like you to swing by the library and take a few pictures, including one featuring Mary Yates and Richard if I can persuade them to be there to meet you."

A slow smile spread across my face. "Mary's here at the castle. She's filling in for Larry for a couple of hours."

Cian nodded. "Excellent. On your way out, you can ask her about the story in person. I can't imagine she'll refuse."

This was true. Recent budget cuts to the library had put Mary's position under threat, and Richard was expecting to hear similar news about the museum's funding.

"They'll definitely say yes," I said, pulling on my jacket. "They won't pass up the chance to get advance publicity. Both the library and the museum need this exhibition to be a success."

I made a mental note to ask Richard about the injured man's uniform and trench watch. I hadn't seen the museum director since I'd taken a peek at the stranger's belongings, and I was keen to know if he'd had a chance to compare the cartridge with examples at the museum.

Cian retrieved the camera from Marcus's desk, ignoring the subeditor's resentful glare at the confiscation of what he felt to be his property. "Get Richard and Mary to say a few words to emphasize the importance of preserving Dunleagh's history," Cian said when he handed me the camera, "and mention the budget cuts when you write the article."

"So I'm not just snapping a photo?" I asked teasingly. "Time and a half for the writing, too?"

"If you get it done before the dress rehearsal, yes."

"Okey-dokey." I handled the camera gingerly and hung its case around my neck. A mammoth electricity bill had forced me to sell my beloved digital camera last month, and I'd been itching to get my hands on this one. "I'm not sure when Richard and Mary will have time to talk to me. Depending on when, I could swing by the hospital for an update on the patient." If I wasn't working in the archives today, I might as well put my afternoon to good use.

Cian inclined his head. "Sounds good. See you later, Dee."

"Bye, all." With a mock bow, I waved to my coworkers and headed out into the dimly lit corridor.

ELEVEN

As I'd expected, Mary and Richard were happy to agree to an interview and photographs. We arranged to meet at the library at three o'clock, which gave them time to have their meeting and me a chance to stop at the hospital and check up on Mr. No-Name. On my way through the courtyard, I spotted DI Bradley talking to the mayor. Despite the lack of rain, I pulled up my hood and increased my pace. The surly Dublin detective was the last person I wanted to meet, especially since I was on my way to finagle an interview with one of the victims in his case.

I made it out of the castle without being waylaid by cops, shooters, or anyone else I didn't care to encounter. After a brief visit to Dunleagh Garda Station to report my phone missing, I arrived at the hospital. Like yesterday, the parking lot was full, and I had to wait for a free space. I wrinkled my nose at the stench of exhaust fumes—a significant disadvantage to traveling via my Vespa instead of a car.

Once I'd parked Mavis, the clock was ticking for my appointment at the library. I jogged across the hospital grounds, dodging people and vehicles. In front of the main entrance, a steady stream of cars and taxis offloaded their passengers. An ambulance roared by me and into the ambulance bay, siren wailing. I swung my backpack over one shoulder and strode through the sliding doors.

Inside the hospital, a line of people waited at the reception desk. I bypassed them and headed left, taking the stairs up to the wards. I didn't know where to find the man I was here to see. My best bet was to try the ward River's friend worked on and throw myself at her mercy. As well as being my sister's best friend, Suzie Quinn was a fellow member of the Historical Murders Club, and I was pretty confident she'd help— if she was on duty.

When I reached the second floor, I turned left and entered St. Patrick's Ward. I peered through the glass at the nurses' station and couldn't resist a fist pump. For what felt like the first time that week, luck was on my side. Her back was turned to me, but Suzie's distinctive auburn hair was visible. I knocked on the door, and she spun around, eyes widening in surprise when she recognized me.

She said something to the other women in the

room, put down the mug she was holding, and opened the door. "Hi, Dee. What are you doing here?"

"Hey, Suzie. Sorry to bother you at work. I'm here to see the man brought in after yesterday's shootings, but I don't know which ward he's on."

Understanding flooded Suzie's pretty face, and she laughed. "Ah-ha. You want to score an interview."

"Of course I do." I glanced around me and lowered my voice. "Preferably without the cops knowing."

"Good luck with that." Suzie tilted her head to one side. "There's a guard outside his room."

Ugh. Of course there was. Why hadn't I considered that possibility? "I don't suppose you want to sweet-talk the guard while I sneak past?"

Suzie gave a bark of laughter. "No chance. I shouldn't even be talking to you now. We're all on strict instructions not to talk to the press."

"I might be here in a private capacity," I countered playfully, "seeing as I rescued him."

Her eyes crinkled. "Nice try, Dee."

"Can you at least tell me where to find him? I can handle the guard myself." This last part was delivered with a bravado I didn't feel, but I'd spent most of my life chancing my arm, as the Irish said, and it often paid off.

Suzie grinned and lowered her voice to a whisper. "I absolutely didn't tell you he's in Room 303 on St. Colmcille's Ward."

I gave her a thumbs-up. "You're a star. Thank you."

"Will you be at the next club meeting?" she asked. "I've been reading up on the Eyre Square murder, but unfortunately, I have to work tomorrow morning."

"I'll be there, although I wish we'd picked a case that wasn't as cut and dried." The case, which concerned a jilted lover who'd murdered his former fiancée at the Royal Hotel on Galway's famous Eyre Square in 1884, didn't appeal to me as material for the Historical Murders Club. I preferred to discuss cases that had never been solved, or ones where the convicted killer's guilt was in question. In this instance, I'd been overruled.

"I found it interesting to research, but I agree with you. There's not a lot of fodder for debate." Suzie glanced over her shoulder. Through the glass of the nurses' station, an older woman tapped her watch. "Sorry, but I have to get back to our meeting. Good luck with your story."

"Thanks. See you soon."

After I left St. Patrick's, I climbed the stairs up to the next floor. I didn't need to check the room numbers to know which was the one I sought. On St. Colmcille's Ward, a stocky man in a police uniform sat in front of a room, reading a newspaper. It was Sean O'Connor, one of Dunleagh Garda Station's junior officers, nicknamed Ken Doll after Barbie's boyfriend. He had the muscular build, square jaw, and swept-back brown hair to match the nickname. We'd been on a date a few months ago, but neither of us had felt the need for a repeat. Still, Sean wasn't the worst person to run into. Although he took his duties extremely seriously, he wasn't the quickest of cats. I should be able to persuade him to slip up and give me information he shouldn't divulge to the press. Whistling cheerfully, I pushed the door open and stepped onto the ward.

My optimism faded a second later. A beautiful dark-haired nurse swept out of the nurses' station. Zosia Kaminski, Lev's sister, was not my favorite person. The feeling was mutual. Although I'd never done anything to her, she regarded me as a figure of fun and never missed an opportunity to take a swipe at me. For some inexplicable reason, she and my sister were close, and I suspected Zosia regarded my move to Dunleagh as competition for River's attention.

Zosia sashayed over to Sean, her slim hips swaying. "Can I offer you a coffee, Sean?"

The young police officer dropped his newspaper onto his lap and stared up at Zosia, clearly dazzled. "An espresso would be great, thanks."

"I'll get right on it." Zosia turned to leave but paused when she caught sight of me. "Well, if it isn't Dunleagh's trusty girl reporter. Rather late off the mark, aren't you? The nationals were here this morning."

I ignored Zosia and focused on Sean. "Hey, there. Long time no see."

Sean glanced my way, and a pained expression

crossed his face. "Before you ask, the answer is no. DI Bradley forbade us to talk to the media."

I disregarded Sean's obvious reluctance to chat and dropped onto the seat beside him. "If you're offering coffee, Zosia, I take mine black with no sugar."

Her lip curled. "Nice try, Dee. The offer was solely for Garda O'Connor."

I treated her to a sweet smile. "In that case, you'd better skedaddle and make it for him, hadn't you?"

Zosia's eyes narrowed at me. "I'll be right back, Sean."

The nurse stalked down the corridor and I turned to the police officer. "How's it going with Bradley at the helm? Are you hoping he'll put in a good word for you with your superiors?"

"How did you—?" Sean flushed and fell silent.

"Only natural you'd want to impress the Dublin detectives. Dunleagh's a small place."

Still embarrassed, Sean gave a stiff nod. "Yeah. I'd like a shot at becoming a detective."

I couldn't blame him for not wanting his career to begin and end in Dunleagh, but his ambition might make it difficult for me to cajole him into giving me information. "Thanks to your presence, I know three things about the patient."

He sighed. "If this is a trick to get me to tell you stuff..."

"First off," I continued, "the man's still alive. There'd be no need for a guard if he were in the morgue. Second, he's recovering well from the surgery. If he weren't, he'd be in intensive care. And third, DI Bradley doesn't think the man is in serious danger from a further attack. If he did, he'd have assigned a police officer with a firearms license, not a regular Guard like you."

Sean attempted his best poker face. He'd never survive a game against Nana and her regular cohort, Big Jim.

"Any news on his name?" I probed, watching him for tells. "Okay, I'll take that as a no."

"But I didn't say anything," he spluttered.

"You didn't have to," I said smoothly, gearing up for my next attack. "Is he awake? Okay, also a no."

Sean squirmed under my scrutiny. "Please, Dee. DI Bradley sent me a message a couple of minutes ago. He's at the hospital and he's on his way up. You'd better scram."

Looked like my stream of good luck was about to run dry. The detective must have left the castle soon after me. I leaped to my feet and tried to peer through the glass partition in the hospital room door, but the frosted glass didn't reveal much. "Can you at least tell me if the guy's expected to recover? I helped him, you know. This isn't just a news story for me."

"Yeah, I heard you were there." He sighed and scratched the back of his neck. "If I tell you, will you leave? I don't want DI Bradley to think I was feeding you sensitive information."

"Of course," I said soothingly. "Just that one piece of info, and I'll be out of your hair."

Sean winced as though the effort of revealing anything to me caused him physical pain. "He's doing well from what I understand, but I can't get more specific."

If I'd had more time, and any hint that Sean knew more than he was saying, I'd have treated him to a brute force attack, Dee-style. Still, I'd squeezed more out of the earnest young cop than I'd anticipated. I'd have to be satisfied with it—for now.

The door to the ward swung open, and DI Bradley strode in. He stopped short when he saw me, his eyes narrowing in suspicion. "We meet again, Ms. Flanagan. Engaging in more amateur sleuthing?"

"I'm a reporter," I countered. "Investigating is my job."

"Who told you the patient was here?" he demanded, shooting an accusatory glare at Sean.

The younger man shrank inside his police uniform. "Not me, sir."

"Having a guard seated outside the door rather gave it away," I replied in a bored tone. "Do you have any news on the man's identity?"

The detective's jaw set in a hard line. "You'll be informed when we see fit to provide the public with that information."

"In other words, you haven't a clue." I shifted my backpack to my other shoulder. "Fair enough. I'll be back, though. The people of this town deserve to be kept up to date on the murder investigation. Many townsfolk are afraid to leave their homes in case a gang of killers is roaming the streets."

DI Bradley ran a hand over his perfectly styled hair. For the first time since I'd met him, I noticed the dark circles under his eyes. "That's what we aim to rule out, Ms. Flanagan. Just let us do our job and don't stir up scaremongering rumors with your newspaper."

I bristled at this accusation. "The *Chronicle* isn't a tabloid paper. We don't embellish stories to increase our sales, or spread unfounded rumors." Frankly, if we did, our finances might be rosier, but I left this part unsaid. "We're a serious news outlet, and we've covered news in Dunleagh diligently for one hundred fifty years."

The detective sighed. "I'm not disputing your paper's age or reputation. We'll hold a press conference this evening. If I have anything to say to you, you'll hear it then."

Along with myriad reporters from the nationals. What I needed was an exclusive, but I wasn't about to get one from DI Bradley. While I was dogged when it came to following up a lead, I also recognized the need for a temporary retreat.

I nodded to Garda O'Connor. "Bye, Sean. See you, Detective."

Resisting the urge to accidentally-on-purpose open

the patient's door and take a peek inside, I forced my feet into motion and exited the ward.

————

Unlike my impromptu visit to the hospital, the interview at the library went according to plan. The library was located in an elegant old building, set back from Dunleagh's main thoroughfare and surrounded by its own gardens. The building had once been a private residence belonging to the British military commander who'd been in charge of the castle during the nineteenth and early twentieth century. In the 1950s, it'd been repurposed as the town's library and now housed thousands of books.

The exhibition on Dunleagh's role in the Irish War of Independence was situated in what had once been the morning room. Mary and Richard had done an excellent job creating a feel for the period without bogging it down with details that would bore the average visitor, and they were delighted to share their enthusiasm for the time period with readers of the *Chronicle*.

Both keen historians, Richard and Mary had pooled their knowledge and resources to put together a unique exhibition featuring museum artifacts, old letters, newspaper clippings, and photographs. They'd carefully selected material that showed how the war was an escalation of tensions that had grown during the

Irish revolutionary period, the most notable event of which was the 1916 Easter Rising.

I'd played a minor role in preparing the exhibition by sorting photographs and through my research in the castle archives, most particularly the back issues of the *Chronicle*, and it was lovely to see the finished product.

I finished the interview by taking a few pictures of the organizers. "Thanks, guys. That was fantastic."

"No, thank you," Richard said. "You've been a great help in getting the exhibition up and running, and we appreciate the press coverage."

"My editor's sudden enthusiasm to give the exhibition front-page billing is entirely thanks to the mayor. Cian is raging over the threats to the newspaper. He's more than happy to provide coverage to anyone or anything threatened by Hyland's plans."

A pained expression crossed Mary's face. "That man has no appreciation for history or culture. He's already slashed the library's funding, and we were on a shoestring budget beforehand. I'm either going to have to take a salary cut or look for another job."

"I'm so sorry, Mary. That's awful."

"The way things are looking, I'll be joining Mary on the job hunt before too long." Richard ran a hand through his curls and pulled an envelope out of the breast pocket of his jacket with the other. "This arrived today."

I took the envelope and withdrew the letter. I scanned the page and let out a slow hiss. "He's evicting you? This is insane," I stammered. "And how does he expect the museum to fit into one small room? What's he planning to do with the other two rooms? More apartments?"

Richard sighed. "Who knows? It's not as if I'm overly attached to my apartment, but it came as part of the job. Without it, and with no salary increase to compensate for the rent I'll have to pay on another place, I can't afford to remain at the museum. Apart from my living arrangements, who's going to pay to see a one-room museum? We rely on ticket sales to keep afloat."

I bit my cheek to stop myself from screaming. "Hyland's out of control."

"Yes, but what can we do to stop him?" Mary asked, fiddling with her hands. "Not everyone in Dunleagh cares about the library or the museum. They'll be fine with the idea of the town making money with luxury rental properties."

My chest swelled with anger. "We have to make the townsfolk care. If they're indifferent to the loss of historical and cultural institutions, we need to focus on money. I can't imagine Hyland's not making a profit on all this wheeling and dealing. If we can prove he's corrupt, then the majority of the town won't stand behind him."

"The man's canny," Richard pointed out. "Proving his dealings are nefarious won't be easy."

"He's smart, yes, but he's also arrogant. He won't

expect anyone to uncover evidence to prove he's taking a slice of the money that's flowing into the town coffers. I have no proof at the moment, but my gut tells me he's on the make."

Mary nodded. "That's my feeling, too. If there's anything we can do to help, let us know."

"Just keep your eyes and ears open. If something is going on, someone must know." I packed the camera back into its case and hung the strap around my neck. "I'd better get back to the paper. I'm supposed to attend the dress rehearsal of Cian's play this evening and I need to get this report typed up beforehand."

Mary laughed. "Good luck. I had the joy of proofreading the script."

"I'm his unofficial historical expert." I pulled a face. "You can imagine how well my suggestions were received."

"No need to tell me," Richard added with a rueful grin. "I'm in the play."

"Would you mind walking me to the gate, Richard? I'd like to ask you a couple of research questions." Research that was entirely to do with the shoot-out, but I didn't elaborate on this part with Mary in the room.

"In that case, I'll get back to work," Mary said. "Thanks again for featuring the exhibition in the *Chronicle.*"

"No problem. Anything I can do to help put the brakes on the mayor's plans, I'm all in."

I meant every word. I had no idea how we'd

overturn Henry Hyland's plans to monetize Dunleagh at the expense of everything I held dear, but I was determined to give it my best shot.

He escorted me to the library door and out into the garden. The strong wind whipped my hood down. I pulled it back into place just as the first raindrops began to fall.

"The rain reminds me of your raincoat and sweater," I said. "I need to get them back to you. Will I bring them by the museum later?"

"No rush. Wait until the Historical Murders meeting." Richard took refuge beneath the arch of the doorway. "What did you want to ask me about? The spent cartridge you discovered?"

I nodded. "Among other things."

"As I suspected, it's definitely an old Mauser round and would have fit the C96." His brow furrowed. "I have no idea why the shooters were using vintage firearms. It's bizarre."

"It's not the only oddity about yesterday's shoot-out," I said. "The man I helped was wearing an old RIC uniform, presumably a replica."

Richard stopped short, his eyebrows receding into his wild mass of curls. "Are you serious?"

"Didn't you notice what he was wearing when you arrived on the scene?"

The museum director shook his head. "I saw he was in a uniform, but I was too shocked by the sight of blood to register what sort."

"Did you and Mary hire actors for your exhibition?" I asked. "If so, could he have been one of them?"

"No." His denial was concise. "It never occurred to me to hire actors, although it's not a bad idea. We'd have had to recruit volunteers in any case. No money to pay for a frill."

"I'd appreciate it if you kept the news about the uniform to yourself for the time being. I'm writing a story for the *Chronicle*, but I told Lou I'd wait until she gives me the okay to publish it."

"Of course. I won't breathe a word. I've already promised the Guards I wouldn't spread the information about your cartridge."

Once again, the wind jerked my hood from my head. I pulled it back into place and secured it with a button. "One more question before I go. Does the museum have any World War I trench watches I could look at?"

"No," Richard replied. "We had a couple many years ago but they're now in museums in Dublin and Cork. We simply didn't have the money to store them correctly. They still emit radiation, you know."

"Yeah, I read that. I asked on the off chance you had one."

"We have two trench watches dating from the Second World War if you'd like to take a look at them, both in storage. By that time, the manufacturers had lowered the amount of radioactive material used in the luminous paint." He regarded me curiously. "Does your trench watch question have to do with your mystery man?"

"Yeah, but it's another detail I'm not supposed to divulge just yet."

He motioned zipping his lips. "I won't say a word. I'll have a look for the watches and set them aside for you."

I leaned up and kissed him on the cheek. "Thanks, Richard. You're a star."

The museum director turned a charming shade of pink. "I'm happy to help. Have a good day, Dee, and try to avoid trouble and shoot-outs."

"One shoot-out was enough for this lifetime, believe me. As for trouble—" I grinned at him, "—I can't make any promises, but I'll do my best."

TWELVE

After Richard returned indoors, I strolled down the path that cut through the gardens, leading to the wrought iron gate. The rain proved to be a light shower and was over almost as soon as it had started, leaving the flowers glistening in the sunlight. The sound of water cascading from the library's fountain soothed me and I stopped to trail my fingers through the basin. The fountain was a stone structure featuring the nine muses from Greek mythology. Apparently, one of the military guys who'd once lived in the house had been a fan of the classics. He'd have gotten on great with my dad.

I shook water off my hand and continued down the path. Pushing open the gates, I stepped onto the pavement, and strode to the spot where I'd parked Mavis. I was just adjusting my helmet when a familiar green-haired figure appeared in front of me. My heart leaped and my hand flew to my chest as if to steady its pounding.

"Yo, Dee." Aido grinned at me. "How's it hanging?"

"Jeez. What's with the stealth act? You gave me a fright."

"Sorry, friend." He jerked a thumb down the street. "I was at my aunt's place, doing some recon on the mayor."

It took me a moment to register what he was talking about. "Oh, right. I forgot Elaine is related to you. I think of her as having no surname, like an Eighties pop star."

Aido chuckled. "She's my mother's sister. We don't share a family name."

"What did she have to say about Henry Hyland's visit to her safe room?"

"Nothing complimentary. Elaine can't stand the guy."

"No surprises there," I said. "Did she have any dirt to share?"

His cheery expression faded. "Nothing we can use in a story. Not without hard evidence. He's allegedly cheating on his wife, but I'm not sure that's sufficient to topple him from power."

"Not in this day and age," I agreed. "Did Elaine say who he's having an affair with?"

"No, but she's bound to know. I can ask her." Aido nodded at the library. "Did the interview go well?"

"Yeah." I patted the camera case. "This little beauty helped me to take a few nice photos. It's so much better than my phone. Mind you, I'd happily swap it for my phone right now. Not having one sucks."

"Understandable. What will you do if it doesn't show up? Get a replacement?"

I heaved a sigh. "I don't have much choice. Apart from the general convenience factor, I need one for work. I still have to set up an interview with James Kylemore, among a million other tasks." How much would a new phone set me back? More than I currently had in my bank account? Probably.

"Naido's got an old prepaid phone at home. I can ask her if she'll let you borrow it."

I couldn't see Aido's taciturn sister doing me a favor, but I nodded and said, "Thanks. I'd be grateful if she would. It'd tide me over until my own phone turns up." Or I was forced to admit it was gone for good and fork out for a replacement.

Aido checked his watch. "Where are you off to now? I told Cian I'd be right back, but I could do with a decent cup of coffee. I'm about to grab a takeaway cup from The Coffee Bean."

A slow smile spread across my face as an idea formed. "If you do me a favor, I'll buy you a double espresso."

My friend cocked his head to one side. "What do you need me to do?"

"I want to try to get into the injured guy's room," I said, "but there's a snag."

"I don't like the sound of this."

"There's a police guard at the door."

"Oh, no." Aido threw his hands in the air. "That DI Bradley dude scares me. I have no intention of winding up in a cell if he catches me breaking the law."

"We won't be breaking the law. Well," I amended, "not exactly. If anyone asks, we're just paying a visit to the guy whose life I saved."

"I don't see the detective buying that story."

"We won't try it if he's there. I promise. The most recent guard on the door was Sean O'Connor. Don't you play hurling with him?" Hurling, a traditional Irish sport, was beloved by the inhabitants of Dunleagh, and Aido was one of the club's best players.

"Sean's a stickler for rules," Aido said. "I won't get past him."

"No, but you could distract him long enough for me to slip past."

He shook his head. "Eda is your best bet. That woman can cause mayhem in five seconds flat."

"Nana's at home." I paused, considering my grandmother's adventures over the last couple of days. "At least, I hope she is. And I definitely don't want her causing a second scene at the hospital. I'm talking about a quiet distraction, preferably one that doesn't involve fire alarms or medical emergencies."

"I guess I can do that," Aido said slowly, doubt written all over his face.

"Brilliant." I shoved the spare helmet at him. "Hop on, and let's get this show on the road."

———

In what felt like a déjà vu moment, I drove Mavis into the same parking space I'd scored earlier that afternoon. Dunleagh General Hospital was still buzzing with activity, especially now that official visiting hours had commenced. Up on the third floor, I peeked through the glass panel of the door to St. Colmcille's Ward. A young plain-clothes police officer had taken Sean's place outside the patient's door. At least, I assumed she was a police officer. Her stern expression indicated she wasn't there for fun.

"What now?" Aido peered over my shoulder. "Want me to turn on the old Lafferty charm?"

"It's worth a try. Whatever you do, get her away from the door."

"Righto."

Whistling a tune, Aido jammed his hands into his pockets and shouldered open the door to the ward. I followed at a discreet distance. Unless DI Bradley had decided I was such a menace to his investigation that he'd issued photos of me to his entire team, this woman wouldn't have a clue who I was. Aido sauntered over to the police officer, and I developed a sudden interest in the whiteboard containing the staff roster. The patient in Room 303 had the unimaginative moniker of Mr. X. Better than John Doe, but not by much. Behind me, Aido had launched in to a full-fledged charm attack. Within what seemed like moments, he'd urged the woman to look at the whiteboard with him, pointing to Mr. X's name and peppering her with questions about the investigation.

The instant her back was to the door, I slipped behind her and made a beeline for Room 303. My heart was in my throat as I turned the handle and darted inside the room. Still breathing hard, I took in the scene. The injured man lay on his bed, hooked up to an IV drip and some kind of medical machine. His eyes were closed, and his dark lashes fanned out over the top of his prominent cheekbones. Although his skin was pale, he looked a lot healthier than the last time I'd seen him. And a whole lot better-looking.

Stealthy as a cat, I moved closer to the bed and took the seat next to him. I swallowed hard. Now what? Should I wake him up? What if he was still unconscious? Tentatively, I reached for his hand.

In the next instant, he was gripping my wrist, his blue eyes boring into me.

"Ouch," I said, trying to pull free from his grasp. "I mean no harm. I just wanted to see how you were doing."

"You can see without touching." The voice was gruff but he relaxed his grip. His cool gaze raked me in an indifferent once-over. Once he'd completed his perusal of my person, he leaned back against his pillows as though unimpressed by what he'd seen. In spite of myself, my cheeks grew warm. "You're the woman from the courtyard," he added blandly. "What are you doing here?"

I slow-blinked. "You recognize me? But you mistook me for someone else yesterday."

He regarded me coolly. "So I've been informed."

As he didn't seem inclined to expand on this statement, it was up to me to press him for details. "Who's Eliza? More to the point, who are you?"

For the first time since he'd grabbed my wrist, his gaze shifted away from me. "She's someone I know."

"I gathered that," I said sardonically, "but who is she to you? Wife? Girlfriend? Sister?"

The guarded look returned. "You ask a lot of questions."

"And you answer few."

A small smile played at the corners of his mouth. "Touché."

I relaxed against the back of my seat, confident now that he wasn't about to rip my wrist out of its socket. "So what's your deal? Who are you, and who shot you?"

His glance strayed to the folded copy of the *Chronicle* that lay on his bedside table. My first-ever front-page feature stared back at me, closely followed by Marcus's preliminary report on the castle shootings. "You tell me, Miss Flanagan," he countered. "You seem to be the expert."

My eyes skimmed over the newspaper. *Of course.* Cian always included the reporter's bio photo if their story made the front page. If Mr. X had read my article, he'd have seen my picture and byline.

"Don't you want your attackers caught?" I asked, leaning back in my chair and treating him to a disinterested gaze to match his own. "They killed another man, you know."

A flash of pain crossed his face. "I heard."

"Then why don't you want to help me? All I want is to get to the truth. And an excellent place to start would be by telling me your name."

A muscle in his jaw flexed. "I don't like journalists. They make money by selling lies."

"Not me. I'm only interested in the truth, as are the Guards." Was it my imagination, or did his expression change when I mentioned the cops? Whatever I'd seen, it was gone in an instant.

A tense silence hung over the room. Finally, the man tapped the folded newspaper. "Is this supposed to be a joke? A new method to make me talk?"

"I don't know what you mean. I wrote what I saw in the courtyard. No more and no less."

A flash of anger broke through the cool indifference in his eyes. He snatched the paper from the nightstand, upsetting a plastic cup of water. He shook out the paper and slammed it down on the bed. "Not content with finding someone who looked like Eliza, you took the trouble to illustrate these photographs."

I scanned the front page. "They're just photos. No one illustrated anything."

"They're colored," he snapped. "Photographs aren't colored. And you said I was wearing a fancy dress costume. The clown was dressed up. I wasn't."

I let out a slow breath. "Okay, then. I guess the blood loss affected your mind."

"And this—" he jabbed a finger at the date, "—is the crowning glory of your little exercise. Are you trying to send me to a lunatic asylum? Is that the new ploy to get rid of me?"

Cautiously, I leaned forward. "That's today's date. Nothing strange about that."

He glared at me. "Only the hundred-year difference."

I stared at him, caught in a tug-of-war between my fascination with what he was saying and my urge to run. "What hundred-year difference? A typing error with the date?"

"Exactly." He underlined the year with a fingertip. "See? 2019. You've made the date a century in the future."

"Wait a sec," I said, comprehension slowly dawning. "You think it's the year 1919?"

His jaw set in a hard line. "I don't *think* it's 1919. I *know* it's 1919. And neither you nor your cohorts will convince me otherwise."

I let out a long breath. "You want to tell me you were walking around in a Royal Irish Constabulary uniform because you think you're living one hundred years ago? Dude, you have issues."

"The only issue I have is being stuck in this bed, tied up to this device." He tugged down the neck of his hospital gown and pulled off the discs that connected to his heart monitor.

"Stop," I cried. "You have to stay still."

"And listen to you try to convince me I'm insane?" His eyes burned with hatred so intense that I moved my chair back a fraction.

"Please, stop. The IV and the heart monitor are for your own good. You've just had surgery, for goodness sake."

He ignored me and pulled the remaining electrodes off his chest, predictably causing the machine's alarm to emit its piercing sound. Any second now, Guards and medical staff would burst in and I'd be rumbled.

"This is ridiculous," I said. "If you wanted to have everyone storm your room, you're going the right way about it."

He opened his mouth to reply, but stopped when the door to his room was thrown open. DI Bradley loomed on the threshold, glowering at me. "I told you to stay away, Ms. Flanagan."

I got to my feet. "So you did. I just happened to stroll by this room and noticed that the door was open."

Behind the DI, a female voice rose. "The door wasn't open, sir, I swear. She must've snuck in."

I shrugged. "Maybe I possess the ability to pass through closed doors."

Zosia pushed past the detectives and ran to the heart monitor. A second later, the awful din ceased. She took in the disconnected electrodes and shot me an accusing look. "Did *you* do this?"

"Of course not. He did it himself. The poor dude thinks he's living in the past—literally. It's not a heart monitor he needs, it's a psych consult."

Red stained the detective's cheekbones. He pointed to the corridor. "Out. Right now. This man needs rest."

I slung my backpack over my shoulder. "Rest, probably. A psychiatrist, definitely. Has he seen someone from psych yet?"

The detective's mouth opened and shut. "I ask the questions here, not you."

"Fair enough. I'm done here, anyway." I wasn't done. Far from it. For today, though, I'd gotten all the information I was likely to get and I'd have to bide my time to hear more. Even if the man was well into crazy territory, there was a story here. I could sense it with every fiber of my being.

I looked over my shoulder at the man I'd come to see. His spurt of activity had drained his energy. He sank back against his pillows, his face a mixture of defiance and exhaustion. For a moment, our eyes clashed. "Maybe rethink the tale you told me, eh?" I said, my tone gentle. "Hope you feel better soon."

THIRTEEN

"What was all that about?" Aido demanded when we reached the parking lot. He'd remained blessedly silent on the walk down from St. Colmcille's ward, which had given me time to mull over my conversation with the mysterious Mr. X.

"Sounds like a title for a novel," I mused. "This case certainly has all the trappings of a Hollywood thriller."

"Huh?" Aido stared at me, perplexed.

I stopped beside Mavis and handed him his helmet. "Sorry. I was thinking aloud."

He took the helmet but didn't put it on. "Before you get on the bike and have a legit excuse not to talk, please tell me what happened in Room 303."

"Totally sounds like a book title." I grinned, but Aido didn't return my smile.

"I'm serious, Dee. After you refused to tell Bradley

what the man said to you, you blew the *Chronicle*'s chance to get an exclusive in with the detectives. Cian's going to blow a gasket. Seeing as I'll be implicated, surely I deserve to know if it was worth it or not."

I sighed. "Yeah, you do. Come on. Walk with me."

I led him toward the hospital gardens and the maze my sister and I had loved exploring when we were kids. A series of wooden benches were positioned outside the maze. I nabbed a free one and checked the seat for dampness before sitting. Aido sat beside me, uncharacteristically subdued.

"The guy's not thinking straight," I said without preamble. "He accused me of being part of a plot to send him to a lunatic asylum. And then he proceeded to tell me he was from the year 1919."

This bombshell blasted Aido out of his moody silence. He blinked several times. "Wow. Bro's got problems."

"Yeah. I feel bad for him. I hope it's a temporary aberration. Maybe caused by the shock of the attack. If not..." I trailed off, meeting Aido's steady gaze, "he has serious mental health issues."

"Why didn't you tell Bradley? It's not like the guy revealed important info about the case, apart from the fact that he's a bona fide fruitcake."

"I don't know." I stared at the ground, unseeing. "I guess it felt like it would be a betrayal. The man's not in his right mind, but he's a victim in all of this. He didn't shoot Mr. Chuckles, and he didn't shoot himself. So why throw him to the wolves? He needs professional help, not a police interrogation."

"Are you sure about that? You said yourself you heard more than you saw, and the Guards have had no luck finding the gunmen. Maybe they've had the lone shooter all along."

"He was carrying a revolver," I said, "which might not have been genuine. The cartridge I found on the ground came from a pistol."

"So he had two guns. Easy enough to shoot the clown with one, hide it, and then shoot himself with the other."

I shook my head. "It all went down too fast for that. Besides, the Guards found no trace of either gun. If they were removed, it wasn't by Mr. X."

"I still think he could be the killer," Aido said, folding his arms across his chest. "Did you have a chance to ask him about the shooters' names?"

"No. The conversation devolved into crazy territory pretty fast, and then Zosia and the Guards burst in."

"Zosia..." Aido's face took on a reverent expression at the mention of Lev's sister.

I rolled my eyes. "You only like her because she's one of the few women in Dunleagh who's failed to respond to your flirting."

Aido grinned. "I like her because she's hot." He must have recognized the irritation on my face because he swiftly changed the subject. "Any chance your brother-in-law might give us details on the autopsy?"

"Not with DI Bradley on the prowl. I'll corner Lev for sure, but not at the hospital." I stood and stretched. "If I'm to get this story written before the dress rehearsal, we'd better move. It starts in ninety minutes."

Aido groaned. "Why did I agree to help with the sets?"

"Masochism," I said simply. "Or the bonus Cian dangled in front of your greedy paws."

He laughed. "Speak for yourself, Ms. Pay-Me-Double. You're as mercenary as they come."

"Needs must," I said, oddly disconcerted by his statement. "I've got to pay the bills somehow. Lord knows we have enough of them."

"Tell me about it." Aido sighed. "I'm half regretting not taking up my aunt's offer to work Saturdays at her café. It brings back nightmares of my school days, but I might have to cave."

As we walked back to my scooter, I tried to figure out what had caused me to inhale sharply when Aido referred to me as Ms. Pay-Me-Double. I wasn't offended. I needed the money, just as he did. But something had triggered a memory and I couldn't quite place what it was.

I was riding Mavis out of the hospital grounds when it hit me. Mr. X had called me Miss Flanagan, not Ms. While I'd been called Miss a few times in other countries, it wasn't common in Ireland, particularly not among people of my generation. Was his use of Miss part of his act? Or was such adherence to historical details a symptom of whatever mental health episode he was experiencing? Or was I simply reading way too much into his word choice? I blew out my cheeks. Regardless of why the man had referred to me as Miss, it was yet another oddity to add to my list of strange occurrences over the last couple of days.

By the time Aido and I got back to the castle, it was pushing five o'clock. Walking over the drawbridge and into the cobblestoned courtyard usually brought a smile to my lips, but the atmosphere today was subdued. Unlike this morning, I forced myself to look toward the Green Archway and absorb the changes since yesterday. Crime scene tape cordoned off the area where the men had been shot. According to Lou, it would stay in place until this evening. A police presence remained, both in the form of uniformed officers who were guarding the crime scene and a contingent of plain-clothes detectives, conspicuous by their authoritative demeanors.

A woman I vaguely recognized as an acquaintance of my grandmother's stood in the middle of the courtyard, talking to one of the police officers. All of a sudden, she pointed at me and began gesticulating wildly. The officer's cold gaze acknowledged my presence before returning his attention to his notepad. I guessed I was the talk of the town today, especially with my eyewitness report on the front page of the *Chronicle*. Finally scoring a front-page spread was awesome, but I'd have preferred it to be for a story in which I wasn't personally involved.

I quickened my pace to match Aido's long strides and he held the castle door open for me. Inside, Larry was deep in conversation with one of the Dublin detectives and didn't notice our arrival. I had zero desire to draw this officer's attention to my presence. Averting my face from the reception desk, I followed Aido through the lobby and up the stairs that led to the North Tower and the *Chronicle*'s offices.

Once we were safely in the newsroom, the tension in my shoulders slackened. I inhaled a deep breath and unpacked my stuff. From the depths of his ratty backpack, Aido withdrew an illicit sandwich.

I slung my jacket over my chair and sat opposite him. "Naughty, naughty."

My friend stared ruefully at the sandwich. "I figured Cian would bend his no-food-in-the-office rule if it meant me skipping dinner and attending the rehearsal."

"I forgot all about food. I'll have to see if I can grab an energy bar from the café on my way to the Great Hall."

Aido inhaled his sandwich at a speed that would

give me indigestion and washed it down with a bottle of ice tea. "Hey," he said, wiping his mouth with a tissue, "I meant to tell you I texted Naido about her spare phone. She'll give it to me tonight. Unless you've heard anything about your phone?"

I grimaced. "Not yet. I told Lou to keep an eye out for anyone handing in a lost phone, and I asked her to tell Seamie to do the same when he's released. I'll gratefully take Naido up on her offer."

"She's not exactly offering it to you," Aido amended with a rueful smile. "I just mentioned I needed to borrow it for a while."

"Ah." Although Aido and I had never discussed his sister's animosity toward me, I'd have been amazed if she'd been willing to do me a favor. "I'm not sure I feel comfortable borrowing it without her permission. She's not exactly my greatest fan."

"It's not personal. Naido doesn't like any of my friends, male or female."

This assertion tied in with my own assessment of the situation. I'd never asked Aido directly, but Nana had mentioned that Naido had depression and codependency issues. According to my grandmother, Aido (Aidan) and Naido (Sinéad) still went by their childhood nicknames for each other at Naido's insistence. I suspected Aido had moved back to Dunleagh after university to look after his sister, but he rarely mentioned his home life and I didn't like to pry.

Marcus bustled into the newsroom, carrying a

stack of printer paper. "Cian's looking for you, Dee. More questions about his script."

I groaned. "I am so not in the mood to deal with *A Fighting Man*. I'll have to sit through it in less than an hour."

Sure enough, I'd barely had time to fire up my computer when the editor's office door swung open. My boss emerged, script in hand, his eyes glazed with manic determination. "Dee, I need a favor."

From the opposite side of our shared desk, Aido mouthed, *Run for your life.*

I pretended to type, ignoring the fact that my computer still hadn't fully booted. "We're due to talk about your play after the rehearsal, Cian. I'm pretty busy working on the exhibition article. Can we—"

"I have a question about the script. It'll only take a minute."

The editor delivered the statement with a finality that told me he wasn't prepared to take no for an answer. Unless I wanted to get suckered into reading his script for the umpteenth time, I had to act fast.

As the man trundled toward my desk, I grabbed my laptop and hurled myself through the door at a speed that would've astounded my jogging partner. "Gotta follow a lead," I yelled over my shoulder. "Back soon."

Make that, "Back in one hour and not a second before."

I bolted down three flights of stairs, not slowing my pace until I'd reached the door to the archives. In the dungeons of Dunleagh Castle, the central heating we took for granted on the upper levels was conspicuously absent—a disadvantage to working for a newspaper that had its offices in a medieval fortress. The pro to the archives' location was that Cian wouldn't follow me down here. According to newsroom gossip, Cian and his sister had seen a ghost in the dungeons when they were kids, and the man still turned white whenever anyone mentioned venturing down to the lower levels of the castle. I didn't believe in ghosts, but even I had to admit that the dungeons gave me the creeps. I unlocked the door to the archives and stepped inside.

In contrast to the damp corridor, the walls of the archives had been insulated during the Eighties and did a reasonable job at maintaining a dry atmosphere. Unfortunately, "dry" wasn't synonymous with "warm." Even in summer, it was freezing down here. The lone source of heat was a portable radiator, and I wasted no time in switching it on. Once I'd ensured I wouldn't freeze to death, I made straight for a haphazard pile of boxes. I extracted an enormous volume and blew a thick layer of dust from its cracked leather cover. With the library story, I hadn't expected to get a chance to get down to the archives today. If I got my article on the exhibition written quickly, this volume of old newspapers would be my reward.

One of the tasks I'd been assigned when I'd started working at the *Chronicle* was sorting the paper's back issues for their long-overdue digitization. Founded in

1869, the *Chronicle* was among Ireland's oldest regional newspapers. The earliest installments had been lost in a fire during the Twenties, but most of the issues from 1895 onward had survived. At some point in the last century, the oldest issues had been bound in a series of thick leather volumes and were stored in sturdy metal boxes. In spite of the chaotic filing system, sorting through the newspapers was a job I enjoyed. It got me out of my open-plan office and back into the hushed silence I'd grown used to during my years in academia.

I placed the enormous tome on the archives' only desk next to my laptop. Spurred on by the thought of spending time perusing old newspapers, the article on the exhibition flowed. Thirty minutes later, I had a decent first draft. I saved the file and closed my laptop with a sigh of satisfaction. I'd read over the article again this evening, but it was as good as I could get it for now.

I grabbed a pen and two of the ever-present A4 notepads from a drawer and turned my attention to the volume of back issues I'd selected earlier. Some of the stories were perfect for my popular weekly blog feature, "This Week 100 Years Ago." My latest installment needed to go live by tomorrow evening, and I hadn't had a chance to prepare material for it. Seeing as I had to go through the back issues to check for mold and other damage, I might as well make the time pull double duty.

The radiator kicked into gear and I was soon

engrossed in a report about a street brawl between priests that had scandalized Dunleagh in 1919, scribbling references to damaged pages on one pad and notes for my blog post on the other. Noting the year brought the mysterious stranger's claims back into consciousness, but I pushed them away. He had a fixation with the past. Some sort of psychosis. That explained the uniform and the revolver and the dogged belief that he was living a century ago. Whatever problems the man had, they were way beyond my areas of expertise. Shoving all thoughts of the injured man from my mind, I returned to the newspapers and immersed myself in my work. When a thump on the door broke the silence, I almost jumped out of my seat.

Aido lounged in the doorframe, the spikes of his green hair brushing the head jamb, and a sardonic smile stretched across his handsome face. "If you can tear yourself away from the dust, the rehearsal starts in five minutes."

"It's nearly six already?" I yawned and checked my watch. "I lost track of time."

"I grabbed this from the café. It looked the least revolting of their offerings. I figured you can eat on the way to the Great Hall." He tossed me a cellophane-wrapped sandwich.

I caught the sandwich one-handed and slowly got to my feet. "Thanks. I need to grab my bag and jacket from the office before we go to the rehearsal."

"Not keen on attending the rehearsal?" Aido asked dryly.

I laughed. "Is it that obvious?"

"Yep. And I left your bag and coat at the reception desk on my way down here. You have no excuse to slink back to the office and hide."

"Frankly, I'd rather hide down here. The archives are more interesting."

"No can do, my friend. You can't be a no-show. Cian's already peeved by your disappearance earlier."

"Can you blame me? The idea of reading that awful play again was more than I could cope with. It'll be bad enough having to give him feedback after the rehearsal." I wrinkled my nose. "He wants me to critique the historical accuracy of the props and costumes."

Aido's forehead creased. "Isn't it a bit late to make changes? The play opens on Friday."

"That's one of my objections. Even if there was time to tweak the costumes, Cian wouldn't listen to any of my suggestions."

"What's your other objection?" Aido's lips twitched. "Let me guess—Bliss."

I rolled my eyes. "Her starring role has totally gone to her head. Sitting through two hours of my mother caterwauling onstage is bad enough, but to do it twice in one week?" I shuddered. "My daughterly duty doesn't extend that far."

"It'll be a train wreck," my friend said cheerfully.

"Cian's plays always are." While I sorted the two sets of notes I'd taken into some semblance of order, Aido leafed through the volume of back issues that lay open on the desk. "Found anything interesting?"

"I sure did. In 1902, a guy named Aloysius Lafferty was in court, accused of driving a donkey and cart 'in an unfortunate state of inebriation.' Any relation to you?"

My friend chuckled. "I'll ask my grandmother, but that totally sounds like something one of my ancestors would do."

After I'd turned off the portable heater, we exited the archives and I locked the door. Aido took the stairs up to the castle's entrance level two at a time, forcing me to hurry to keep up.

"Dude, in case you haven't noticed, I'm shorter than you."

My friend snorted but slowed his pace. "Not by much, and it definitely doesn't hold you back. You took off like a gazelle when Cian wanted you to read over his play."

"Ha. Wait until you *see* said play. Then you'll feel my pain."

When we reached the ground floor, Larry was on duty at the reception desk.

"Hey, Larry." I nodded toward the digital reader in his hands. "Good book?"

The older man leaned back in his chair, making it

creak under his bulk. "It's about the Honour Bright murder. Have you heard of that case?"

Aido screwed up his forehead. "The Dublin sex worker who was shot in the Twenties?"

"That's the one. A police superintendent and a doctor were tried for the crime but acquitted."

"You should suggest the Honour Bright killing to the Historical Murders Club," I said. "Richard was looking for ideas at our last meeting."

In the distance, the church bells chimed the hour. I didn't bother to stifle my groan.

"We'd better get going," Aido said, "or Cian will kill us."

The security guard retrieved my bag and jacket from behind the desk. "Are you two off to Bliss's rehearsal?"

My lips twitched. "We're on our way to the play's rehearsal, yes."

Larry's unrequited crush on my mother had endured thirty years, multiple rebuffs, and the quelling presence of a wife. Larry was just one of my mother's many male admirers. Meanwhile, I was single with no dating prospects. I swallowed a sigh. I had no idea how she did it.

"I'll be at the play on opening night," Larry continued. "The missus has a supporting role. She'd kill me if I missed the premiere."

"At least someone is enthusiastic about seeing the play," I murmured when Aido and I moved away from the reception desk. "The last thing I feel like doing is watching half of Dunleagh cavort on stage for ninety minutes."

Aido grinned. "Think of the amusement factor. The best part will be watching the mayor prance around stage, convinced he can act."

"If he delivers his lines in the same smarmy monotone that he uses to deliver his speeches, I'll be asleep within two minutes."

He laughed. "Tragic but true."

"How did you get roped into attending the rehearsal? I get that you helped create the sets, but you're not part of the crew during performances, right?"

"Correct. Cian's paranoid about the play turning into a fiasco. He wants me in the hall as a backup crewmember. If someone doesn't show up, I'll take their place. And if something goes wrong with the sound or lighting, I'm to help fix the problem."

We reached the door to the Great Hall. Voices floated through it, some muffled, others distinct. "I don't suppose you thought to bring a hip flask?" I asked. "Preferably one filled with vodka?"

Aido grinned. "Sorry, but no."

I squared my shoulders and reached for the door handle. "Okay. Let's do this thing."

FOURTEEN

The Great Hall of Dunleagh Castle was a typical example of late medieval architecture. The hall was twice as long as it was wide, with a high, arched ceiling —a marked contrast to the low-ceilinged rooms in the rest of the castle. To my right, a series of long windows faced the courtyard. The wall opposite bore an array of flags, coats of arms, and heraldic mottos dating from the castle's first iteration right up to the early twentieth century. At the far end of the hall, the dais had been transformed into a stage. A fire burned merrily in the enormous fireplace next to the dais, but most of the heat in the room was provided by strategically placed radiators.

The Great Hall was one of my favorite places in the castle. This evening, it buzzed with activity. Fold-down plastic chairs, presumably the same ones Larry had used yesterday to hold back the old folks from the crime scene, had been arranged in rows on either side of the hall with a narrow aisle running between them. I scanned the rows and whistled as I took in the number of people present.

"How did Cian persuade this number of people to attend the dress rehearsal?" I whispered to Aido. "Surely he's not paying them all to sit through his play."

"A bunch are from the most recent tour group. I heard Cian mention he'd offer them a chance to see the play."

A cardboard cloud chose this moment to make a rapid descent to earth, forcing a crewmember to jump off the stage or risk a whack on the head.

Cian leaped to his feet from his front row seat. His unruly ginger hair looked even wilder than usual. He'd replaced his uniform of rock T-shirts and jeans for an ill-fitting suit. "For heaven's sake, Mark," he yelled. "Make sure the sky is secured properly. And Jane, move the tree to the left, not to the right. It needs to look like a forest."

While our editor barked last-minute orders at crewmembers, Aido and I slid into the back row, staying close to the exit. "Guess we're not late after all," he said. "I don't see this play starting for another few minutes. Not if the scenery's falling down."

I discreetly unwrapped the sandwich and took a bite. "Aren't you supposed to write a review of the play for the paper?" I asked between mouthfuls.

Aido grimaced. "Alas, yes. I'll have to praise the play and the performances to the skies or face life as an unemployed outcast."

"I'm not sure if I should thank you or curse you for reminding me of the rehearsal. Cian would've been a bear had I missed it, but I love working down in the archives. It relaxes me."

My friend wrinkled his nose. "I don't know how you can stand it. The dust gets me every time. Plus the place gives me the creeps."

"It's nice and quiet. An added bonus is that the back issues project is giving me a ton of material for my blog."

Aido's phone vibrated to the sound of an incoming text. He swore under his breath. "I thought I'd turned it off." He rummaged through his bag and pulled out his phone, glanced at the display, and frowned. "It's from Cian. Apparently, one of the cast members is causing problems and he wants me to stand in for him."

"Whoa. How are your acting skills?"

"Well, I was in a couple of school plays. I had the starring role of a tree in one, and played a pillar in the other."

"Wow. No lines at all?"

"Absolutely none." Aido got to his feet, a cheeky grin plastered across his face. "Wish me luck."

I gave him a double thumbs-up. "You've got this."

Aido sauntered down the aisle to take up whatever role Cian had in mind for him, and I returned to the vital task of finishing my sandwich. I'd just swallowed the last bite when a familiar voice boomed into my ear, sending my heart into a skitter.

"Hello, love. Shove over, will ya?"

Nana leaned on her cane. The goggles she'd worn yesterday were back in place, and she'd jazzed up her look since I'd last seen her with the addition of a generous application of teal-green lipstick. Behind her stood Dottie and their friend Big Jim. Although age had added a stoop to his broad shoulders, Big Jim stood around six-feet-five-inches.

Elaine, Aido's aunt and the proprietor of the dubious eatery beloved by Dunleagh's seniors, brought up the rear. She was a large, solidly built woman of an indeterminate age whose fashion sense hadn't recovered from the horrors of the Eighties. Shoulder pads and sequins were staple components of her wardrobe. Tonight's outfit consisted of a royal blue trouser suit with shoulder pads so wide they made her V-shaped. Completing the look, Elaine's platinum-blond permanent was combed and sprayed into an unmoving updo. She smiled when she saw me. "Hello, Dee," she said in her raspy smoker's voice. "Where's my nephew?"

"He's been conscripted into the cast."

Elaine's rumble of a laugh made several spectators turn around in their seats. "Good luck to him. You couldn't pay me enough to appear in one of Cian's plays. I'm only here to provide refreshments during the interval."

I frowned. "Won't the castle café take care of that?"

"Cian owed me a favor. I made sure my crew got to serve the food and drink during the play's run." The corners of her eyes crinkled in amusement. "With the Guards roaming the castle, I'm looking forward to getting plenty of insider information. My customers like to keep up to date on town gossip."

"Good luck. The Dublin crowd is a tight-lipped lot."

Elaine chuckled. "No one's tight-lipped after a cup of my rum punch. Come by my stand during the interval and try a cup."

"I might just do that." I shifted my attention to Nana. "Did you forget your glasses at Big Jim's again? You had them on this morning."

"Ah, no. I noticed I see better through these and thought I'd wear them to the play."

As one did. "Okay then." I stood and made to move up the row.

"Oh, no." Nana shook her head, making her purple curls bounce. "We want a good view of the action. Let's go to the front."

I stared down the hall. "Um, Nana, those seats are all taken."

"Not for long." Before I had a chance to react, she was on the move, the cane swinging from side to side in a menacing fashion. Dottie and Big Jim hurried to catch up.

I put my head in my hands and groaned. "I can't watch."

"You might as well join her," Elaine said, ever the pragmatist. "Eda will use any means necessary to get those seats."

"That's precisely what I'm afraid of." I grabbed my stuff and stepped back into the aisle. "Are you coming?"

Elaine shook her helmet of hair. "I need to get moving on the food prep. I'll see you at the interval."

"See you then."

I rushed down the aisle to catch up with Nana and her friends. My grandmother walked straight up to the front row, which was occupied by a group of people I didn't recognize. Probably members of the tour group Aido had mentioned. Nana sniffed the air, paused, and pointed under one of the seats with her cane. "There's another one, Dottie," she roared at a volume fit to make the windows shake. "That's the fourth rat I've seen in here tonight."

"Rats?" A woman in the front row clutched her companion's arm. "Are you sure?"

Nana nodded sagely. "There it goes. Do you see it shooting under your friend's seat?"

Instead of looking, the woman screamed and jumped on top of her chair. The cheap plastic wasn't designed to bear her weight, and the chair folded in on itself, trapping its occupant before crashing to the ground.

"There's an infestation of vermin in this hall," Nana yelled, ignoring the woman's plight.

The tourist's friend had by this time gotten to his feet and attempted to release her from her plastic prison. The only way to get her out of the chair was to force the two halves apart, and he and Cian applied themselves to the task. The crack that had appeared in the back of the chair prior to the woman's fall now groaned under the pressure of two men pulling at it. The back broke away from the seat. The woman was shot out of her trap and landed face-first in front of the stage. Eyes wild with fear, she scrambled to her feet. "Over there," she shouted. "I think I saw a rat."

This outburst was sufficient to oust the rest of the front row from their seats. "I can't stand rats," one woman cried, clutching her handbag to her bosom.

"There are no rats in the Great Hall," Cian said in exasperation. "We have regular checks from pest control. We wouldn't be allowed to conduct tours if the castle was infested with vermin."

"If they're like the rats we had in here last year, they spread irritable bowel syndrome. Sure, we were all down with it, weren't we, Dottie?" Nana made the sign of the cross. "I hope it hasn't returned."

"Irritable bowel syndrome isn't contagious." Cian turned desperate eyes on me. "Can't you stop her?"

"No chance," I said without a shred of guilt. "She's on a roll."

The woman who'd gotten trapped in her chair was in hysterics, flailing her arms and wailing. "I saw another one," she gasped between sobs. "Over there by the piano."

"I'm pretty sure that's Mrs. McClure's Chihuahua," I said, but no one paid me a shred of attention.

"I'm getting out of here," the chair victim announced, breaking into a trot. "I'm going to Lanzarote next week. I don't want to catch that bowel thing."

Her companions followed suit, and a flurry of feet echoed against the stone slabs of the hall floor as the visitors raced to safety.

Big Jim picked up the wreckage of the broken chair and regarded it thoughtfully. "I'll toss this one."

"Why, Eda?" Cian asked, more a broken man than a fighting one. "If I'd known front row seats were so important to you, I'd have reserved a few."

"No worries," she said in a cheery tone. "I got it sorted."

"Seriously, Nana," I whispered when we were all seated. "That was outrageous."

"Sure, don't I want a good seat to see my Bridget's performance?"

"It's called arriving early. You should try it

sometime. Did my mother sort out the mobility scooter issue?"

"Shush now." She patted me on the arm. "The play's about to start."

"I'll take that as a no." Sighing, I mentally added the scooter mess to tomorrow's to-do list and leaned back in my seat to watch the action unfold onstage.

———

A Fighting Man was even worse performed than written, which was saying a lot.

"What possessed me to agree to sit through this play?" I murmured to Nana as the second act shuddered through its midpoint scene.

"At least Bridget looks good," Nana replied, "even if she's spent most of the time in her knickers."

This was only a slight exaggeration. While my mother's character occasionally wore stylish pre-flapper era dresses, she'd spent a number of scenes draped across sofas, wearing night attire made from a flimsy gauze. Regardless of her costumes, even I had to admit that Bliss could act. Not that she had stiff competition from the rest of the cast. The mayor was a ham actor and frequently missed his cues, blithely speaking over characters. Poor Richard had been cast as my mother's effeminate confidante. He'd been provided with a pair of trousers so tight at the crotch that I expected them to split every time he moved. He must have had a similar fear, as he had difficulty delivering his lines while moving across the stage in an unconvincing mince.

At last, the makeshift curtain fell and the audience had a temporary reprieve. I breathed a sigh of relief. "Good grief, that's bad. I'm tempted to try Elaine's rum punch just to get through the second half."

"Elaine makes a great rum punch," Nana said, getting to her feet. "Especially when she spikes it with poteen."

"Rum and poteen?" I shuddered. "Maybe I'll take a rain check on the punch after all."

Elaine and her staff had set up serving tables in the castle's reception area. An array of plain sandwiches was arranged on one table, along with self-serve carafes of coffee and tea.

Aido sidled up to me, clutching a plate of ham sandwiches and looking dapper in an old-fashioned postal uniform. "Take my advice and skip the coffee. It's worse than the play."

"Hey, you. Nice costume. I haven't seen you on stage yet. Where have you been hiding?"

"Helping with the sound effects." He indicated his outfit. "I'll deliver a telegram in the second half."

The creak of the castle door opening drew my attention. DI Bradley stood in the entrance, flanked by a subdued-looking Lou and one of the plain-clothes police officers who'd been outside the castle this afternoon. Silence descended over the crowd as everyone craned to get a good look at the Dublin detectives.

DI Bradley scanned the throng before his gaze settled on me. "Ms. Flanagan. We'd like a word."

I swallowed hard and darted a questioning look at Aido. He returned my unspoken query with a "beats me" shrug. My pulse quickening, I crossed over to the detective. "I'm here to watch the play," I said, my voice not quite steady. "Whatever you want to ask me, you'll have to make it quick."

His smooth smile didn't meet his eyes. "I'm happy to take this down to the station, Ms. Flanagan."

I released the breath I'd been holding and crossed my arms over my chest. "Fine. Fire away."

"I understand that you and the dead clown had an altercation yesterday."

I'd seen this line of questioning coming, but not DI Bradley's timing. "So? We didn't like one another. No crime in that."

"When one of the party winds up dead and the other is the only witness, it might well be a crime."

I unfolded my arms, aware of our audience listening to every word. "Come on. I didn't care for the guy, but I didn't want him dead."

"You filed a complaint about him last month." He delivered this as a statement, not a question.

"Yes. Lou—Sergeant Healey—knows all about that."

"So yesterday's argument with the man wasn't your first," DI Bradley continued.

"Well, no."

"Several witnesses say you threatened to spray him with an illegal substance."

"What the—?" A memory stirred. "Oh, that. I showed him a hairspray can and told him it was pepper spray. I just wanted him to back off and let me go to work."

"I'd like to see that hairspray can." DI Bradley held out a hand.

Muttering under my breath, I opened my backpack and found the offending object. "Until Mr. Chuckles got up in my face, I'd forgotten I owned this. I needed it as part of my Halloween costume."

The detective removed the cap, aimed the can toward the wall, and pressed down on the nozzle.

"Smells like hairspray to me," Lou said.

DI Bradley's nostrils twitched. "Even hairspray can cause damage if sprayed into someone's eyes."

"Look, I said the part about the spray in the heat of the moment. I had no intention of using it."

The man handed the hairspray can back to me. "Maybe not. However, it's a mighty fine coincidence that a man you admit you threatened wound up dead an hour later."

"He didn't die of hairspray inhalation," I pointed out. "Are you accusing me of shooting the guy? I've never handled a gun in my life, not even the ones in the museum."

DI Bradley pounced on this claim. "And yet you were able to identify the weapon the injured man was carrying. The same weapon that mysteriously vanished before the Guards had a chance to remove it as evidence."

"I'm a historian. I recognized the gun he was holding was a revolver and figured out it was a Webley RIC later. I still don't know if it was the real deal or a fancy fake."

"We'd like to continue talking to you at the station," the detective said smoothly. "Feel free to contact a legal representative."

"Are you arresting me?" I demanded, feeling my legs begin to shake. "For what?"

His tight smile made me feel queasy. "At the moment, you're simply helping us with our inquiries."

"Dermot, is that you?" My mother's melodious lilt floated across the room. Her lithe figure followed, cutting a path through the crowd. She was still in the gown she'd worn in her last scene, and she'd wrapped a lacy shawl around her delicate shoulders. She raised an eyebrow in question to me and then shifted her focus back to the detective. "I'd know your voice anywhere. How are you? What are you doing in Dunleagh?"

DI Bradley's face was frozen with shock. "Bliss?"

"Yes, it's me." She stood on her tippy toes and

kissed him on the cheek. "You're looking well. Still keeping up the yoga routine?"

To my surprise, a genuine smile broke through the detective's stern demeanor. "Every day. Yoga keeps me grounded. I'm hoping to attend another of your retreats in the spring."

My mother clapped her hands together as though she were a child who'd just received the holiday gift she'd wanted all year. "Wonderful. I'll be delighted to see you there." She moved to my side. "Have you met my daughter, Dervorgilla?"

My cheeks burned at the sound of my full name. "Just Dee will do," I muttered. "The other's a bit of a mouthful. DI Bradley and I are acquainted, Mother. In fact, he was just about to arrest me."

Bliss's full lips formed a perfect O of surprise. "You're not serious, Dermot. Whatever for?"

The man's cheeks turned redder than mine felt. "She's a person of interest in the murder that occurred yesterday, Bliss. You must understand—"

"Nonsense," my mother said, still all wide-eyed disbelief. "My daughter put her life at risk helping the men who'd been shot. For all she knew, the shooters would come back to finish the job. You should give her a medal for bravery, not arrest her."

"Hear! Hear!" Elaine shouted, raising a glass of her infamous punch. "We should nominate Dee for mayor."

"What's that?" Henry Hyland exclaimed from his

position by the reception desk, where he was holding court among a group of his friends. "I'm not dead."

"So we see." Elaine's dry delivery elicited a round of laughter from the crowd.

My mother used this distraction to her advantage. She slipped an arm through DI Bradley's and dragged him in the direction of the Great Hall. "Why don't you stay for the play, Dermot? The second half is about to begin, but I'm in several scenes. I'd love to hear your thoughts on my performance."

"Well, I—" He looked back at his colleagues, clearly flummoxed by the situation and hoping for a lifeline. Neither Lou nor the other woman said a word.

Bliss patted his arm. "I won't take no for an answer. And you must join me for drinks after." With these words, she swept him into the Great Hall.

I stared after them, open-mouthed.

Lou cocked her head to the side. "How does she do it? I need tricks from Bliss on how to charm that man. So far, all I've managed is to dig myself into a very large hole that he's determined to fill with paperwork."

The female detective laughed. "His bark's worse than his bite. You'll be fine, Sergeant Healey."

The bell rang, announcing the end of the interval. We all filed into the hall and reclaimed our seats. When I reached the front row, Nana was already settled in her chair and chatting with Dottie, Big Jim, and—incongruously—DI Bradley.

"I'm thinking of getting a boob job," she said at a brain-splitting volume.

This unexpected pronouncement startled me out of worrying over my possible arrest. I straightened in my seat and stared at her, examining her wizened face for signs of more than the usual dose of Flanagan family madness. "What did you say?"

"And I thought I was the one with a hearing problem. I said I want breast enhancement surgery." Nana enunciated each syllable and increased her volume by several decibels. "Sure, if they're going in to fix my heart, they might as well fix my girls."

Heads in the audience swiveled in our direction, their owners wearing expressions of horror or amusement. I swallowed a groan. Nana was generating more entertainment than the dire theater production could ever hope to achieve.

Cian glared at us. "Shush. The curtain's about to go up."

The second half of the play was no better than the first. The mayor, who played an English lord and one of my mother's love interests, discovered she'd been supplying the Irish rebels with intelligence stolen from his office. His portrayal of the betrayed lover was hilariously unconvincing. My mother's performance carried each of their scenes and led up to the final confrontation.

The mayor's impassioned plea for her to betray her comrades seemed to go on forever. Given the number of times he fluffed his lines and insisted on repeating them, it probably had. I stifled a yawn and stole a glance at my watch.

"I'll never betray my country." My mother drew a pistol from the folds of her nightgown and pointed it at the mayor. "I'll kill you first."

The mayor, momentarily startled out of character by the sight of the weapon, recollected himself and pulled a revolver from his coat pocket. "Not if I kill you first."

My mother threw back her head and laughed. "Shall we see which of us is the better shot?"

In the next instant, the crack of gunfire rang through the hall, leaving a plume of smoke rising from my mother's pistol.

The mayor, finally appearing to grasp this acting lark, clutched his chest. "You've. Shot. Me." His knees buckled and he lost his balance, pitching forward onto the stage floor.

"That last bit wasn't half bad," Nana announced in a stage whisper, "but the rest of his performance was like watching Kermit the Frog perform Shakespeare."

The demise of the mayor's character elicited a hearty round of applause from the audience. Like me, they were probably breathing sighs of relief that the play was over. Up on the stage, my mother remained frozen, gun still cocked. She didn't move to take her bow or show any sign that the play had limped to its conclusion. Was Bliss taking method acting a step too far? I'd read the play many times. Unless Cian had changed the script yet again, that was the last scene.

And then everything seemed to happen at once. My mother let out a strangled cry, and the pistol clattered to the ground. She staggered toward the mayor with outstretched arms and dropped to her knees. One hand reached out to touch him, and jerked back as though she'd experienced an electric shock. "Blood," she said faintly, still staring at the man's prone form. "I've shot Henry."

Cian leaped out of his seat, his face panic-stricken. "You can't have. The pistol wasn't loaded."

My mother held up her hand, now stained with red. "The blood's real, Cian. I think...I think I've killed him."

FIFTEEN

My mother's pronouncement heralded complete pandemonium. With a strangled cry, Cian jumped onto the stage, quickly followed by DI Bradley, who ran to the mayor and checked him for a pulse. Richard sprang from behind the scenes, disregarding his tight pants. As he raced over to the body, an audible rip of tearing fabric echoed through the hall. The museum director stopped short of the corpse, realizing his predicament. In a futile attempt to avert disaster, he yanked at his waistband. The extra strain on the fabric extended the tear to the left side of the crotch, revealing more of the museum director than I'd ever wished to see.

"Who knew Richard went commando?" Nana roared. "I'm glad I wore my goggles."

"Oh, for heaven's sake," I cried. "Can't you see something's wrong?"

"I can see several wrong things, love, starting with your mum's flimsy outfit. If I wanted to see Bridget in her knickers, I could have stayed at home. Now Richard flashing the crowd is a sight I can get behind."

I strained to see the action on the stage, but DI Bradley blocked my view. I got to my feet and hopped onto the dais. I sidestepped the growing crowd around the mayor and grabbed my mother's discarded shawl from a chair. Richard stood motionless at the front of the stage, shoulders hunched, his hands trying to conceal his exposed bits. I threw the shawl around his waist and tied it at the side, sarong-style.

He gave a brief inclination of his head, shame rolling off him in waves. "Thanks, Dee," he whispered. "There's only so much I can cover with my hands."

I squeezed his arm. "Take heart. It might have happened on opening night. Then you'd have flashed the entire town."

He gave a low laugh. "You certainly know how to comfort a man when he's down. I'll go get dressed. I can't face giving a corpse CPR two days in a row."

"Looks like DI Bradley's got that well in hand," I said, my tone somber. "Go get dressed and we'll get out of here."

Clutching the shawl around his waist, Richard shuffled behind the scenery. I closed the space between my mother and me. She kneeled by Henry Hyland's prone form, her complexion ashen, goose bumps covering her bare arms. DI Bradley's grave demeanor told me his assessment of the mayor's condition matched Richard's. He addressed the audience in a carrying baritone. "Is there a doctor in the house?"

"Dr. Moriarty is in the play," I said. "At least, his wife mentioned he had a role."

Aido stepped out from behind a cluster of fake trees. "He was supposed to play my character, but he and Cian had a last-minute falling-out and I stepped in to take over the part."

"Does anyone have his number?" I called out to the audience. "He might still be at the castle."

Doubtful, but as no one else was proclaiming their medical expertise, it was worth a try.

DI Bradley pressed his phone to his ear and rattled off instructions to emergency services. When he ended the call, his expression was grim. "I have to ask everyone to stay in their seats. I don't want anyone to leave the castle."

Conversation buzzed around the hall, the hum rising and falling. The audience had come for a show, but no one had bargained for one this dramatic. Having exited their seats in the back row, Lou and the plain-clothes detective were busy keeping the audience back from the action. Even without new additions, the stage was uncomfortably crowded.

I took my mother's arm and helped her to her feet. She trembled at my touch, and I fetched a blanket from the sofa that formed part of the set. "Can I take my mother to get a drink, Detective?" I asked, wrapping the blanket around Bliss's shoulders. "She's in shock. I promise we won't go farther than the refreshment stand outside the hall."

DI Bradley looked up from his position on the floor. "Yeah, okay. Just stay in the castle. We'll need to talk to your mother. And don't let her wash her hands."

"I won't. And thanks."

I urged my mother into motion and navigated the step down from the dais. "One of Elaine's rum punches will do you good."

I had no idea whether or not this was true, but I felt compelled to fill the silence. My mother and I weren't close, and comforting her was an alien concept. Bliss had a penchant for extravagant hugs and air-kisses, which I took pains to dodge, but she'd never been the sort of parent to invite confidences. She lived in her own bubble of positivity, far removed from reality and apparently oblivious to a myriad of crises. Until tonight, I'd never seen her distraught. Not once, in spite of two failed marriages, several unsuccessful business ventures, and numerous threats from creditors. Tonight, her childlike confidence that the universe would provide had taken a nosedive.

I hurried Bliss past the front row, where Nana was struggling to get to her feet, aided by Big Jim. I didn't stop to wait for them. Instead, I dragged my mother down the aisle and got us out of the Great Hall. I breathed a sigh of relief when I saw Elaine leaning against the reception desk, fishing a piece of nicotine gum out of a pack. "It's the only way to get me through the evening," she said when she spotted us. "I can't smoke in here."

Elaine gave Bliss a once-over and her expression changed from bland indifference to concern. "Is that blood on your hands? What happened? Did another part of the scenery collapse?"

The woman managed to compress her questions into one run-on sentence. Impressive.

"There was an accident," I said. "The mayor was shot."

Elaine's jaw descended. "You're not serious? I thought he was all hot air when he was blathering on about enemies out to get him."

"It was an accident," I repeated, glancing at Bliss. My insistence on the accident theory rang hollow even to my ears, but it was what my mother needed to hear. "The pistol used in the final scene must have been loaded with a real bullet."

A pistol that had looked suspiciously real. I'd swear that Mr. X's weapon had been a revolver, but Richard was adamant that the cartridge I'd found came from a pistol. Could Bliss's stage prop be the weapon that had killed Mr. Chuckles? If not, how many vintage weapons were floating around the castle?

"That doesn't sound like an accident to me." Elaine grabbed Bliss and hauled her to one of the refreshment tables. "Sit yourself down." She shoved Bliss onto a chair. "I'll get you a cup of my punch. You'll take one as well, Dee."

Before Elaine could pour the drinks, Lou emerged from the Great Hall, a resigned look on her face. "I have to test you for gunshot residue, Bliss. It'll only take a moment."

"Isn't it obvious she'll have it on her hands?" I asked. "We all saw her pull the trigger."

"Doesn't matter," Lou replied. "We have to do it anyway."

While the police officer repeated the procedure she'd performed on me yesterday, Elaine poured generous helpings of her punch into four mugs and shoved one at me. I sniffed at the concoction and drew back. "Do you really add poteen in with the rum?"

Elaine tapped her nose and winked. "It's a secret family recipe."

Lou sealed the pack containing the samples she'd taken from my mother's hands and placed them in a container. "We'll need to ask you some questions, Bliss. I'm afraid it'll have to happen at the police station. You're not under arrest, but we have to treat the shooting as a potential crime until we can prove otherwise."

Unless they could prove otherwise... "Where were the props stored?" I asked. "Anyone could have tampered with the pistol, or replaced a fake with the real deal."

Bliss shivered and drew the blanket tighter around

her shoulders. "I'm not sure. I didn't pay attention to the props."

The door to the Great Hall opened, and Aido emerged, still in his costume. He ushered a now fully clothed Richard into the reception area.

"Do either of you know where the props were stored?" I asked. "I'm wondering where the pistol was before and during the play."

"And who had easy access to it," Lou added. "Far too many people for my liking, I suspect."

"Most of the props are part of the stage set," Aido replied. "Limited space and all that. As far as I know, the pistol was always stored in the jewelry box that Bliss took it from in the second last scene. After that, she had it hidden in her costume."

"We practiced that scene a million times." My mother's voice was lackluster. "I don't know how a real bullet got into the pistol. I understood the gun was a fake."

"It was no fake." Richard addressed Lou. "The pistol belonged to my grandfather. Cian wanted to use authentic props wherever possible."

"Surely you weren't firing blanks onstage?" Lou demanded. "Not at close range?"

"The gunshot was just a sound effect," Aido interjected. "At least, it was until this evening. I helped Cian program the sounds."

"He's right," Richard added. "We made sure the pistol was never loaded."

"It was loaded tonight," I pointed out. "No one's confirmed it yet, but the mayor looked dead to me."

"He is," Lou said quietly. "We're waiting for the paramedics to arrive, but they won't be able to help him."

"How can this mistake have happened?" My mother's panic-stricken eyes looked at each of us in turn.

Bliss in panic mode was triggering my anxiety. I pulled air into my lungs and tried to keep calm.

"I have no idea what went wrong." Richard slumped against the refreshment table. "I checked the pistol during the interval." He caught the change in Lou's expression. "Not to see if it was loaded— although I did check, and it wasn't. It's a valuable piece. Cian strong-armed me into lending it to him for the play and I've been nervous ever since."

Lou pulled a notepad and pen from her pocket. "I'm aware that Mayor Hyland upset a lot of people since taking office. So is DI Bradley. After yesterday's shootings, Hyland was at pains to provide us with a pile of poison pen letters he'd received, plus a list of everyone he claimed had a grudge against him."

Past caring what it contained, I took a swig of Elaine's punch. It tasted vile but I relished the burn in my throat. "Let me guess. We're all on the list."

"Apart from Elaine, yes."

Elaine wheezed with laughter. "I couldn't stand the man. I'd be honored to be on that list. I didn't tamper with that pistol, though, and I didn't write him threatening letters."

Lou screwed up her nose. "The list is long enough as it is without adding your name. At any rate, we have to question Bliss, and we need to talk to Dee about Charles O'Rourke."

"I keep forgetting the clown had a real name." Bliss reached for her mug and downed the contents in one long gulp. "Wasn't he a civil servant before he became a clown?"

"He was?" I blinked. "I've only ever known him as a mediocre street performer."

"O'Rourke worked for the town council for a while," Lou supplied. "He was the personal assistant to a former mayor. I'm blanking on the name, though. Maybe one of you locals know."

"You've become such a fixture in Dunleagh that I forget you're not from here, Lou." Elaine refilled my mother's mug. "Charles worked for Mayor McElligott back in the late Eighties."

The police officer snapped her fingers. "McElligott. That's the name."

The syllables rolled off Lou's tongue in her soothing Northern lilt, dislodging a memory from my mental storage facility. What was it? My pulse quickened.

"Funny to think he was once mayor," Bliss said, toying with the handle of her mug. "He doesn't seem the sort."

"He's not. More's the pity. Every mayor we've had since has been on the make." Elaine shoved a plate of sandwiches at me. "Want one? You might as well. I'll have to chuck them at the end of the night if they don't find homes."

I took a ham and pickle sandwich on autopilot, my thoughts racing. "Can you repeat the mayor's surname, Lou? Only say it slowly this time."

The urgency in my voice startled her. She stared at me as though I'd sprouted a second head. "Why?"

"Please. Just humor me."

She blew out her cheeks, then shrugged. "Okay, then. McElligott. Happy now?"

I slammed my mug onto the refreshment table and tossed the uneaten sandwich to Aido. "Can I have a word with you in private, Lou? It's important."

The police sergeant jerked up from contemplating her notebook. "Uh, sure. We'll go into Larry's office."

Ignoring the curious murmurs from the rest of the company, I marched into Larry's office. Lou followed me at a cautious pace. "So," she said once she'd closed the door. "What's going on?"

I paced a restless rhythm in front of the desk. "Remember you asked me what Mr. X said when I asked him who'd shot him?"

"Yes. You said it made no sense."

"It didn't. Until now. You're from Donegal, right?"

She slow-blinked. "Yeah. Letterkenny, born and bred."

"Mr. X, the dude in the RIC uniform, has a Northern accent."

"I've noticed," Lou said dryly. "Not that it's helped us identify him."

"When I heard him say the name of the person who'd shot him, he could barely breath. The syllables poured out in a jumble. They sounded something like Ma-hell-gut. Hearing you pronounce the name McElligott, I think that was what he was trying to say."

A frown line appeared between her brows. "Are you sure?"

"I couldn't swear to it beyond a reasonable doubt, but it's a lead worth following."

Lou ran a hand through her short hair. "I'm drowning in leads, Dee. What do you think all the admin work I mentioned is about? DI Bradley has Eoin and me chasing down missing persons all over the country, as well as pursuing everyone on the mayor's long list of enemies. Given what happened tonight, we're assuming the mayor's claim he was the intended target of yesterday's attack is correct. That means Mr. X and Mr. Chuckles were collateral damage."

"But you don't know that for sure. The mayor's shooting could have been an accident. My mother didn't fire a real bullet intentionally, and I don't think anyone would sabotage a stage prop to get rid of Henry Hyland."

Lou closed her eyes briefly and exhaled a sigh. "Look, I'm not dismissing your suggestion. I'll pass it on to DI Bradley. All I'm saying is that we can't jump every time a member of the public has a hunch."

"This is more than a hunch," I insisted, frustration adding sharpness to my voice. "I was the only person the man spoke to before he passed out, and I asked him a direct question about who'd shot him."

"You said yourself the man was disoriented. He mistook you for someone called Eliza. How do you know he was answering your question? He might have been saying anything."

"True, but my gut tells me differently."

The police officer scribbled a note in her notebook and replaced it in her pocket. "Like I said, I'll pass it on to the team. I'll be sure to ask a few questions. Maybe this former mayor and his relatives can shed information on the matter. I just can't say when we'll get around to it. Tonight's priority is questioning everyone involved with the play." She glanced at her watch. "A task I should get back to. Will you accompany Bliss to the station?"

"Sure." Another interrogation session with DI Bradley and his team was the last thing I needed, but I couldn't exactly refuse. Besides, being at the station gave me the opportunity to keep an eye on Bliss.

"I'll check with DI Bradley. If he gives me the okay, we'll go now."

I followed Lou out of Larry's office. By this time, the group around Elaine's refreshment table had expanded to include Nana, Dottie, and Big Jim. The golden oldies were lashing into the punch, and Bliss's bleary-eyed look indicated she'd followed suit. This didn't bode well for her trip to the police station. Lou returned to the Great Hall, and I reclaimed my seat beside my mother.

"I predicted turbulence for all zodiac signs in my latest horoscopes," Bliss said in a tremulous voice, "but I had no idea I'd be involved in a violent death."

I resisted the temptation to roll my eyes. Whatever was in Elaine's punch, it had revived my mother. Bliss making every situation all about her was par for the course.

"Has anyone confirmed the mayor is dead?" I asked. "I'm assuming he is."

"The paramedics arrived while you were holed up with Lou. Not that they can do anything for Hyland." Nana tut-tutted. "He was an awful man but he didn't deserve to die like that. When I get hold of the person who set up my Bridget, I'll put them in the morgue alongside Hyland and Mr. Chuckles."

"Lev will be kept busy." I picked up the mug I'd abandoned earlier and took a swig. I didn't like the punch, but I needed something to distract me. With my mother cast as the mayor's unwitting killer, Cian's play had turned into a horror show.

"What did you want to talk to Lou about?" Elaine demanded, her blue-mascaraed eyes brimming with curiosity. "You got all mysterious. Are you trying to accuse Dunleagh's favorite former mayor of murder?"

"What's that?" Dottie cupped her ear. "Who does Dee suspect?"

"I don't suspect anyone," I insisted. "The name McElligott sounded familiar."

"Well, of course it does," Nana said, shoveling a sandwich into her mouth. "What's he got to do with the mayor cocking up his toes?"

"The connection was with the clown, actually. Or the man I helped yesterday to be precise. He said something when I asked who'd shot him. It sounded like nonsense at the time, but hearing Lou say the name McElligott made me wonder if that was what he was trying to say."

"Well, that's a turn up for the books," Nana said, perking up. "Are you sure that's the name you heard?"

"No, but it's a lead worth pursuing. Do you know where Mayor McElligott lives? I'd like to pay him a visit."

"No need." Big Jim piled sandwiches onto his plate and winked at me. "I'm right here."

"Wait...*you* were mayor of Dunleagh?" I couldn't wrap my head around the image of my grandmother's disheveled poker-playing companion as mayor.

"I was indeed."

"And Mr. Chuckles was your personal assistant?"

Big Jim grimaced. "That he was. For a while. I caught him reading confidential documents and fired him on the spot."

I hesitated for a moment, searching for the right

words. "Any idea if one of your relatives had a grudge against Henry Hyland?"

Big Jim's rheumy eyes moved from his sandwiches back to me. "The only living McElligott in these parts is me, and I didn't shoot anyone."

SIXTEEN

In a twisted cosmic joke, the morning after my mother gunned down the mayor dawned bright and sunny, heralding the hottest day we'd had so far this summer. To my surprise, I'd slept well, in spite of the hours of grilling we'd endured at Dunleagh Garda Station. After a brief tussle with my conscience, I decided that attending the Historical Murders Club breakfast was what I needed to take my mind off last night.

I managed to shower and sneak out of the house without encountering Nana or Bliss, neither of whom I could face before a good breakfast and a liter of coffee. Bliss's subdued state was a new experience for me, and Nana's excitement over yesterday's drama was grating on my nerves.

I rode Mavis to the seafront and chose a parking space close to the promenade. This early on a Saturday morning, the place was almost deserted.

Only a few tourists were up and about, squeezing in the sights of Dunleagh before driving to their next destination. A gentle breeze blew in from the sea, ruffling my still-damp hair. I inhaled the salty air, relishing its taste and smell. Seagulls called to one another on the shore, and the soothing lap of the waves calmed me. Close proximity to the sea was a huge plus to living in Dunleagh, and I squeezed in a swim whenever I could. Today, though, I'd have to content myself with a stroll down the promenade. I had a long list of places to be, and my first port of call was The Coffee Bean.

My friend Amy's café was the antithesis of Elaine's greasy establishment. Instead of the grimy framed pictures of long-dead Irish heroes that lined Elaine's walls, The Coffee Bean had opted for a nautical theme. The café's name was spelled out in seashells above the door, and a huge anchor sat under the large bay window. When I walked inside, I was hit with the twin aromas of freshly ground coffee and sizzling bacon. I exhaled a sigh of pure pleasure. This was my definition of paradise.

In spite of the early hour, the café was busy. Amy had shoved several tables together for the Historical Murders Club meeting, and most of the seats were already occupied. Mary Yates sat in a window seat, wedged between Larry and Orla Tierney. The young pathologist looked ill from stress. What was bugging her? Was my suspicion that she was involved with her boss correct? It would explain her discomfort at sitting next to his wife.

My gaze shifted across the assembled company. Suzie wasn't there, and neither was Zosia. Dared I hope the other nurse was also working? I had no desire to put up with her jibes this morning. At the end of the table, sat Anna Jobson, a young librarian with a massive crush on Aido. Across from Anna, Elaine tucked into a stack of pancakes.

"What's this?" I asked teasingly. "Have you ventured into enemy territory?"

Elaine, unabashed, stuck her fork into her breakfast. "It pays to check out the competition. I can't be having anyone rival my Coronary Classic, now can I?"

A smile spread across my face at the comparison between Elaine's greasy mess of a signature dish and Amy's fluffy pancakes. My smile turned into a laugh when I spotted Richard and Aido on the other side of the table, rocking a Battle of the Bands look. Aido wore his usual punk uniform. Richard, clad in a red open-necked shirt and skintight leather pants, looked like a member of a Seventies metal band.

Aido was in full morning-person mode. "Hey, Dee. Great to see you."

"We didn't expect you to show up," Richard said, "but I'm glad you came. It'll do you good to have a distraction."

Elaine patted the free seat beside her. "Sit yourself down."

My good humor faltered when I spotted the woman seated on the other side of the free space. I'd happily skip breaking bread with Aido's surly twin sister, but she and her brother often came as a package deal.

Naido scowled at me through her fringe of lank brown hair. I don't subscribe to the myth of the magical makeover that transforms people's appearances, their self-confidence, and their love lives. However, if anyone in this world needed an intervention, it was Naido Lafferty. She paid less attention than she should to personal hygiene and wore the same handful of shapeless garments day in, day out. Everything about the woman screamed depression. My heart ached for her, but she was hard work. Her open hostility made it easier to avoid her than to engage. Which, of course, was her intention.

"Morning, Naido," I said. "Mind if I sit here?"

Naido's only response was a grunt. I dropped onto the seat next to hers and tried not to take offense when she moved her chair as far away from me as she could get and still have access to her plate.

I opened my backpack and removed a plastic bag. I passed it across the table to Richard. "Your coat and sweater. Thanks for letting me borrow them."

"No problem at all," he said. "I'm glad they came in useful."

I reached for the menu and addressed the others. "How did you sleep after last night's drama?"

"I took a sleeper." Richard rubbed his unshaven jaw. "It didn't do much good."

"Two mugs of my punch and I was a goner," Elaine supplied between mouthfuls.

Aido spread a thick layer of butter across his toast. "I slept like a baby. You?"

"Surprisingly well, all things considered."

Naido peered at me from beneath her thick brown fringe, triggering an image of Cousin Itt from *The Addams Family*. "You're like the kiss of death these days. How many dead bodies have you found this week?"

Oh, boy. I was so not in the mood to deal with Aido's snarky sibling. "Two. And your point is?"

"Dee didn't kill either of them. We don't know who offed the clown, and the mayor..." Aido trailed off, realizing what he was about to say.

"And the mayor was shot by my mother," I finished for him, "using a stage prop that she didn't know was loaded."

"A stage prop supplied by me." Richard stared at his unbuttered toast. "I never should have let Cian borrow Granddad's pistol."

"Don't blame yourself," I said. "It wasn't your fault."

The museum director looked up at last, his expression somber. "Wasn't it? I keep going over yesterday evening in my mind. To be frank, I was more concerned about the value of the pistol than its potential as a deadly weapon. I checked it during the interval, yes, but my examination of the magazine was cursory at best."

"You'd have noticed if it contained bullets," I insisted. "You'd have registered that something wasn't right, even if you merely glanced at the magazine."

"Exactly what I told him," Aido said. "Even if he performed the check on autopilot, he'd have noticed a bullet."

Naido toyed with her fork and regarded the museum director with a combative attitude. "Didn't Mayor Hyland threaten to evict you and cut your pay?"

Elaine snorted with laughter. "That fella threatened to evict loads of people, love. Richard was just one of many to fall victim to Henry Hyland's building plans."

"Do you seriously think Richard resorted to murder over his job?" I demanded. "You've known him how long?"

She sniffed and glared at me through her sheepdog hair. "No need to be so touchy. I was only saying what everyone else in town is thinking. Dozens of people had a reason to want Hyland out of the way, and Richard is one of them."

"She's right," Richard said quietly. "It is what everyone's thinking."

Aido's sister returned her attention to her scrambled eggs. My stomach growled at the sight of them. At that moment, Amy appeared, looking clean and efficient in a brown apron and a T-shirt emblazoned with the café's logo. She placed a large cappuccino before me. "Morning, Dee. I thought you could do with a coffee. You've had quite the week."

"Thanks, Amy." I dumped a generous spoonful of brown sugar into my cup and stirred.

"Lovely to see you, Dee." Amy drew closer to our table and lowered her voice. "We're all hoping this business with the mayor is cleared up soon for your mother's sake. How's Bliss holding up?"

"Not well," I said. "I've never seen her properly rattled before."

In spite of the warmth of the café, Amy pulled her cardigan tight around her chest. "I can't believe we've had two murders in as many days. Mayor Hyland's death was murder, right? That's what everyone's saying."

I nodded. "I can't see how it could have been an accident. No one loads bullets into a pistol by mistake."

Amy shuddered. "What an awful thing to happen."

"Not really," Naido said through a mouthful of eggs. "No one liked Mayor Hyland."

Her brother shot her a warning look. "No one wanted him dead, though."

Naido snorted. "Yeah, right. Only half the town, including his wife."

Amy caught Aido's imploring gaze and deftly steered the conversation to my order. "Do you want your usual, Dee?"

My usual consisted of scrambled eggs and bacon with a side of fried tomatoes and a large freshly squeezed orange juice as my nod to proper nutrition. "Yes, please."

After Amy left to take care of my order, Aido pounced on his sister. "You can't go around saying things like that. Until the Guards find the killer, everyone's under suspicion, but it doesn't do to go upsetting people by pointing it out the whole time."

"Don't you mean *killers*?" Naido asked through a mouthful of food. "Dee's report said there were at least two shooters in the courtyard."

Aido shot me a look of exasperation. I shrugged. "She has a point. It's too late to pussyfoot around the matter. We all know Henry Hyland upset half the town, and I heard several male voices and too many shots for there to have been one shooter the day Mr. Chuckles died."

"I say we compile a list, like we do for our Historical Murders cases." Elaine raised her voice and addressed the rest of the club members. "What do you think, lads and ladies? Up for a little contemporary sleuthing? This week in Dunleagh's a lot more interesting than that boring Eyre Square Murder. Will we have a show of hands?"

Everyone raised a hand, some more tentative than others.

"That's settled then," Elaine said with a decisive air. "Let's clear Bliss's name as well as Richards."

"It's not a bad idea, I suppose." Aido sounded less than convinced. "We do a decent job at analyzing murders."

"Historical murders," I pointed out, "with no personal stakes involved. Shouldn't we leave the investigating to the police?"

Aido laughed so hard he choked on his coffee and Richard had to pound him on the back. "You're a hypocrite, Dee Flanagan. You couldn't wait to sneak into Mr. X's room to dig for information."

"And you were quick to persuade Lou to let me examine the cartridge," Richard added.

Aido looked at Richard and then to me. "What cartridge? Does this have something to do with Dee's freak-out at the museum the day of the shootings?"

"Was it in the missing evidence bag?" Naido asked, shoveling toast into her mouth and spraying crumbs over the table.

I breathed in sharply. "You know about that?"

The woman shrugged. "Orla mentioned it yesterday. A rumor connecting you to its disappearance is making the rounds."

Elaine's words carried down the table. Orla's pale

cheeks turned scarlet. *Great.* As I'd suspected after talking to Mary yesterday, word had spread. A sinking feeling in my stomach depleted my appetite. Cian would be furious if he discovered I'd known about this and not told him. I'd text him the moment our meeting was over.

"I didn't steal anything," I insisted. "Lou won't be pleased everyone knows about the missing evidence bag."

"Orla and Mary have already told us what was in the bag, but they didn't actually see the stuff," Elaine said. "Can you elaborate?"

I threw my arms in the air. "Fine. Seeing as the news is already all over town." I addressed this last bit at Orla and Mary, both of whom had the good grace to look abashed.

By the time I'd finished filling them in on the RIC uniform, Mr. X's revolver, and the contents of the mysteriously vanishing evidence bag, even Naido was paying attention.

Aido leaned back in his seat. "Whoa. I had no idea there were so many antique firearms floating around Dunleagh. Did the cartridge Dee found come from the pistol Bliss fired?"

Richard shook his head. "Not possible. My grandfather's pistol is a Smith & Wesson Model 1913. It takes a different cartridge to the one Dee found. My best guess for the weapon that fired Dee's cartridge is a Mauser C96."

"It all sounds like gibberish to me," Aido said, "but I'll take your word for it. Let's compile that list Elaine suggested and go from there." He pulled a tablet from his bag and swiped a fingertip over the screen. "I say Cian is the number one suspect. I like the dude, but we know he fought with the mayor, and Hyland was killed during a performance of his play."

"But did he kill the clown?" Mary asked. "The two murders have to be connected."

"Not necessarily," Naido replied. "Coincidences do happen. It seems rash not to consider the possibility that we're dealing with two separate crimes."

Naido volunteering an opinion that wasn't a sarcasm-laden insult took me off guard. I took another sip of my cappuccino and considered the point. "She has a point. We should keep an open mind."

The woman regarded me with suspicion but made no further comment.

"Two murders in two days is a massive coincidence, though," Larry said. "Even if they're not connected, someone set up Bliss to fire that gun."

"You don't think she did it deliberately?" Orla ventured, shooting me an apologetic look. "Sorry, Dee, but we can't leave Bliss off the suspect list just because she's your mother."

"I know." I sighed. "Add her name to the suspect list. And put down mine as well. I stood to lose my job if Hyland's plans for the newspaper came to fruition."

"And you fought with Mr. Chuckles," Naido

added with a hint of malice. "That puts you in the frame for both murders."

I gritted my teeth but didn't contradict her. "That's true."

"Okay," Aido said, "if Dee goes on the list, so does everyone else who works at the *Chronicle*, including me. We all stood to lose our jobs if Cian couldn't afford to pay us."

Elaine whistled. "This is going to be a long list."

"Then there's me," Richard said. "No, I didn't do it, but we have to add my name. I stood to lose my job and my home and I handled the pistol shortly before Bliss fired the fatal shot."

"To be fair, anyone in the cast, crew, or audience could've tampered with the pistol," Aido pointed out. "Everyone was milling about during the interval, and we were all focused on you once DI Bradley showed up."

"That's true," I mused. "We'll have to add the library staff to the list. Their pay's already been cut and a couple will be let go by the end of the year."

"Fair enough," Mary said. "Put my name on the list."

"And mine," Anna Jobson added. "I suppose we should put down Cathal Byrne as well."

"Is he the guy who works with you?" I asked. "Kind of dorky-looking?"

"That's Cathal," Aido supplied. "I went to school with him."

Amy reappeared with my breakfast and cast a glance at Aido's tablet. "What's this? Are you lot making a list of murder suspects?"

"Yeah," I replied. "The only thing we know for sure is that my mother shot the mayor with a pistol that should've been unloaded. We don't know who put bullets into the pistol, but there are plenty of people with a grudge against Henry Hyland. Apparently, he received several threatening anonymous letters before his death. Any idea what sort they were or who sent them?"

I scanned the table for reactions, but no flash of telltale guilt showed on their faces.

Richard pursed his lips. "Who knows? There are plenty of potential candidates."

"Anyone on our list of suspects could have sent the letters," Aido said.

"As for what sort," Elaine interjected, "I heard they were the type you read about in books. Letters cut and pasted from magazines."

I filed this information away for future reference. "Thanks, guys."

Amy slid my plate onto the table. "This is a departure from your usual meeting discussions, no?"

"It's what's on everyone's mind." My wry smile was more for my benefit than anyone else's. I'd decided to attend the breakfast because I thought it would distract me from the murders. However, I couldn't muster annoyance that our conversation had taken this turn. At least compiling a list of suspects was proactive and made me feel slightly less helpless.

"I'm glad I didn't bail," Naido added. "I thought today's meeting would be a snoozefest."

The bell above the café door jangled, and a fresh influx of customers strode in. Amy smiled. "Back to work for me."

While Amy served customers, we continued adding names to our suspect list. By the time I'd polished off my breakfast, we had twenty-four names, including the mayor's wife and son.

I drained my coffee cup and considered the names. "Wow. I knew Hyland was unpopular but I hadn't realized the extent to which he'd annoyed people. Just about everyone I know in Dunleagh is on that list, apart from Nana and my sister and her family."

Richard took the tablet from Aido and scanned the list. "How do these people have a connection with Mr. Chuckles? Was he also a target? Or was he simply in the wrong place at the wrong time?"

"Here's what bothers me about connecting the two murders, even though I know it makes sense to do so." I drummed my fingertips on the tabletop and considered my next words. "We can all agree that two shootings in less that forty-eight hours, both involving vintage firearms, is a massive coincidence. That said, Mr. Chuckles was gunned down in broad daylight. It was a direct attack, and the more I think about it, the less convinced I am that he was killed by mistake. He was wearing a clown costume, for goodness sake. Kind of hard to miss, no? On the other hand, the mayor was shot onstage using my mother as an unwitting accomplice. That's sneaky and indirect and indicates a different personality type to the person behind the clown's death."

"Right." Aido toyed with his coffee cup, his forehead creased in thought. "And that begs the question if Mr. Chuckles was just collateral damage and the real target was your pal, Mr. X."

"Exactly. One of them probably was in the wrong place at the wrong time, but which one? We need to find out if the clown had enemies—" I caught Naido's smirk, "—apart from me. And we have to discover the mystery man's identity."

"Not sure we can do much about Mr. X," Elaine said, "but I can ask around about Mr. Chuckles."

"No, leave that to me," Naido said. "The clown was friendly with my boss."

Naido was an indie game designer who made ends meet with a part-time job at a photography studio. Her boss, a slimy-looking individual named Ger Hayes, fit my expectations of anyone who'd have called Mr. Chuckles a friend.

"Okay, you tackle Hayes about the clown. Maybe Aido can talk to the mayor's wife. See how grief-stricken she is and if she has any more names to add to our list."

Aido groaned. "Why me? Sally Hyland's a pain."

"Yes, but she's a pain who likes you." When she wasn't at a health spa or hobnobbing with the golf club set, Sally Hyland organized fancy fundraisers. We'd covered one such event at her home a few months ago. She'd been rude to me and absolutely poisonous to the caterers but she'd positively gushed over Aido.

"I'll quiz Hyland's staff," Larry said, grinning. "Subtle, like. Although I can already tell you that none of his staff liked him."

"Huge shocker," I said dryly. "At this stage, finding someone who liked him would be a surprise."

"Who do you want to question, Richard?" Aido asked.

"He could question all of us at the library," Mary volunteered, "and we could question him."

"Yeah, that makes sense," Richard replied. "I have to go to the library later anyway to put the finishing touches to the exhibition. We'll chat then."

"I thought I'd swing by the hospital," I said. "See if Suzie knows more about Mr. X."

"Not keen to ask Zosia?" Naido shot me a sly glance. She was well aware of my dislike of Lev's sister and was for some inexplicable reason on cordial terms with the woman. I wouldn't go so far as to describe them as friends—Naido didn't do friends—but I'd seen her offer Zosia something dangerously close to a smile at our club meetings.

"I suspect Suzie will be more forthcoming," I said

dryly. "And while I'm at the hospital, I'll try to corner Lev and get updates on the autopsies."

"Won't they be straightforward?" Naido blew her fringe out of her eyes. "Like, they were both shot. The cause of death is clear."

"Yeah." Aido's frown deepened. "I don't see much point in wasting time in the morgue, unless you want to follow up on the missing evidence bag."

I did intend to check up on the bag, but I was less interested in the missing evidence than I was in following up on Mr. X's strange claims. The guy had to be crazy, but maybe there was a grain of truth in his outlandish claims. Perhaps he was connected to a War of Independence fan group or had some other traceable interest in the past. As Lev was the only doctor I knew well at Dunleagh General Hospital, I hoped to use him to get info.

"You never know what Lev might tell me," I said. "It's worth a go."

"Before you go haring off asking questions—" Aido shot his sister a significant look, "—Naido has something to give you."

With a great show of reluctance, she pulled a mobile phone from the voluminous folds of her tunic and shoved it at me. "Don't lose it."

I took the phone and examined the old-fashioned model. "Thank you. I've felt lost without a phone."

The other woman muttered something inaudible that I suspected was an uncomplimentary comment about me. I pocketed the phone and pulled my purse out of my backpack. "I'll pay up and get going. Want to chat tomorrow?"

"Yeah," Aido said. "That'll give us a chance to start asking questions."

"Sorry to love you and leave you, but my schedule today is crazy." I laid money on the table. "I'm going to head to the archives and put in a couple of hours on the digitalization project. Then I'll swing by the hospital. Do you need me at the museum later, Richard?"

With the exhibition about to open, my usual Monday and Saturday morning volunteer slots had been flexible.

He shook his head. "Not unless you want to come by. You've gone way over your hours this month already."

"I was happy to help." I stood and gathered my stuff, my mind already on the questions I wanted to ask Mr. X. "Thanks for the unorthodox meeting, people. Happy sleuthing."

SEVENTEEN

After leaving The Coffee Bean, I rode Mavis to the castle and put in a solid couple of hours in the archives. The Guards were everywhere except the dungeons, a fact for which I was grateful. I had no desire to bump into DI Bradley and his colleagues again. Even Lou was low on the list of people I wanted to meet. She'd be fuming that the news of the missing evidence bag had leaked. I hadn't stolen the evidence, but I'd been the last person who'd admitted handling the bag before its disappearance.

My inner sense of guilt was at the fore. If I hadn't snuck into the storage room, would the bag have been stolen? Had my curiosity drawn the shooters' attention to Mr. X's personal effects? If Mr. X hadn't been their intended target, why bother stealing his stuff? I gave myself a mental shaking. My current train of thought was leading me nowhere. What I needed to do was focus on my work and add another two or three hours to this month's pay. I took a deep breath and tackled the huge volume of back issues on my desk.

Once I'd sorted another stack of old newspapers to send for digitalization, I packed my stuff and left the archives. After I grabbed an energy bar at the castle's café, I got Mavis and headed for Dunleagh General. It was after twelve when I strode through the hospital doors. As always, the registration desks were a hive of activity. A sea of white-coated doctors, blue-clad nurses, and a plethora of patients moved in and out of my line of vision. I took the stairs up to St. Patrick's Ward and knocked on the door to the nurses' station. There was no answer. I glanced at my watch and paced the corridor. What now? I could head right up to Mr. X's room, but I wanted a heads-up from Suzie before I tackled whoever was standing guard today. I was on the verge of giving up when I spotted my quarry, staggering under the weight of a pile of paperwork.

"Hey, Suzie. Want a hand carrying those files?"

She laughed when she recognized me. "Hey, you. Have you taken up residence at the hospital? I caught sight of you down in reception this morning."

I slow-blinked. "That's not possible. I just arrived."

Suzie's brow furrowed. "Are you sure? I was certain it was you. Your hair's pretty distinctive."

On impulse, my hand strayed to my mane of wild curls, which were barely contained by a hairband. "It definitely wasn't me."

The nurse looked perplexed. "Okay. I must've been mistaken. Maybe you have a doppelgänger."

"With the wild things that have been happening in Dunleagh this week, nothing would surprise me."

Suzie passed me three of the files. "Are you here to ask me awkward questions again?" she asked, leading me back toward the nurses' station.

"Of course." I held open the door and she lunged in, dumping the files on a desk. I added mine to the pile.

Suzie wiped a sheen of sweat from her forehead and darted a look around the empty room. "Okay, make it quick. What do you want to know?"

"How's Mr. X?"

Her smile was smug. "Don't you mean Mr. Sweeney?"

I sucked in a breath. "You've identified him?"

"He identified himself."

"Don't leave me hanging," I said, bouncing from foot to foot. "I want all the deets."

"There's not a lot to tell. Apparently, he woke up this morning and had his memory back. His name is Matt Sweeney. He's a teacher from Donegal and he'd just moved to Dunleagh the day of the shooting. He's due to fill in for your sister's maternity leave when the kids go back to school in September."

I sagged against the desk, oddly deflated. Could the mysterious Mr. X's story be so banal? What about his old-fashioned uniform and gun? "He's the replacement history and Irish teacher?"

"It seems so. He's new to town, hence no one recognizing him." Suzie shoved a stray strand of hair behind her ear and gestured at the mountain of folders. "I'm sorry, Dee. I have to get back to work. Matron will have kittens if I don't finish this paperwork."

I straightened. "Right. I'll let you get on with it. Thanks for the update."

Leaving Suzie to her folders, I exited the nurses' station. While I walked down the corridor, I turned what I'd learned over in my mind. Mr. X was a secondary school teacher, not a time traveler from the year 1919. Not that I'd believed his wild story. Of course I hadn't. Still, his explanation for being in Dunleagh was a letdown. Was I glad the guy had his memory back? Sure. Did I wish his story wasn't quite so pedestrian? Definitely.

I paused at the stairs, first looking down at reception, and then up to the floor above me. Was there any point in tackling Mr. X again? It'd take me a while to get used to thinking of him as Mr. Sweeney—I'd grown attached to the Mr. X moniker. What excuse did I have to visit him? Suzie hadn't provided any reason for his RIC uniform. Surely that was a question worth asking? He'd gone to a great deal of trouble to acquire an accurate costume, right down to the detail of the trench watch—a watch that had his initials engraved on the back. No, Mr. Sweeney definitely had questions to answer. After taking a deep breath, I climbed the stairs to St. Colmcille's Ward.

This time, no one blocked my entrance to Room 303. Either the man's self-identification had eliminated him from suspicion of Mr. Chuckles's murder, or the Guards had decided he was in no danger from a further attack. I checked the corridor for any stray police officers but only saw a nurse carrying a tray into a room further down the ward. I lifted my hand and knocked on the door before entering.

Zosia posed beside the bed, her nurse's uniform emphasizing her ample curves. A seductive smile played at the corners of her mouth, and she was laughing at something Mr. X had said. They both looked up when I walked into the room. Her smile turned into a smirk. "Here to interrogate my patient again? Visiting hours don't start until three."

My gaze swept past her and latched onto the man I'd come to see. "I was hoping Mr. Sweeney would give me a moment of his time."

He met my gaze and amusement tugged at the corners of his mouth. He looked better than the last time I'd seen him. Color was back in his cheeks, and his eyes appeared livelier. Although his IV was still in place, he was no longer hooked up to the heart monitor. I took this to be a positive sign.

"I don't think—" Zosia began, but the man cut

her off.

"It's fine. I'd like to speak to Miss Flanagan. Alone, if you don't mind."

Indecision flickered across her beautiful face. "Visiting hours don't start for another hour," she repeated with a stubborn jut to her jaw.

"Surely you can make an exception for the woman who saved my life?" The patient's smile warmed me to my toes, and it wasn't even directed at me.

Zosia cast me a look laden with venom. "Fine," she snapped. "Dee can stay. Don't blame me if she wears you out."

"And a cup of tea would be lovely," he added.

For a moment, I thought Zosia would object. Instead, her mouth formed a hard line and she stalked out of the room.

After she'd left, I pulled a chair over to the side of the bed. "Thanks for agreeing to chat with me."

"No, thank you for coming to see me." A lock of brown hair fell over his forehead and he blew it out of his eyes. "I owe you an apology. I made some rather unusual statements yesterday. None of them were true. I can only assume the blood loss confused me."

I took in his cool and collected demeanor. His words were reasonable. Far saner than anything he'd said yesterday. *And yet...* "No worries. I'm glad you're feeling better." I grinned. "And I hear you have a name that's neither John Doe nor Mr. X."

His smile didn't quite meet his eyes. "That's right. I'm Matt Sweeney."

I held out a hand. "Nice to meet you, Matt. I'm Dee."

His handshake was firm, and his deep blue eyes gave little away. "I'll be teaching school as of September. Irish and history."

"So I've heard." I settled back in my chair and pulled a paper notepad and pen from my bag. "Do you mind if I ask you a few questions? We didn't exactly get off to a great start yesterday."

A dark flush crept over his cheekbones. "No. I'm sorry about that. What would you like to know?"

"Let's start with an easy question." I uncapped my pen. "Why were you at Dunleagh Castle on Thursday?"

"I wanted to speak to your boss."

"Cian Egan?" I frowned. "Did you have a story for the *Chronicle*?"

"No. I'm interested in amateur dramatics. I wanted to see if he had a part for me in his play."

If Matt Sweeney delivered his lines as convincingly as he told this tale, he was a terrible actor. "Is that why you wore the Royal Irish Constabulary uniform?" My voice rang with skepticism. "And the old-fashioned watch engraved with your initials? To get into character?"

"I'm interested in the time period of the Irish War of Independence." His cool gaze raked my face. "I understand that's something we have in common, Miss Flanagan."

"Dee, please. I'm only ever called Miss Flanagan when people are annoyed with me. Ditto Ms. Flanagan."

I laughed, but Matt's only reaction was a perplexed stare. "Mizz?" He cast me a quizzical look. "Don't you mean Missus? Are you married?"

"No, I'm not married." I waited for a beat. "Ms., as in the default form of address for a woman?"

Still no response.

"An honorific that doesn't denote marital status?" I continued, scanning Matt's blank face for clues. "Surely you've heard of it before?" My laugh rang hollow. "It's only been common since before I was born."

His Adam's apple bobbed. "Uh, naturally. Of course I've heard of it. I'm sorry. I'm still confused after my—" He gestured to his upper chest, which was still swathed in bandages.

"Right. Of course." A wave of guilt flooded over me, warring with my suspicions. Was I harassing an innocent man? Or did Matt Sweeney know more than he was saying about the shoot-out? I swallowed past my doubts. "You must be on strong pain relief."

He latched onto this lifeline with palpable enthusiasm. "Yes. The medication is making me drowsy."

"I won't keep you long, so." I gave him a reassuring smile. "I have just a couple more questions."

He cleared his throat. "Before we get to those, I believe you're something of an expert on the War of Independence?"

In spite of my best efforts not to blush, my cheeks warmed. "I know quite a bit about it, yes."

"I don't suppose you can recommend some books on the topic? I'd like to read new material on the subject before school starts."

"Sure. I'll send you a list. Can you give me your email address?"

A frown line appeared between his brows. "I'm afraid I can't remember my house number."

"Not your snail mail address. I can email you the list." No reaction. Bizarre. Was the guy having some sort of episode? "Um, do you need me to call the nurse?"

Matt straightened in the bed. "Not necessary. Yes, I'd like your list. If you could write it down for me, I'd be delighted."

I digested his words. The guy was an odd character. What was his issue with email? Even my grandmother preferred it to regular letters. "I'll get you the list. Is the internet connected yet in your new place?"

He blinked. "Excuse me?"

"The internet," I repeated. "Do you have it set up already?"

"No." He delivered the word quick as gunfire. "Not yet."

"When you do, you can look up my history channel. I have lots of blog posts and videos about Ireland during the War of Independence. Maybe you'll find material to use for your classes."

He swallowed, darting a nervous glance from side to side. "Perhaps you can tell me more over dinner," he blurted. "I'd like to invite you out to say thank you for helping me."

"I did what anyone else would've done, and probably less efficiently than most. I was just glad you didn't need CPR."

The blank expression slid over his features again, as though he was trying to hide his reaction to my words. This man flustered me, and I had the sneaking suspicion that he knew it. I shifted my gaze to his bed covers and tried to marshal some semblance of composure.

"All the same," he said softly, "you were there and you helped. I'm grateful."

The longer this conversation lasted, the more convinced I was that he was trying to distract me from his strange responses to my questions. I drew in a breath and posed another. "Who shot you?"

Matt raised both shoulders in a shrug and winced when his injured side protested against the sudden movement. "I have no idea. I assume they were after the other man."

"Mr. Chuckles," I filled in. "Well, that was his stage name. Why do you say the shooters were after the clown?"

"I can't think of a reason anyone would want to shoot me." His delivery was less credible than Mayor Hyland's attempts to act.

"When we were in the courtyard, you mistook me for a woman named Eliza. You clearly thought she was in danger. And when I asked you if you knew the gunmen, you said a word I couldn't understand at first, but that I now believe was the surname McElligott."

For the briefest of moments, shock registered in Matt Sweeney's deep blue eyes. Then his protective shutters slammed down. "I have no idea what I said. The shock of my injury must have affected my mind."

"The watch you were wearing had your initials engraved on the back, plus those of the gift giver. Is Eliza E.R.?"

"I bought the watch from an antique shop. I wasn't aware my initials were on the back, but I assure you, it was merely a coincidence."

I tapped my pen against my notepad. "Why don't I believe you? What are you hiding?"

"I'm not hiding anything, Miss—" he treated me to an ingratiating smile, "—sorry, Dee."

"Did Big Jim McElligott have anything to do with the shooting?" I probed, determined to shock him into another unguarded response.

My tactic worked. "Big Jim McElligott?" he spluttered. "I don't know anyone of that name."

"He's the former mayor of Dunleagh."

Matt scrunched up his forehead. "The man who was killed last night?"

"No. Big Jim was in office long before I lived in Dunleagh. The man who died yesterday was Henry Hyland."

"I haven't heard of him, either."

I raised an eyebrow. "Really? Didn't he have to sign off on your new teaching position?"

Actually, I wasn't sure if the mayor played any role in staffing decisions for Dunleagh's schools, but I wanted to see how Matt Sweeney would react.

His face remained a blank mask. "Yes, of course. I didn't pay attention to the name."

"Your new internetless home—where is it?"

The mask relaxed. "I've moved into an apartment on—" he hesitated a fraction, "—Prince Albert Street."

I looked up from my notepad. "Prince Albert Street? I don't think I know it."

His Adam's apple bobbed, but his face remained otherwise impassive. "It's the street adjacent to the school."

I scribbled a note, mostly to allow myself time to think. I could picture the street he meant, but I couldn't recall its name. Prince Albert Street struck a wrong chord, though. Why would he lie about a detail I could easily verify? I blew out my cheeks. The dude had been more convincing when he'd told me he was alive one hundred years ago.

Matt Sweeney opened the drawer of his bedside table and extracted a mobile phone. "Can I have your telephone number, please? I'll contact you about dinner after I'm allowed home."

"Sure. I'll have to give you a couple of numbers, though. My own phone is missing, and I've borrowed a friend's device to tide me over." Calling Naido a friend was a stretch, but her brother fit the bill, and she'd only allowed me to borrow her phone for his sake. I scribbled both numbers on a blank sheet of my notepad and tore it free. "Here you go."

He took the proffered piece of paper with a smile. "Thank you. I'll be in touch."

"Can I have your number?" I nodded to his phone. "Just in case I end up buying a new phone with a different SIM card."

Panic flitted across his face. "Uh, certainly."

Matt Sweeney picked up his phone. A few awkward swipes later, beads of sweat had formed on his upper lip. I scrunched up my forehead. If I didn't know better, I'd say the man had never handled a mobile phone in his life.

"New phone?" I asked, nodding at the device.

"Yes. I'm still getting used to it." He swiped a finger across the screen again and again, muttering under his breath.

I raised an eyebrow. This was one weird dude. "Do you need help?"

"Yes, please. I seem to have forgotten how to use this. The blow to my head..." He trailed off, suddenly finding his fingertips fascinating.

I took the phone, which was thankfully unlocked, and located his phone number. I transcribed it into my notepad. "Thanks, Matt. I have it now."

He shoved the phone back into the drawer and collapsed against his pillows. "I'm sorry, Dee. I think I should sleep."

I eyed him with suspicion. He looked tired, yes, but not enough to match the exhaustion in his voice. Was I reading too much into the situation? The dude had taken a bullet, after all. What did I know about recovery from a gunshot wound? And I had no idea what medications were pumping through his veins. Maybe his odd behavior was a side effect. In spite of these totally logical conclusions, I didn't buy them for a second.

I packed my notepad and pen into my bag and got to my feet. "Thanks for your time. I'll let you get some rest."

His warm smile caught me off guard. "Goodbye, Dee. Thank you for the visit. I'm looking forward to our dinner. I'll contact you when I'm released from the hospital."

"Sure." I shifted my bag from one hand to the

other. "I might drop in some research material before then if you're interested."

A twinkle lit up his eyes. "I'd like that very much."

To my embarrassment, my face grew warm. I was usually pretty good at controlling my emotions, especially around men. Why did this guy throw me off balance? I wasn't used to the sensation, and I didn't like it. I returned the smile with a quick nod and closed the door to Room 303 behind me.

Out in the corridor, I spotted Zosia heading my way, carrying a tray with Matt's tea. She'd only included one cup. I bit back a laugh. Typical Zosia. I hadn't expected she'd include me in his tea party. I hastened down the corridor, keen to avoid another encounter with the nurse. The only member of the Kaminski family I was interested in talking to right now was Lev. I'd run down to the basement and pump him for info on the morgue's two VIP guests.

Once I'd harassed my brother-in-law, I'd turn my attention back to the mysterious Matt Sweeney. He was hiding something. I was sure of it. Whether his subterfuge concerned the murder in the courtyard or his reasons for moving to Dunleagh, I couldn't tell. Either way, I intended to find out.

EIGHTEEN

When I reached the ground floor, I spotted Lev walking up from the basement. He radiated exhaustion. His trim, marathon-trained body was thinner than usual, and the dark circles I'd noticed under his eyes the other day were verging on black.

"Hello, favorite brother-in-law," I said, meeting him at the top of the stairs. "You're a walking ad for contraceptives."

"I'm your only brother-in-law," he replied with a wan smile. "And please feel free to come over and do the good-aunt thing once in a while. It might buy River and me some sleep."

I cocked my head to the side. "Is it still Poopageddon at your place?"

He scrunched up his nose. "'Fraid so."

"Then no way. Call me when the kids are better.

Actually, scratch that. Call me when they're toilet trained. I deal better with older children."

Lev laughed. "Better than what? You run whenever a child comes near you."

"Hey, you don't want me babysitting. Trust me. Last time I looked after a friend's kid, I had to duct tape him into his nappy."

He regarded me, aghast. "How is that even possible? Nappies come with self-adhesive fasteners."

I shrugged. "It's a talent. I don't deal well with the preschool crowd. Hey, do you have time to talk?"

A pained expression crossed over his face. "Does it involve you interrogating me?"

"Of course. I'll sweeten the deal by buying you one of those gross pastries you like from the cafeteria."

He rubbed his eyes. "Yeah, okay. I could do with a sugar shock."

We walked to the hospital's cafeteria, a grim room with the permanent smell of boiled cabbage. I opted for mineral water, and Lev got a double espresso and a sticky Danish pastry. When we were seated, I let him take a couple of bites before going in for the kill.

"So..." I cupped my chin with my hands and leaned forward. "Any news on the clown and the mayor?"

Lev swallowed a mouthful of Danish. "They're still dead, if that's what you're asking."

"Dude, I want details on the bullets. Same weapon? Make and model? That sort of thing."

He took a sip of his coffee and grimaced. "This stuff gets worse every week. I wish the hospital would cough up for a decent coffee machine. Okay, here's what I know. We extracted a bullet from Mr. Chuckles. It was exactly as you'd predicted: an old-fashioned round, most probably from a Mauser C96."

I nodded. "That matches the cartridge I found in the courtyard. What about the mayor? Different weapon?"

"Yeah. The bullet went through him, but the Guards said it matched the pistol your mother fired. Some kind of Smith & Wesson."

"Richard said it was a Smith & Wesson Model 1913 and that it needed a different cartridge to the Mauser C96."

"I'll take your word for it." Lev took another bite of his pastry.

I thought while he chewed. "Anything else interesting come out of the autopsies?"

"No," he said, wiping crumbs off his mouth. "The mayor had heart disease. Otherwise, he was in good shape. Mr. Chuckles had diabetes, but that didn't contribute to his death. The post-mortems confirmed what we already suspected: they died of cardiac arrests brought about by blood loss."

"Blood loss caused by their gunshot wounds," I added.

"Yeah, exactly." A sly smile crept across his tired

face. "I do know something that might interest you, though."

I perked up instantly. "Go on. Don't leave me in suspense."

"Have you heard your mystery man now has a name?"

"Yeah. I've just been to see him. He's called Matt Sweeney."

"The surgeon pulled bullet fragments out of his shoulder. I hear they're suspected to be from yet another vintage firearm. I'm blanking on the model, but it definitely isn't the same one used to kill Mr. Chuckles, nor is it the pistol Bliss fired last night."

The air left my lungs in a gasp. "Wow. I *knew* I heard several male voices in the courtyard. This proves there was more than one shooter."

"From what I've heard, the Guards are working on that theory."

My mind spun with possibilities and questions. "Do you know if they're still trying to connect the mayor's death with the courtyard shootings?"

Lev shrugged. "I have no idea. I presume so. How many killers can we have in Dunleagh?"

"Right," I mused. "And how many townsfolk can have a target painted on their back? I still think Matt Sweeney might be the original target. There's something odd about that guy."

My brother-in-law grinned. "Zosia tells me he's mighty hot."

I rolled my eyes. "She would." Not that I didn't think exactly the same thing, but I'd never admit to liking the same man as Lev's sister.

Lev checked his watch and drained his coffee cup. "Duty calls. Sorry I couldn't be more help."

"No worries. Thanks for taking the time to fill me in."

We stood, and Lev put his tray back on the conveyor belt.

"One last thing," I said as we retraced our steps to the staircase that led to the basement. "What's Orla Tierney's deal? Is she having a relationship with Dr. Moriarty?"

Lev's surprise was genuine. "That's news to me. He's fond of her, but he's like that with all young women."

"Not me," I retorted. "He made that very clear."

"Okay, *most* young women," Lev amended with a chuckle. "He likes playing the protective fatherly figure."

"He's allegedly horrible to his wife," I pointed out. "Clearly, his protective nature doesn't extend to her."

My brother-in-law shrugged. "I don't know much about his marriage. He hardly ever mentions his wife."

"Getting back to Orla: she signed for the evidence bag that went missing. Any reason to suspect she took it?"

Lev gave a bark of laughter. "No way. Frankly, she

doesn't have the imagination to sabotage a criminal investigation."

This assessment of Orla's character fit my impression of the woman. "Is she under stress of any kind? Nervier than usual?"

My brother-in-law's lips twitched. "Orla's always close to the edge. Medicine is a stressful job, and I'm not sure she's cut out for the pressure. She's highly strung, yeah, but I can't see her stealing evidence."

"What about the others who were on duty the day the bag disappeared?"

"Moriarty's a bear, but I can't imagine he'd steal the bag. What reason would he have?"

"I don't know," I mused. "Did he have a grudge against Mr. Chuckles?"

"Are you asking if Dr. Moriarty killed the clown?" Lev's headshake was emphatic. "He was on duty all Thursday morning, and I was with him most of that time. There's no way he could've snuck off to the castle and shot Mr. Chuckles."

"What about Henry Hyland? Any animosity between him and your boss?"

"Not that I know of. The hospital was one of the few institutions in Dunleagh the mayor couldn't interfere with, and I don't know if Moriarty even knew him personally."

"And the third person who was on duty on Thursday morning? A guy, if I recall correctly."

Lev nodded. "Jack Finch. He's an intern. He

assisted Orla on a post-mortem. Again, I know of no reason Jack would want to steal evidence or harm either the clown or the mayor. He's new to Dunleagh and probably didn't know either of them."

"And you?" I caught his horrified look. "Sorry, I have to ask."

"I didn't go near the storage room all morning, and I definitely didn't shoot anyone. Satisfied?"

"No, but I'll have to work with what I've got." I wrinkled my nose. "I'm still under suspicion for the missing evidence, and Bliss has to live with the fact that she fired the shot that killed the mayor."

"How's she bearing up?" he asked.

"Not well. I haven't seen her yet today, but she was a wreck last night. At least she has an alibi for the clown shooting."

Lev sighed. "Let's hope this new police crew can crack the case and find the real killers. Everyone's on edge until they do."

"Yeah." I gave him a quick hug. "Thanks for the chat. Take care of yourself."

I left Lev to return to his job in the morgue and I walked back to Mavis. The sun beat down from the cloudless sky, giving the impression that it never rained in Ireland. I checked my backpack for my spare raincoat, just in case. I'd learned not to trust the Irish sun.

Before I hopped on my bike, I took out Naido's phone and looked up the school where my sister worked. I checked all the streets near it, but none were called Prince Albert Street. The one I assumed Matt Sweeney lived on was Michael Collins Street, named after one of the leaders during the War of Independence. Bizarre. If Matt was as interested in the time period as he claimed, he should have found the street name memorable. Frowning, I shoved the phone back into my bag and headed into town.

Tourists poured out of shops on the main street, and the strand was packed with sunbathers. I breathed in the salty air. I'd join them, just as soon as I'd finished a little sleuthing into Matt Sweeney. I drew to a halt outside the library. The sweet scent of garden flowers greeted me when I opened the gate, but I had no time to stop to admire them. I hurried down the path and entered the house. Mary Yates was on the main desk when I strode in and she waved to me. I wasn't in the mood to chat, but I was also clueless as to where to find what I was looking for.

"Hi, Dee. How's your mum?" Mary asked the instant I reached the desk.

I grimaced. "As well as can be expected."

She clucked her tongue. "It's awful. I can't believe whoever is behind these killings is local. We've never had problems with violence here before."

This wasn't entirely true, as I well knew from my job at the *Dunleagh Chronicle*, but I didn't have time to argue the point. "Can you help me locate old maps of

Dunleagh? Preferably from the time around the War of Independence?"

Mary adjusted her glasses. "I can indeed. Richard and I considered using one for our exhibition, but we simply didn't have space. In any case, not much has changed in the layout of the town."

"Right." I tried to keep the impatience out of my voice. "Would you mind showing it to me?"

"Certainly." Mary stood and walked at what seemed an agonizingly slow pace. She led me to a small room upstairs and sat me at a wooden table. From one of the shelves, she withdrew a cardboard cylinder. "Here we go." She unrolled the map and laid it on the table. "Do you need anything else?"

"No, this is fine. Thanks, Mary."

She glanced at the stairs. "I'd better get back to the desk. Leave the map here when you're finished. I'll put it away later."

After she left, I took out the magnifying glass I used in the castle archives. It didn't take long to locate the secondary school. It was on the same plot of land as the modern building, although it had then been a boys' school, not the coed facility we had today. I shifted the magnifying glass to the left, searching for the street that must be where Matt Sweeney had his apartment. And there it was.

My heart lurched in my chest. The map was dated 1915, and the road I knew as Michael Collins Street had then been called Prince Albert Street.

I jumped up, almost toppling my chair. My pulse pounded in my neck, brushing against the pain threshold. Barely able to breathe, I grabbed my stuff and descended the stairs at breakneck speed. Ignoring Mary's questioning call, I barged past her desk and ran all the way back to my bike. I shoved my helmet over my hair and revved the engine.

I'm pretty sure I broke several rules of the road on the ride to the castle, but I was barely aware of my surroundings. Somehow, I reached the castle in one piece. When I legged it over the drawbridge, the courtyard teemed with tourists. I left my manners at the castle gates and pushed past, taking no notice of the shouts of protest I left in my wake. I barreled by Larry at reception and raced down to the archives. With trembling hands, I located a volume of back issues. The words blurred as I skimmed the pages, searching for an entry that might not exist.

And there it was, smack bang on the front page of the 20 June 1919 issue of the *Dunleagh Chronicle*. "Ambush at Dunleagh Castle Leaves Three Dead." A grainy photograph accompanied the article, showing several men on the ground of the castle courtyard. Barely breathing, I moved my magnifying glass across the words. The gist of the article was this: a band of Irish rebels had attacked the police barracks at Dunleagh Castle, killing three RIC officers and wounding five. At the time of the article's printing, the attackers were still on the run. The officers killed were listed under their rank, first initials, and surnames. I ran my finger over the yellowing paper, hardly believing my eyes. The highest-ranking officer killed was listed as District Inspector 2nd Class M. Slattery.

I slumped onto a chair, hyperventilating. Matt Sweeney had claimed to be from 1919. Matt Sweeney had worn a uniform belonging to a District Inspector 2nd Class. Matt Sweeney's initials matched both M. Slattery's and the original owner of the trench watch. I held my head in my hands and tried to steady my breathing. I was going mad. I couldn't possibly believe the man I'd saved had been alive one hundred years ago. And M. Slattery had been killed in the ambush. M. Sweeney was very much alive.

My mind swam with conflicting thoughts. I shoved my belongings back into my bag and left the archives. I wasn't sure how I made it back to the reception without falling back down the stairs. From the side of my eye, I caught a glimpse of Larry talking to a petite woman at the reception desk. I trundled past, still sifting through what I knew.

"Dee?" A woman's voice halted my chain of thoughts.

"Bliss?" I blinked at my mother, now recognizing Larry's companion. "What are you doing here?"

An ethereal smile wafted across her elegant features. "Looking for you, darling. Want to walk and talk?"

"Uh, sure." My mother seeking me out voluntarily was a novel experience. There had to be a catch.

We stepped outside the castle and into the courtyard. The herd of tourists had thinned since I'd arrived—a tour must be in progress. My mother glided over the cobblestones and arranged herself on a free bench, crossing one slim leg over the other. I lumbered after her, feeling every inch the elephant to her mouse.

Bliss patted the seat beside her. I dropped onto it and we sat in semi-companionable silence for a long moment. Finally, the tension became too much for me. "What's up?" I demanded. "You didn't come here to chitchat."

"No, I needed to ask Larry about arranging transport for the mobility scooters."

"I'd happily blocked those from my mind. You know Nana's is doctored to go faster than the speed limit, right?"

My mother's half shrug barely lifted one shoulder. "That doesn't surprise me. At any rate, Larry is working on a solution."

I gave a bark of laughter. "In other words, you offloaded the responsibility onto him."

"I didn't want to talk to you about the scooters," Bliss said, deftly avoiding a response to my statement. "I find myself in a bit of a dilemma."

"In other words, you're up to your chin in excrement and you want me to dig you out."

Bliss wrinkled her tiny nose. "Really, Dervorgilla. Must you be so crude?"

"Must you be so vague?" I countered. "Come on, Bliss. Out with it. What do you need me to do?"

My mother folded her hands on her lap. "I made a mistake when I spoke to the Guards last night."

I narrowed my eyes. "You lied to them?"

"Of course not. I merely failed to mention a fact they might find...interesting."

"So you lied by omission. What about?"

Her hand fluttered to her throat. "Dermot—DI Bradley—assumed I returned from my yoga retreat yesterday. That's not strictly true."

Frustration rose in my throat, almost choking me. "Something's true or it's false, Bliss. I saw you come home yesterday. Are you saying you returned before that?"

"To Dunleagh, yes. To your grandmother's house, no." She sighed and fiddled with her moon necklace. "I got back on Thursday morning, but I went to my studio first."

My mother's studio was located several kilometers south of Dunleagh. It was little more than a roadside shack, but Bliss adored it and often spent nights there. Mostly, I suspected, to avoid Nana and me.

"Why? I thought the retreat lasted until Thursday night."

"It was supposed to, but I received a phone call from my landlord and that rather put me out of sorts.

As I wasn't the retreat leader this time, it wasn't a problem for me to slip away early."

"Your landlord?" I stared at her, open-mouthed. "As in Henry Hyland?"

Bliss inclined her head. "Yes. He called to inform me that I had to be out of my shop in two weeks."

The words hit me in the solar plexus. So that's what Henry Hyland had meant when he'd mentioned my mother's rent. "Whoa. Didn't he need to give you more notice if he wanted to gut the place and turn it into luxury apartments, or whatever it was he had planned?"

"Normally, yes, but I was a little behind with my rent."

"A little behind? Is this Bliss-speak for hadn't paid it in months?"

"Shush," she said. "People will hear you."

"Why didn't you tell Nana and me you had money troubles?"

My mother raised one slim eyebrow. "You two have enough money problems of your own. I didn't want to add to the burden. Besides, I thought I could turn the situation around, especially with the start of the tourist season."

I considered her words. "Why did you return from the retreat early? What difference could a day make?"

"I wanted to talk to Henry." She stared at her hands. "To reason with him."

"You spoke to Henry Hyland on Thursday?" A prickling panic crept over my skin. "When?"

Her hand strayed back to the necklace. "I was in his office when the clown was shot."

I gasped. "Seriously, Bliss? It didn't occur to you to mention this before?"

"You were clearly annoyed with me when I got to Mum's house yesterday," she replied, on the defensive. "I didn't think it was the best moment to bring up my imminent eviction."

"Fair enough, but where were you when I was calling for help on Thursday? I was yelling my head off and no one came."

"I didn't hear anything, darling. When the fire alarm went off, I left the building. I had no idea you were involved."

"Apart from the mayor, did anyone you know see you at the castle?"

My mother sighed. "I don't know. Henry's secretary was out of the office when I arrived. And when I left the castle, everyone was focused on the scene of the crime."

"You can't rule out that someone recognized you," I insisted. "There were dozens of tourists milling about, not to mention all the people who work at the castle."

"Exactly. That's why I wanted to talk to you." She cast me a beseeching look. "What should I do?"

"What you should've done last night. Tell the Guards about Hyland's call and say you visited his office on Thursday. You know what Dunleagh's like. Someone will have seen you, and it'll get back to the police. Much better coming from you than from an outsider."

Bliss tugged on her necklace. "I know you're right. I just feel it'll look bad."

"It'll look worse if you stay silent."

She made to get up. "I'll go now. Try to catch DI Bradley if I can. Dermot's a reasonable man."

"Hang on a sec. Before you go, there's something I wanted to ask you."

She turned back and regarded me with an air of distraction. "What?"

"You know you said the planets were out of alignment?"

"They always are around the time of solstices and equinoxes."

"What effects does the lack of alignment have on Earth?"

"Well," she mused, "the walls between worlds are thinner at those times. It shows in odd weather developments and in the behaviors of plants and wildlife."

"When you say 'walls between worlds,' could those include different times?" My voice cracked as I formed the words of my next question. "Like, could people move from one time period to another?"

Far from laughing in my face and calling me crazy, my mother considered the question before responding.

"I suppose it could, yes. It's long been rumored that time portals exist."

"Are there any in Dunleagh?"

"Not that I know of, but it wouldn't surprise me." She gave me an odd look. "Why do you ask?"

I took a deep breath. Should I tell her? My suspicions about Matt Sweeney were wild. Surely even my unorthodox mother would tell me I had an overactive imagination?

Before I could make up my mind, a stampede of feet over the cobblestones jerked me out of my reverie.

DI Bradley stood before us, flanked by two plain-clothes officers. My stomach sank when I clocked his grim expression, and it went into free fall when he held up a piece of paper. "Bridget Flanagan, I have a warrant for your arrest."

NINETEEN

The hours following Bliss's arrest seemed interminable. After my mother left with DI Bradley, I contacted the only solicitor I knew in Dunleagh, and he put me in touch with a lawyer who specialized in criminal law. Once I'd secured my mother legal representation, it was almost seven o'clock in the evening. I followed her to the police station on Mavis but was turned away by Lou. As the station was brimming with people waiting to be questioned about the murders, including an anguished-looking Cian, I couldn't blame her for not wanting me cluttering up the premises.

Apart from twirling my thumbs on a bench outside the station, there wasn't much else I could do to help, so I drove home. On the drive, I went over the events of the last few days. I didn't believe my mother had intentionally killed the mayor, however upset she was over her eviction. Rash acts of violence were at odds with her character. Bliss was a born optimist and a shameless manipulator. She'd have done exactly what she'd said she'd done: tried to sweet-talk the mayor into giving her an extension, and kept on trying until he gave her what she wanted. She wouldn't have shot him dead during a dress rehearsal.

As for Matt Sweeney, the more time passed since I'd read the entry in the *Chronicle* back issue, the sillier I felt for entertaining the time-traveler theory. It was absurd. The street name business would have a logical explanation. Perhaps the change was relatively recent and older residents still called it by its original name. One of them must have referred to it as Prince Albert Street in front of Matt, and he'd latched on to the wrong name.

When I got back to Nana's house, she was out. I'd contacted her after Bliss's arrest and left a message, but I hadn't received a reply. Still, someone was bound to let her know her daughter was behind bars, particularly if Nana was where I suspected. *Elaine's* was a hotbed of gossip, and Nana's friends would waste no time in spreading the news. Deciding I was fit for nothing but my bed, I opted for an early night, but tossed and turned for hours.

After what felt like days of trying and failing to sleep, a monumental crash reverberated through the house. I sat bolt upright in bed, my heart in my throat. What now? Had Nana come home tipsy and upset the coat stand again? I stole a glance at my alarm clock.

The luminous dials informed me that it was five-thirty in the morning. Rather late for Nana to come home, even by her hard-partying standards. I tossed my bedclothes aside and went to investigate.

Out in the corridor, the sounds of gentle snoring floated from beneath my grandmother's bedroom door. Maybe she'd knocked something over in her sleep. I'd better make sure it was nothing flammable. I padded to her room and had my hand on the door handle when another crash jerked my head to the side. This time, the bang was accompanied by male swearing. My limbs froze. A man was prowling downstairs. I crept back to my room before recalling I'd left my phone in the kitchen. Nana never remembered to bring her phone upstairs, and the landline had been disconnected after we'd failed to pay last month's overdue bill.

I glanced at the staircase and considered my options. If the man downstairs were part of the clown-shooting gang, surely he'd be a little subtler? A third crash, followed by a groan of pain, made up my mind. Whoever was down there was no master criminal. I grabbed the spare walker that Nana kept at the top of the stairs and made my way downstairs. The place was in darkness, and I had to rely on memory to feel my way to the kitchen. Suddenly, a pair of shining green eyes leaped through the air. I screamed. The man screamed. And I brought Nana's walker down over his head.

Shaking, I groped across the wall for the light switch. Yellow light flooded the room, making me blink. Mellie, Nana's cat, stared at me defiantly from her perch on the kitchen counter. On the floor, a man moaned in pain and tried to disentangle himself from the walker. He turned his face toward me, and I noticed a familiar red leather phone case clutched in his hand.

I sucked air through my teeth. "Gary?" I exclaimed. "What are you doing here? And why do you have my phone?"

———

Five minutes later, Gary sat across the kitchen table from me, clutching an ice pack to his forehead and moaning with pain. "You nearly brained me, Dee. What were you thinking?"

"I was thinking that a strange man was prowling around my house in the dead of night without an invitation." I folded my arms across my chest. "Give me one good reason I shouldn't call the cops."

Gary touched his rapidly swelling eye and winced. "The Guards are busy dealing with your mum and your boss and about half the town. With a nutter on the loose killing people, they have enough to do."

"True, but that doesn't give you an excuse to break into our house and scare me half to death. Is this an insurance scam like the one you pulled for your grandmother? And what's my phone got to do with it?"

Gary regarded me dolefully through his one good eye. "I'm here to return your phone."

"Which you just happened to find lying around," I said, my voice dripping with sarcasm. "Did you shove me into the pit?"

"Sorry about that, Dee. I didn't mean for you to fall in, I swear."

"Then why push me forward? I was on the very edge. What did you expect would happen?"

Gary's blank one-eyed gaze stared back at me. "I didn't really think it through. When Eda called, I—"

My heart thudded in my chest. "Back up a sec. My grandmother called you? Do you mean when she and Dottie wanted a lift home? That was *after* I fell."

"No, Eda called me earlier that morning. She wanted a lift out to the farm, and Gran came too."

"So the tractor ride story was a lie." I sank back in my chair and tried to make my sleep-deprived brain function. "Why didn't she tell me you'd driven them? And what does my phone have to do with any of this?"

"I dunno, Dee. I don't ask questions. Eda asked me to get your phone and delete some photos. I did what she asked, but then she was all mad because you landed on your face."

My racing heart skipped a beat. "Which photos?"

He shrugged. "All the ones you'd taken recently. There were a few of the sky that looked like you'd used a purple filter on them. I deleted all of those. Only, Eda was mad that you got hurt."

I rolled my eyes and grabbed the phone. I scrolled through my recent photos. Sure enough, all the ones I'd taken in the courtyard the day of the clown's death were gone. I leaned back in my seat and wracked my tired mind. "Why did Nana want these photos deleted? Couldn't she have waited and taken my phone that evening while I was asleep?"

Gary's perplexed expression didn't alter. "Eda said it was urgent and couldn't wait. She gave me a hundred euro and told me what to do."

"A hundred euro?" Nana didn't have that kind of cash to throw around. Why were the photos so important to her? "Did you tell her that deleting the photos from my phone wouldn't delete them from my cloud storage?"

Another shrug. "Your grandmother didn't mention anything about that. I just did what I was told. No more, no less." In other words, the cloud storage business hadn't occurred to Gary. Even if it had, he didn't have the brainpower to explain it to Nana.

I shoved my chair back. "Out. Right now. Or I will call the Guards."

"What about the ice pack?" he whined. "You gave me a right clobbering."

"Keep the ice pack." I pointed to the front door. "Just leave."

Gary complied, grumbling about crazy old ladies

and crazier cats. Mellie hissed and arched her back when he passed.

I scratched her under the chin. "Good girl. You have excellent taste."

At the door, Gary looked over his shoulder. "Sorry about the fall and all. I didn't mean to hurt you."

"I believe you, but if you ever sneak into my house again, you'll have more than my grandmother's walker over your head. Understood?"

Gary swallowed. "Got it."

I slammed the door on him and stalked back to the kitchen. Mellie had returned to her basket and curled up in a ball. I glanced at the kitchen clock. It was nearly six o'clock in the morning. Going back to bed seemed pointless. I could try waking Nana and shake answers out of her, but my grandmother slept like the proverbial log. Alternatively, I could use the time to work on my history channel. I sighed. Neither option appealed to me.

Beside Mellie's basket, I spied my running shoes. Maybe I should take the hint and go jogging before I faced the day. The exercise would clear my head. Before I talked myself out of it, I ran upstairs and pulled on my running gear.

After I'd put on my running gear, I left Nana's terraced house and jogged down to the beach. I wasn't fond of running on sand, but I loved the winding path next to the strand. It followed the curves of the shoreline for several kilometers and was my favorite place to run. This early, the dog walkers weren't yet out, and I had the path to myself. The crisp morning air was damp against my skin, and the blue sky hinted at a sunny day ahead. The beauty of the day elicited a pang of guilt. I was free to enjoy the nice weather, yet my mother was stuck at the police station, accused of murder.

Never the world's fastest runner, I pushed myself to the max and pounded my troubles onto the hard ground. Running at a rapid pace forced my overactive brain to calm down. I ran hard for three kilometers, finally slowing to a more comfortable pace when I neared a large house set on a rolling hill. I slowed to a jog, allowing my heart rate to come down and my breathing to settle into a more comfortable rhythm.

I adjusted my sunglasses and took in the view. The house on the hill was a lavish Tuscan-style villa, complete with its own clock tower and outdoor swimming pool. Only people with more money than sense had outdoor pools in Ireland. Like the house, the ornamental garden was too fussy for my tastes, but it fit its owners perfectly—this was the Hyland residence.

Intent on my examination of the house, I wasn't paying attention to the track ahead. I jogged straight into a man approaching from the other direction, sending him flying against the fence that separated the path from the Hyland property.

"Watch where you're going, you crazy—" The man

stopped, stared at me, and began to laugh. "You're that crazy woman's daughter."

His laughter turned into hiccups, and he sagged against the fence, sliding to the ground in slow motion. Now that I'd regained my balance, I recognized the guy. It was Rob Hyland, the mayor's son. And he was drunk. There was no trace left of the cocky bravado he and his friends had displayed at Seamie Dean's cockfight. In his bleary-eyed dishevelment, the kid looked younger than the twenty-two or three I guessed him to be.

I dropped to the ground beside Rob and unscrewed my water flask. After taking a long swig, I handed it to him. He took it and drank deeply before returning it to me. "Your that Flanagan woman's daughter," he repeated, but without the hysterics of earlier.

"I am." I took in his exhausted face. "And you're the mayor's son."

He nodded. "Or was. Not sure what the correct tense is now."

"I'm sorry your father's dead," I said softly.

Rob snorted. "If that's true, you're the only person in Dunleagh who is."

"I'm not saying I liked him," I amended, "but I didn't want him to die."

The boy let out a long sigh. "Same here. Still, it's strange thinking the old man's gone."

For a couple of minutes, we fell into a semi-comfortable silence, neither of us knowing what to say next. Finally, I got to my feet and held out a hand to Rob. I hauled him into a standing position, but he swayed and clutched the fence for support.

I shoved my water bottle into its holder. "Come on. Let me walk you home. I don't want to risk you falling into the swimming pool and drowning."

Rob held up a finger and squinted at me through one eye. "I'll have you know I'm an excellent swimmer."

"When sober, I'm sure you are."

It took several tries to get Rob over the fence, and one attempt ended with me landing flat on my face. Getting Rob up the hill involved more fun and games. At one point, he decided that rolling down the slope would be a barrel of laughs, but I managed to keep him in an upward motion. By the time we crested the hill and reached level ground, I was panting from the effort of hauling a heavily built six-foot male up a steep incline.

"Do you have your key?" I asked, struggling to get back my breath. "I'll help you get the door open."

"It'll be fine." Rob's eyes crossed, and he staggered into a pillar.

Yowza. That had to have hurt. Somehow, I steered him to the back door and helped him insert the key into the lock. "Will you make it to bed?" In his current state, he'd probably fall down the stairs and break his neck.

He treated me to a drunken grin. "No worries. I'll crash on the living room sofa."

"If you're sure…" I regarded him with trepidation. The last thing I wanted to deal with was another dead body.

"It's all good." He hiccupped and swayed at an alarming angle. "Did your mum kill my dad?"

I hesitated a fraction of second. "She fired the pistol, yes, but she didn't know it was loaded. It had never contained bullets when they'd practiced the scene."

Rob nodded. "Anyone could have slipped the bullet into the gun."

"Any number of people, yes." I reached out and squeezed his arm. "Take care of yourself. And lay off the booze, eh?"

"Aye, aye captain." He gave me a mock salute and staggered into the house, leaving the door ajar.

I sighed and glanced at my watch. Even with this unexpected detour, I had plenty of time to get home and shower before anywhere in Dunleagh opened. I'd better wait until I was sure Rob was safe before taking off. He crashed into a piece of furniture in what was presumably the living room, swore, and then fell silent. A minute later, loud snores emanated from Rob's direction. Smiling to myself, I reached for the door handle.

The creak of footsteps on the stairs sent me leaping back from the door. For reasons I couldn't explain, I dropped into a crouching position. Why did I care if Sally Hyland found me at her house at six-thirty in the morning? She'd understand when I explained I'd escorted Rob home. I moved to stand up, only to freeze in place.

Whispered voices floated down the stairs, one female and one male. The woman must be Sally Hyland, but who was the guy? Not Rob. He was still snoring merrily in the living room. The footsteps grew closer.

"Well, really," the woman said. "Rob must have come home drunk again and left the door wide open. I don't know what to do with that boy."

"Don't be too hard on him, Sally," her companion said. "He's just lost his father."

Sally Hyland's bitter laughter grew closer. "Gunned down by that silly Flanagan woman. What a way to go."

I scanned the garden in search of a hiding place. I'd left it too late to reveal myself now. With seconds to spare, I dove behind a rhododendron bush. An instant later, Sally and the man emerged through the back door. She was facing him and blocking his face from view.

"I wish you could stay," she said in a low voice. "I mean, it can hardly matter now, can it?"

"Don't be ridiculous, Sally. Even if the Guards have arrested the Flanagan person, her defense team will look for anyone with a reason to kill Henry. Why should we provide them with a reason to focus on us?"

"I know you're right, but I'm sick of waiting." She pulled him into her arms.

While they kissed, I extracted a flower from my nostril and willed myself not to sneeze. After what seemed like forever, they broke the embrace.

"I'll call you later," the man said. "If I can manage to slip away, I'll come to see you."

Sally murmured something in return, but too low for me to discern her words. Finally, she stepped away from her lover and went back into the house. I shifted position and angled to get a look at Sally's companion.

My eyes nearly popped out my head. *Well, well, well.* Charles Moriarty snuck to his silver BMW and opened the door, careful not to slam it when he slid behind the wheel. If I leaped out and confronted him, what excuse would he use for being there? A professional visit? I bit back a laugh. Sally Hyland wouldn't call a pathologist if she were feeling down after her husband's death. No, this was a visit of the most personal nature, as evidenced by that passionate kiss.

An upstairs window twitched, drawing my attention away from the car. Still clad in her scarlet nightgown, Sally waved at Dr. Moriarty as he slid down her driveway at a sedate crawl. When the car was out of sight, she let the curtain fall, ending my morning's entertainment.

Neither Dr. Moriarty nor Sally had admitted to her husband's murder, but they clearly didn't want anyone looking too closely in their direction. Sally Hyland was already on the suspect list I'd compiled with the Historical Murders Club members. Charles Moriarty was a new addition. We'd dismissed him because he hadn't had the opportunity to kill Mr. Chuckles, but he'd been at the castle before the dress rehearsal. Had he decided to murder his mistress's husband by proxy? And did this mean the two murders were unconnected after all? And had I been wrong about Dr. Moriarty having an affair with Orla?

I descended the hill and jogged home, turning these new questions over in my mind. I'd reached no conclusions when I reached my grandmother's house, but the run had taken the edge off my anger. I showered, dressed, and crept out again without waking Nana. I was still steaming over Gary's revelations, but now wasn't the moment to confront her. I needed time to calm down and process my thoughts. No way had Nana intended me to get hurt. That part was all on Gary and his stupidity.

What I didn't get was why she'd want to destroy the photographs. To be precise, I couldn't think of a reason for her to care about the pictures that didn't involve my crazy time-traveler theory. The wind didn't hold people prisoner. Gunmen didn't vanish into thin air. Nothing I'd experienced in the courtyard on Thursday morning made sense. I was working hard to find a logical explanation, and I had the sinking sensation that talking to my grandmother would torpedo my efforts.

I'd mentioned the strange wind and sky to Nana right before I'd left to collect Aido from Seamie Dean's farm. I was pretty sure I'd even shown her some of the photos. I didn't recall her taking a particular interest in what I'd said, but perhaps I'd been mistaken. Why else the mad rush to get Gary to drive her and Dottie out to the farm, not to mention the lies about their reason for being there? Burning with questions, frustration, and ill-concealed irritation, I hopped on Mavis and drove to the one place I might find answers.

TWENTY

I arrived at Dunleagh Library just as the duty librarian unlocked the door. I marched inside and made a beeline for the section on the town's history. After I'd claimed a desk, I settled down with a bunch of books and got to work. It didn't take long to discover that Prince Albert Street had been built during the reign of Queen Victoria and named after her husband. In 1952, the town council had decided to rechristen the street after Michael Collins, a War of Independence hero. Almost seventy years after the change, it was unlikely that anyone would call the road by its old name. Besides, Republican sentiment ran strong in this part of the country, and people were happy to eradicate all trace of British rule in Ireland.

Unfortunately for my mood, this little detail did nothing to allay my suspicions about Matt Sweeney. Sighing, I went back to the bookshelves. A volume on the War of Independence caught my eye. It was one I'd read and enjoyed. I fingered the spine, thinking hard. If I borrowed a couple of books on the subject, I'd have an excellent excuse to pay Matt Sweeney a visit today. I selected two books for Matt, and three on the history of Dunleagh Castle. Preoccupied, I returned to my desk, almost crashing into a library patron en route. The spiky green hair clued me in immediately. "Aido? What are you doing here?"

"Researching vintage firearms." My friend struggled under the weight of a pile of books. He dumped them on the desk beside mine and wiped his forehead. "Guess I underestimated their weight."

"Or overestimated your strength," I shot back with a grin.

We both laughed, earning us a shush from the librarian in charge.

"Are you researching the guns for a *Chronicle* article?"

"Purely personal interest. These murders intrigue me. And with your mum in the frame, I thought it'd be worth reading up on the murder weapons." He glanced at my books. "What's your angle?"

"Same as yours, more or less. I wanted to know more about the castle during the time it housed the police barracks."

Aido flopped onto a seat. "Does this have to do with the guy in the hospital and his old-fashioned uniform?"

"Sort of." Better to be vague than blurting out my wild theories. "I had quite a morning, by the way." I sat beside him and proceeded to fill him in on Gary's story, leaving out all mention of time travel, and continued on with the Rob Hyland interlude and Dr. Moriarty's visit to the Hyland house.

"Wow," Aido said when I'd finished. "And all that happened before seven o'clock? My news seems dull in comparison."

I shot a glance at the librarian's desk, but it was empty. "What have you discovered?"

He beamed at me. "Quite a lot, actually. It segues nicely with your story. I paid a visit to Sally Hyland yesterday, using the *Chronicle* as an excuse."

I propped my chin up with my hands. "Go on."

"She shed a few tears but didn't appear to be devastated by her husband's untimely demise. When I pressed her for names of people who might've wished the mayor harm, she was vague and dismissed herself as a potential suspect by saying they had an open marriage and neither of them cared what the other got up to."

"That sounds more like a marriage of convenience than a happy open marriage, but whatever."

"Yeah, maybe. Sally likes her trinkets, and Henry Hyland needed a traditional family life to appeal to the voters. Either way, if they tolerated one another's affairs, the Dr. Moriarty angle is less suspicious."

"Perhaps, but I'm not convinced. Even if the Hylands had an understanding, did the Moriartys?"

Aido's crack of laughter earned us a disgruntled cough from the duty librarian, now back at her desk. He lowered his voice to a whisper. "You can't seriously think Mary offed the mayor."

I shook my head. "If she wasn't okay with the relationship between her husband and Sally Hyland, she'd target one or both of them, not Henry Hyland."

"Assuming Mary is a psycho killer," Aido added, "which I seriously can't see."

"Me neither, but I wasn't thinking of *her* as a potential suspect. What if Charles Moriarty didn't want to be Sally's other man? What if he wanted to leave his wife and for her to leave Henry? That would give him a strong motive for murdering the mayor."

"Yes, but what was his motive for offing Mr. Chuckles?"

"He didn't kill Mr. Chuckles, at least not if Lev's alibi is to be believed. The more I think about it, the less convinced I am that the two murders are connected. What if someone used the vintage firearm angle to confuse the Guards?"

Aido considered my words for a moment. "I guess it's possible."

"Just unlikely," I added, "which is probably what the mayor's killer wants us to think. We need to take another look at our suspect list and divide everyone into two columns: one for the mayor's murder, and the other for the courtyard shootings."

"Then the guy in the hospital is back in the frame." He pounded the desk with enough force to threaten his precarious pile of books. "I always thought he was dodgy."

"You barely saw him," I pointed out. "As it happens, I agree that there's something off about his story. Did you hear he's got his memory back?"

"Naido told me, but she didn't catch the name."

"Matt Sweeney. He's allegedly my sister's replacement teacher for the new school year."

"Allegedly?" Aido raised an eyebrow. "You don't believe him?"

"I'm sure he's hiding something, but his story must check out. If it didn't, we'd have heard by now." *Apart from the small matter of the street where he lives...* "Listen, can I ask you a favor?"

"Shoot." He winced. "Sorry. Poor word choice."

I chuckled. "It's fine. Really. Could you ask around about Big Jim's ancestors? Or anyone called McElligott who lived in Dunleagh around a hundred years ago? I'd like to know if any of them had a police record or history of violence."

Aido's eyes widened. "Uh, okay. I can do that. Why do you need to know?"

"I'm working on a blog piece about Dunleagh in 1919." This part was correct. Big Jim's relatives being its focus was stretching the truth.

"That's oddly specific," Aido said. "Why that year in particular?"

"The blog post will be part of my War of Independence centenary special. I want to look at events as they unfolded exactly one hundred years ago."

"Okay. I can do that. Maybe Big Jim will help. He loves a chat."

"And ask Elaine. She's a fountain of knowledge about Dunleagh, past and present."

He scribbled a note onto his writing pad. "Will do. What about the murders? Do you want to set a time with Richard to go over our list again?"

He didn't mention involving his sister. I wasn't surprised. Aido liked a quiet life. He'd noticed the tension between Naido and me and wanted to avoid conflict. "Yes, let's see if Richard has time to talk to us after tonight's club meeting. In the meantime, I'm going to do a little investigation into Matt Sweeney's past."

"And research your article." Aido indicated the mountain of books in front of me.

I flushed. "Of course." *No need to mention they're one and the same...*

My friend cracked his knuckles. "Okay. Better focus. Break in forty-five minutes?"

"Deal."

I reached for the first book from my new stack of research material and skimmed the table of contents, followed by the index. I followed this process for the second book, finally striking gold with the third. The author included a brief passage on the 1919 ambush, not naming the officers involved but mentioning that local rebels were suspected of being behind the attack. Could the local rebels include a man named McElligott? Pushing the book aside, I checked the remaining volumes on the table. Neither contained a reference to the ambush. Our forty-five-minute productivity sprint wasn't quite over, but I had an idea where I might find the information I wanted.

Leaving Aido engrossed in a book about War of Independence weaponry, I returned to the ground floor and headed for Mary and Richard's exhibition. When I walked into the room, Richard stood before a presentation board, adjusting the angle of a printed piece of text.

"Hey, you," I said. "How's the last-minute prep coming along?"

"Well, thanks, but I'm a perfectionist. I like to make sure I haven't forgotten any essentials." A look of concern creased his face. "How's your mother?"

"No news today. I'm hoping that's a positive." I forced a smile. "She has a lawyer now."

"I heard." Richard's expression darkened. "I can't believe the Guards think Bliss deliberately shot the mayor. It's ridiculous."

"I hear they gave you and Cian another grilling."

"Yeah." He grimaced. "Not that we could add

much more than we'd already said in our statements. I spoke to Cian when they finally let us leave the station. He's a wreck. Apart from the fact that his play was used as a vehicle for murder, the play can't open. After all the work he put into it, he's devastated."

"I can imagine."

I coughed to disguise a giggle, but Richard caught my expression and grinned. "It's a dreadful play, but Cian poured the last few months into finishing it. After all the iterations the play went through, it's a shame it can't open as scheduled."

"Every version I read, he'd changed stuff, just not the parts he should've altered."

"I proofread an early draft of the script, and it was totally different from the end product." He checked himself, aware of what he'd just said. "Not that any version involved murdering the mayor. I still can't believe it wasn't a horrible accident. Many people disliked Henry Hyland, me included, but I can't imagine anyone killing the man."

"Someone did. The bullet didn't magically appear in the pistol." I checked my surroundings and lowered my voice. "Is Mary here?"

"No. She's due in an hour. I wanted to get a head start before the official opening at eleven."

I glanced around, but no one was within hearing distance. "What can you tell me about Mary's husband?"

Richard's expression spoke a thousand words.

"He's an awful man. Arrogant, demanding, and treats Mary like dirt."

"Do you think he's unfaithful?"

He eyed me curiously. "I haven't heard rumors to that effect, but it wouldn't surprise me. Why do you ask?"

"I think he's involved with Sally Hyland."

"Good grief. I didn't know that. Well, if Mary has any sense, she'll wait to start divorce proceedings until after his uncle dies."

"What do you mean?" I asked, intrigued at this sliver of information.

"Charles Moriarty's uncle owns a hotel chain. The man's elderly, and Charles is his only heir."

"That gives him an excellent motive to want to end his marriage to Mary before he comes into his inheritance."

"Yes, but not necessarily a motive to kill Henry Hyland," Richard said.

I contemplated the matter for a minute. "What about Sally Hyland? Maybe she wanted her husband out of the way to leave her free to marry Charles. The prospect of his inheritance would suit her very well."

"But that leaves the awkward matter of Mary. Sally can't marry Charles unless he gets a divorce or Mary dies. And Mary is still very much alive."

"True." I exhaled sharply. "Every time I think I'm getting closer to the truth, there's a catch."

"Story of my life." Richard resumed fiddling with

the board. "The moment I've got it all together, the entire house of cards comes crashing down."

"Will the mayor's death have any impact on the decision to downsize the museum?"

"That remains to be seen. Hyland's deputy is less obsessed with building projects and more inclined to open a book every once in a while, but I'm not holding my breath."

I moved to another exhibition board, this one containing photographs of Dunleagh Castle. "I haven't seen these pictures before."

"I added them yesterday," Richard said, rearranging pieces of text. "The ones you chose are marvelous, but I noticed we hadn't included photographs of the castle. Given the pivotal role it played during the War of Independence, it seemed a shame."

I stepped closer to the board, my attention riveted on one particular photograph. It was a group shot of around twenty RIC officers, presumably residents of the barracks. The year listed beneath the photo was 1918. I peered closer. The man on the far left of the back row reminded me of someone. An icy sensation crept over my skin. I had to be hallucinating. *There's no way...* "Where did you find these pictures?" I asked, my eyes never leaving the photograph. "They weren't in the boxes you gave me to sort."

"No," he replied, distracted. "They were in with the barracks files."

I twisted to face him. "Files relating to the RIC barracks are in the museum?"

Richard looked sheepish. "A few years ago, all the files were sent to a central repository for storage. I guess we missed a couple of boxes."

I snatched the photograph from the board. "Can I borrow this? I can't explain why, but trust me when I say it's important."

Richard looked doubtful. "We need it for the exhibition."

"I promise I'll find a suitable replacement. I'll go to the museum right away and look in the box you gave me." I closed the space between us. "Please, Richard. It's important."

"Well," he said, not sounding convinced, "I suppose I can rearrange the board until we find a substitution."

On impulse, I kissed him on the cheek. "Thank you so much."

I raced upstairs, grabbed my bag and the books for Matt, and left a flummoxed Aido surrounded by his research books and mine. Five minutes later, I'd checked out the history books and was back at Mavis. I drove into the town center, stopping at a shabby green-fronted shop by the waterfront. After I'd parked, I leaped off my scooter and barged in the shop door, out of breath and apparently out of time.

Naido stood behind the counter of the photography studio, tapping her watch. "We're about to close, Dee. We only open for two hours on Sundays."

"What kind of service is that? It's the tourist season." I slammed the photograph onto the glass countertop and pointed to the police officer at the far left of the back row. "Please, Naido. I need your help. Can you enlarge this photo for me? Specifically, can you zoom in on this man's face?"

Curiosity conquered her desire to annoy me. She took a long look at the photograph. "I guess so."

"Awesome. Can you do it today?"

She cracked up laughing. "Are you joking? That sort of job takes time. We're in the middle of wedding season."

"Please. I'll pay you extra."

Naido shrugged. "No point. I'm behind in getting wedding photos touched up and developed. Unless you're planning to replace my annual salary, try another store."

"There is no other photo specialist in town."

She sniffed. "Then I guess you're stuck with me and my schedule."

"Okay," I said, admitting defeat. "Do my photograph when you have time, but please get to it soon."

She shoved a form at me. "Fill this in. Name, address, phone number."

"But you know my contact info," I protested. "I live two streets away from you."

"I don't care. Every customer fills in a form. Either fill it in or leave."

With a sigh, I complied, pausing only to take a few shots of the photograph with my newly-returned phone. I handed the form back to Naido, along with her spare phone. "Here you go. Huge thanks for letting me borrow it. I owe you a coffee."

Naido sniffed but pocketed the phone. "I did it for Aido."

"I know, and I'm grateful. Your brother's a good friend." I took a deep breath. "Maybe you and I could—"

She held up a hand, effectively halting my flow of speech. "Forget it, Dee. There's no need to bribe me. I said I'd deal with your photograph, and I will."

"But I'm not—" Her glower stopped me midsentence. "Fine. Thanks again for the phone. I'll let you get back to work."

When I emerged from the shop, tourists and school kids flocked past me, forming a neat line down to the beach. I checked my phone. Two text messages, both from Aido. I hit his number on speed dial.

"Where are you?" he demanded the instant the call connected. "You shot out of here like the joint was on fire."

"Long story. Any luck with the research?"

"Nothing interesting on the old guns, but I took another look in the history section, this time for books on the Royal Irish Constabulary."

"And?" I prompted. "You found something?"

"Yes." His voice oozed with pride. "A John McElligott was suspected of involvement in the Dunleagh RIC ambush, but never charged with the crime."

My chest rose and fell in time to my rapid breathing. "I knew there had to be a connection."

"How did you guess?"

"I'll...explain. Later. Anything else about John McElligott?"

"Only that he was accused of killing a British army general in 1920 and died in prison on a hunger strike."

"Thanks, Aido. That's excellent info." I checked the time. "I'm going to head to the castle and put in a couple of hours at the museum. Want to meet later for coffee?"

"Sure," he said. "Say, around three at the castle café?"

"See you then."

I disconnected and slid the phone back into my bag with shaky hands. The deeper I dug into Matt Sweeney's initial crazy claims, the more likely they seemed. I squeezed my eyes shut and tried to steady my breathing. Chasing wild theories wasn't helping get my mother out of jail. I had a feeling my grandmother knew more about Matt Sweeney than she'd revealed so far, and I intended to confront her with my suspicions later. For now, I needed to stay focused. That meant treating the two murders as separate crimes and coming up with a plan to prove my mother innocent.

In the distance, the church bells chimed the hour. Eleven o'clock. A plan of campaign for the day formed in my mind. First, I'd drive to Dunleagh General and pay a visit to Dr. Moriarty. At the moment, he was my prime suspect. He had a temper, as illustrated by his fight with Cian prior to the dress rehearsal, and he was probably having an affair with the mayor's wife. Dr. Moriarty had motives both to sabotage Cian's play and to kill his love rival. After I'd tackled the doctor, I'd drop off the books to Matt, and then deal with my grandmother. Nana was chaotic in many areas of her life, but mealtimes weren't among them. She ate lunch at precisely one o'clock every day, mostly at home. If I timed my trip to the hospital right, I'd be back home in time to pounce on her and demand answers.

TWENTY-ONE

All was quiet in the basement when I arrived. I knocked on the door to the pathology offices. Orla Tierney answered. She looked worse than Lev. Black circles weighed down her eyes, and her pale skin looked gray from fatigue.

She stared at me for a moment, confusion warring with exhaustion. "Hello, Dee. Lev's not here. It's his day off."

"Actually—" I stepped closer and lowered my voice, "—I'm looking for your boss."

"He's in the middle of an autopsy, and he's due to leave as soon as he'd done. Maybe try tomorrow."

I mentally cursed the man for having the audacity to slice open cadavers right when I showed up. Judging by Orla's expression, I must've sworn out loud. "Sorry," I said. "It's been a lousy week."

Tears filled her eyes, and she took a step back into the pathology department.

"Hey, are you okay?" Surely she wasn't grief-stricken over the mayor? Or was she upset because she'd found out about Dr. Moriarty and Sally Hyland? I raked my memory for information about Orla's background but came up blank. Although she was a regular attendee at the Historical Murders Club meetings, she was quiet and didn't often add to our discussions.

Orla swallowed and lost the battle to keep her emotions in check. "I'm sorry," she managed between sobs. "It hasn't been a great week for me, either."

"Come on." I took her arm and marched her into her office. "Want to tell me what's up?"

She shook her head, and her tears came hard and fast. I took a packet of tissues out of my bag and handed her one. After she'd dried her eyes and blown her nose, she seemed to calm down somewhat. "I think I need to talk to the Guards."

My pulse quickened. "What about?"

"I did something incredibly stupid on Thursday. I don't know what possessed me." She blushed. "Well, I do, but it's embarrassing to talk about it."

"Practice on me. I'm not the police. If it is a matter for the Guards, you'll have said it out loud at least once already before you speak to them."

She took a deep breath. "The missing evidence bag."

Oh, boy. Here we go. "What about it?"

"I...sold it." With this pronouncement, Orla's heavy sobs resumed.

I slow-blinked and pushed the packet of tissues across the desk. "You *sold* it? Do you mean, someone offered you money to give it to them?"

"Yes." Orla took another tissue. "I know it was wrong, but I have debts, and the extra three hundred euros will get me through the month."

"You were paid three hundred euros to hand over the evidence from the courtyard shooting? By whom?"

"I don't know. A man showed up soon after you and your grandmother left. Sort of thuggish-looking, but he was polite enough. He offered me a wad of cash in return for the bag." She uncapped a bottle of water on her desk and took a long drink. "It was a moment of weakness. I'd just had a text from my landlord, complaining I was short on the rent. I'm already way overdrawn and I didn't know what to do."

"Did this thug have a star tattoo on his neck?" I demanded, my anger growing by the second.

Orla looked surprised. "Why, yes. Do you know him?"

"Oh, yeah." My fingers curled into fists. Not only did I know Gary, I had a fair idea who'd sent him to bribe Orla. Between paying Gary to steal my phone and bribing Orla, Nana must've drained her savings account to destroy evidence relating to the courtyard shootings. No wonder she'd been poking at Mr. Chuckles's mortal remains. The question was *why*.

I got to my feet. "I won't tell the Guards what you did, but I intend to talk to the person behind the theft."

Orla opened a drawer in her desk and pulled out her purse. She extracted three crumpled hundred-euro notes. "If you know the man who paid me, take the money and give it back to him. I don't want it."

I hesitated for a second before taking the cash. "I'll make sure the evidence bag gets to the Guards, one way or another."

She blew her nose again and released a sigh. "Thanks, Dee. You have no idea how worried I've been. Getting this off my chest is a huge relief."

Not only had she gotten it off her chest, but she'd also pushed the responsibility of sorting out the mess onto me. Still, I had to confront Nana anyway, so it wasn't that big of a deal.

"What are you going to do to sort out your financial situation?" I asked.

A tired smile spread over Orla's face. "Work. Dr. Moriarty knows I've been having a hard time, and he offered me extra shifts."

So he wasn't a total dragon? Interesting. "Speaking of your boss, do you know if he's—" I tried and failed to find a delicate way of putting it, "—seeing a woman who's not his wife?"

The woman turned beetroot and fiddled with her watchstrap. "Why do you ask?"

"I have reason to suspect he's seeing the mayor's wife."

No flicker of surprise registered on Orla's features. She bit her lip. "I know he's seeing someone," Orla said at last. "At least, I suspect he is. There've been a few instances of him telling his wife he's working late when I know he's not. In fact, those have been the extra shifts he's given me."

"But you don't know the woman's name?" I prompted.

She shook her head. "No. I suppose he met Sally Hyland at the golf club. It's a sport he enjoys, but his wife doesn't play."

"You're probably right. Thanks for the info." I pocketed the money. "And the cash. I'll see it gets back to its rightful owner." Better still, I'd use it to pay our overdue electricity bill.

After I left Orla, I ascended the stairs to St. Colmcille's Ward. Matt was sitting up in bed when I arrived, watching TV. He looked up when I walked in, and a broad smile suffused his face. "Hello, Dee."

"Hello, Mr. Mystery." I dropped the library books onto his bedside table. "I borrowed a couple of books on the War of Independence for you. Not sure how you'll read them with one good arm, but neither is available as an ebook."

His face looked blank. "Oh, right. Thanks for the books."

"The whole digital book revolution left you behind, eh?" I dropped onto a chair, eyeing him closely. "Kind of like Dunleagh renaming Prince Albert Street in the 1950s. You didn't get the memo?"

Beads of sweat formed on his forehead. "I'm still confused after my—" He indicated his injured chest.

I snorted. "Yeah, right. I don't know what your deal is, but I don't buy your story. Unless you've lived the life of a hermit since birth, you must've used a smartphone before. Your efforts the other day were those of a total newbie. Heck, my two-year-old niece could do a better job."

"I'm not fond of modern technology," he said, averting his gaze.

"I bet you aren't." I folded my arms across my chest. "Want to tell me what you know about John McElligott?"

Matt started as though I'd electrocuted him. "I don't know what—"

The door to his room flew open, and Zosia glided over to the bed. She treated Matt to a beatific smile and plumped up his pillows. "Is Dee bothering you again?"

"I am rather tired," Matt replied, not meeting my eyes.

"I'm not surprised. She can be tiresome." Zosia turned to me. "Once again, you've snuck in outside visiting hours. Time to leave, Dee."

I grabbed my bag and stood. "Fair enough, but I'll be back. You might want to rethink your responses for next time, Matt. I'm going to keep digging."

"I wish you wouldn't." His words were barely audible. He raised his head and regarded me with his deep blue eyes. "Some things are best left alone."

"Two men are dead," I snapped. "I wasn't fond of either of them, but they deserve justice. I intend to keep looking until I find answers."

I stomped out of Room 303, my temper simmering. I'd had enough of non-answers, half responses, and outright lies. Whatever was going on, I needed to know the truth. I took the stairs down to the entrance level two at a time and almost collided with a woman at the bottom. "Sorry," I said on autopilot. "Oh, it's you."

Lou stood before me, tiredness etched across her thin face. "Hi, Dee. You're in a hurry."

"Yeah. Sorry about that." I shoved a stray curl behind my ear. "Any news on my mother?"

Lou's bleak expression provided the answer before she opened her mouth. "Nothing good, I'm afraid. I like Bliss, but the evidence is stacked against her. She was overheard arguing with the mayor in his office the day of the castle shootings. The timing lets her off the hook for the clown murder, but it puts her in the frame for the mayor's killing."

"But she didn't do it. I'm not particularly close to Bliss, but I know her well enough to say she doesn't have a violent bone in her body."

"She threw a paperweight at Hyland," Lou said. "It left a dent in his office wall."

My shoulders sagged. "Oh."

"I'm sorry, Dee, but Bliss had the means, motive, and opportunity to kill Henry Hyland. Everyone in the audience saw her pull the trigger."

"Okay, but you said yourself she's not a suspect in the clown's killing. Does that mean you're treating the two cases as separate?"

"DI Bradley hasn't found a connection between Bliss and Mr. Chuckles, or between her and Matt Sweeney. We're still looking, but we have to consider the possibility that the mayor's murder was an entirely separate incident."

"What about his business dealings?" I demanded. "Have you looked at those?"

Lou cast me a quelling look. "Of course we have. The Hylands' finances weren't as rosy as the picture they painted for the public. Your hunch about the mayor taking a slice of the profits for the various building schemes was spot-on. Still, we haven't found anything linking his business deals to his death."

"Anyone could have tampered with the pistol during the interval," I pointed out. "Not just my mother."

"But could they?" Lou shook her head. "Richard's pistol is an old model. It requires a specific sort of cartridge. Not everyone would know that, and very few people could get access to the correct type of cartridge."

"If Richard owned the pistol, surely he has matching cartridges."

"Yes, but he keeps them under lock and key."

"He could've brought one with him the night of the dress rehearsal." I squirmed even thinking about Richard being the killer but it had to be said.

"He could have, yes, but he swears he didn't. I'm not ruling him out as a suspect, but at the moment, Bliss is the most likely candidate. I'm sorry I don't have better news."

I took a deep breath. "I'll just have to keep looking for evidence to clear my mother. I know she didn't intentionally kill the mayor. Have you looked at other motives for his death? I suspect his wife was having an affair, for example."

Lou's mouth quirked. "Sally Hyland's had several affairs, as had her husband. We're looking into whoever is her latest fling."

"I can help you there." I gave her a smug smile. "Dr. Charles Moriarty."

My friend's eyes popped. "Seriously? That old stick? How do you know?"

"I'm a reporter," I said, deadpan. "I have investigative skills."

Lou put her hands on her hips. "We're friends. Cut me a break, please. I need a carrot to offer DI Bradley."

I burst out laughing. "Okay, fine. I saw him sneaking out of her house this morning."

Over the next couple of minutes, I outlined my adventurous morning run, deftly avoiding all mention of Gary, Nana, and the disappearing evidence bag.

Lou beamed at me. "This is fantastic information. Thanks so much, Dee. Charles Moriarty wasn't on our radar at all, apart from his role performing the post-mortems on Hyland and the clown."

"Now it's my turn to ask you for a favor..." I drummed my fingers against my thigh.

She laughed. "Go on. What do you want?"

"Can I visit Bliss at the station?"

"I don't think that'll be possible," Lou said. "We have several hours before we need to charge her or let her go. DI Bradley won't let her have visitors during that time, apart from her solicitor."

"Can I at least call her? Please, Lou. I have a lead on the missing evidence bag. If that pans out, you'll owe me big time." I didn't add that the lead was my grandmother and that I had no intention of telling the Guards she'd colluded to steal evidence.

"A lead?" Lou's gaze sharpened. "Tell me more."

"I can't be sure it'll work out until later today. If I'm right, it'll make a magical reappearance at a location I'll communicate to you in advance."

Lou crossed her arms over her chest. "I don't like the sound of this plan. What have you done?"

"I've done nothing." I paused. "Yet."

"Your grandmother…" The police officer pulled at her blouse collar and let out a yelp of frustration. "I knew she had something to do with the missing bag. That woman is an absolute menace, on and off her dodgy mobility scooter."

I held up my palms. "I'm not saying Nana was involved, and I won't tell you anything that might incriminate her. However, if you want the evidence bag back, it's possible I can get it to you."

"Gah. Eda Flanagan is a pain in the rear." Lou let out a hiss. "Fine. If you stumble across the evidence, please send it my way. I don't suppose you know what happened to the revolver you say Matt Sweeney had the day of the shoot-out?"

I raised my shoulders in an elaborate shrug. "No, but it just might end up in the evidence bag."

Lou raised her head and straightened her shoulders as if she'd reached an important decision. "All right, Dee. We'll do it your way. But if I find any link to the bag and your grandmother, she'll be joining your mother at the station."

"You won't find a link." I'd make sure of that. "Oh, and Lou—handle the bag with care. I'm almost certain the Matt Sweeney's watch contains radium."

Her jaw made a slow-motion descent. "Are you joking?"

"Nope. Don't break the watch face and you'll be fine."

Lou's eyes were wide. "That's not reassuring."

I grinned at her. "Just think of the fun you'll have when you drop that bombshell on DI Bradley."

Her phone began to vibrate. "Speak of the devil. I have to take this call, Dee. I'll see what I can do about the phone call with your mother. Any news on the evidence, I want to know immediately."

I stuck out my hand. "Officer, it's a deal."

TWENTY-TWO

As I'd predicted, Nana was at home eating lunch when I strode in at one o'clock. Mellie was stretched out at her feet, basking in a sliver of sunlight. She glanced up when she saw me. "Hello, love. You're just in time. Want some stew?"

"No, I don't want stew. What I do want is answers." I slammed the three hundred-euro notes on the table in front of her. "Starting with these."

Nana regarded the cash with disinterest. "Gary mentioned he'd had a close encounter with my walker. I suppose you got Orla Tierney to cave too."

I paced around the kitchen, beating a restless tempo on the tiles. "Why, Nana? Why did you want to destroy the photos I took the day of the shootings? Why bribe Orla to sell you Matt Sweeney's personal effects?"

My grandmother chewed on a mouthful of stew

before responding. "I was hoping to keep you out of this mess. I had no idea that eejit would push you into the pit at Seamie's place. That was definitely not part of the plan. All I wanted him to do was destroy the photographs you showed me of the sky the day the clown died."

"What's so special about the sky?"

She regarded me with amusement. "You didn't find it unusual?"

I flushed. "Well, yeah."

"Did you notice anything peculiar about the wind?"

"If you're asking me, you know I did." I dropped onto the chair opposite her. "What did it mean? What happened that day?"

"Do you remember what your mother said about solstices and equinoxes?" Nana asked. "She mentioned the walls between worlds being thin at those times. That's true."

"Do those walls include paths to other times?"

Nana nodded. "I always said you were a clever girl."

"I'm a mad one if I'm entertaining this theory," I countered.

"I'm sure you've heard of time portals."

I narrowed my eyes. "Are you trying to tell me there's one in the castle?"

"Oh, undoubtedly," Nana said airily. "They're not objects like a stone ring or that nonsense. They can appear anywhere at times of great stress. They occur most often in places with a long history, and almost always around the time of a solstice or equinox. Actually, I prefer to call them cracks in time than time portals, but that's splitting hairs."

In spite of my determination to remain calm and collected, a shiver snaked down my spine. I dropped onto the seat opposite Nana. "Are you saying a crack occurred in the courtyard on Thursday morning?"

"Exactly. What you witnessed, or half witnessed, was a battle played out one hundred years ago."

My pulse quickened. "The ambush on the RIC barracks in 1919? Was that what was happening?"

"I believe so, yes. The clown was collateral damage. He was simply in the wrong place at the wrong time—in every sense of the term."

"What about Matt Sweeney?" I asked. "How does he come into this unlikely tale?"

"His story is more complicated," Nana said. "He's what we call a Displaced. He stumbled through the gap between times and can't get back."

I poked at a crack in the tabletop. "Did you help to fake Matt's identity?"

Her head bobbed. "Indirectly, yes. We've been expecting a new arrival for some time, but we didn't know precisely when he'd arrive, nor what year he'd come from. I got word on Thursday morning that an arrival was imminent, and when the mayor burst into

Elaine's place, babbling about you and a gunfight, I put two and two together."

"So your determination to get a look at the shooting victims wasn't mere curiosity?"

She shook her head. "As I said, we were expecting a new arrival, and I was alarmed to hear you were involved with the crack in time. Until Thursday, I'd had no idea you were a Guide."

"Who's *we*?" I demanded. "My mother? River?"

Nana let out a bark of laughter. "Goodness, no. I love them dearly, but they're no Guides. You and I are."

Frustration rose in my chest. "What's a Guide? Like a tour guide for lost time-travelers? Please tell me you're joking."

"You witnessed an open crack in time, love, and you lived to tell the tale." Nana toyed with her stew. "If you weren't a Guide, you'd have ended up dead like the clown."

"Fantastic. So I witnessed an open time portal and a murder we can never solve because the shot was fired one hundred years ago. The Guards will love that theory."

"The Guards can never know." Nana's placid demeanor vanished. "I'm serious, Dee. This information stays between you and me. Not even your mother and sister know about our role in time travel."

My jaw clenched. "*We* don't have a role. *I* did not

agree to participate in whatever madness you've got yourself mixed up in."

"I know, but there's no denying the truth. Your mother helps people through her crafts and meditations. Your sister is a gifted teacher—literally. I dabble with herbal remedies, but my true calling is as a Guide for the Displaced. You've inherited this gift from me. I wish you hadn't, but there it is."

Nausea washed over me, and the room seemed to spin. "No way. I want nothing to do with time travelers."

"I didn't want to involve you." She gave a tired sigh. "I tried everything I could think of to keep you away from this mess, but it was no good. You took care of Matt Sweeney's new identity and fake background. Or, to be precise, you *will* take care of it."

The memory of my conversation with Suzie Quinn played in my mind like a film reel. "When I visited the hospital yesterday afternoon, Suzie was convinced she'd seen me at the reception desk earlier in the day— the same day Matt Sweeney miraculously regained his memory. Are you telling me I went back in time to provide him with a false identity?"

The corners of my grandmother's mouth drooped. "Unfortunately, yes. I wanted to keep you out of this, but I couldn't create the false identity on my own. Once Gary screwed up the phone-stealing business, I knew I couldn't rely on him to help. I can only assume that you'll agree to take care of the problem at some point in the near future."

"But I won't." My fingernails bit into my palms. "I'm telling you here and now that I won't have anything to do with whatever nonsense you're involved with."

"We know that you will, though. You came back in time and supplied Matt with his new identity." A wry smile tugged at the corners of her mouth. "It makes sense. You have both the brains and the contacts to create a credible false identity in the twenty-first century."

In spite of my anger, I laughed at the absurdity of this statement. "What contacts? I'm a historian and a part-time journalist. I don't have underworld connections." I massaged my temples. "And I definitely can't time travel."

"Under certain circumstances, you can—" Nana's solemn expression was at odds with her usual upbeat attitude, "—as can I. With technological advances, it's not easy for me to help the newly Displaced. I don't have the computer skills to hack into databases and create fake IDs. It's not like it was back in my day."

Curiosity warred with my outrage. "Are you telling me you've done this before? You've helped people from other times?"

My grandmother looked away. "Yes, and it brought me nothing but misery. Being a Guide is a difficult gift to have."

"It sounds like more a curse than a gift."

Her laugh rang hollow. "You're not wrong, love. I'd hoped it would skip a few generations. Take my advice: stay away from Matt Sweeney. You have the gift, but you also have free will. You'll do your duty at the appropriate time and get him his false identity. Once that's done, you can opt to walk away."

"When am I supposed to get the guy his fake ID? Please don't pull a Bliss and be vague. I want precise information."

Nana rose her shoulders in a tired shrug. "I don't have the answers to give you. You shoved a letter through the letterbox yesterday. That was when I knew the game was up."

"I sent you a letter from the future?" My laugh sounded hysterical. "What fabulous news did I impart? Winning lottery numbers, I hope."

"The letter told me to start your training this summer," Nana said seriously. "And also that Matt's revolver is no longer in our time."

I glared at her. "The one you stole the day of the shoot-out?"

Her eyes widened. "I didn't steal his revolver. I assumed everything he owned would be in that evidence bag."

"So who took it? The revolver didn't get up and walk out of the castle." I put my head in my hands and groaned. "This is insane, Nana. Please tell me you're going senile and making it all up."

Nana tapped the side of her head. "Sorry, love. I maintain a healthy regime of gin and poker. My brain's well preserved."

"The free will part you mentioned is sounding more and more dubious, especially if I'm supposed to undergo some sort of training."

"The training is the only way you'll be able to travel through time and back again on the same day," Nana said gently. "We know that you'll get Matt Sweeney his papers and disappear. That means you had training. What you do after you deliver the papers is your choice. My recommendation is that you have nothing to do with the man. Neither of us needs to see him between now and you delivering those papers."

I closed my eyes and tried to steady my breathing. My grandmother's admission that my time travel theory was correct freaked me out. What bothered me more was her reluctance to get involved with Matt Sweeney. It wasn't like Nana not to throw herself headlong into an adventure. Whatever she'd experienced with time travelers in the past, it must've made an impact. "Will you tell me what happened the last time you helped a Displaced?"

"No." The response was emphatic. "Not today. Just take my advice and give the man a wide berth. I'll prepare the materials for your training, and you concentrate on getting your mother out of jail."

I retrieved my backpack from the floor and got to my feet. "Believe me, I'm on it. But this conversation isn't over, Nana. I want to know more about Guides and Displaceds. And you need to give me the evidence bag. I've arranged to get it to Lou. As long as she doesn't find indisputable proof that you took it, she won't ask questions."

"It's behind my armchair. I'll get it for you now." She stood and shuffled to the living room. "Just get Bridget home, please."

"I'll do my best." I slung my backpack over my shoulder and followed her. "If the bag's on the floor, I'd better get it. I don't want another trip to the hospital with you."

"Cheeky mare," Nana said, chuckling. "While you're down there, see if you can find my missing knitting needle."

I moved Nana's armchair away from the wall and dropped to my knees. Sure enough, the blue plastic evidence bag was behind it, along with a broken bracelet, a half-empty packet of chewing gum, and a full bottle of gin. I placed the last item on Nana's side table. "Missing knitting needle indeed. This was what you were after."

Her eyes grew large in mock surprise. "Well, I never. Fancy that being down there?"

I peered inside the bag. At first glance, everything that should be there was present and correct. "I'll contact Lou and set up a handover point."

"Before you run off to the Guards, would you mind giving Dottie and me a lift to the castle? We can use

Bridget's car. I'd drive us, but I'm a bit hazy on where I left my driver's license, and Dottie won't make left-hand turns." Nana pulled a face. "She insists on making us take a circuitous route whenever she's behind the wheel."

I eyed my grandmother with suspicion. "A bit hazy, eh? Why do you need to go to the castle?"

"The mobility scooters. Bridget asked Larry to deliver them to us, but there's still no sign of them. Dottie and I are fed up waiting. We decided it was time to take action."

I sighed. "All right. Let me contact Lou, and then we'll get moving. Returning the evidence bag is my priority."

Nana shook her head. "Where did I get a granddaughter who's such a stickler for rules?"

I dropped a kiss onto her papery cheek. "Someone's got to play the straight man in this comedy duo."

TWENTY-THREE

Arranging a handover was easy. Lou ate lunch at The Coffee Bean, making sure she snagged an outside table. I cruised by on my way to the castle. I'd concealed the evidence bag in a spare backpack and gave it to Lou through the car window. She shot a suspicious look at Nana, but didn't say anything. Her relief at the return of the evidence was palpable—the reappearance of Matt Sweeney's personal effects would score her points with DI Bradley.

Once I'd done my civic duty, I aimed the car for the castle. I parked and escorted Dottie and Nana over the drawbridge and across the courtyard. I deposited them in front of the main entrance.

"We might nip into the café for a slice of fruit cake," Nana winked at Dottie. "I'm still feeling peckish."

"How is that possible?" I asked. "You had two large helpings of stew."

My grandmother patted her stomach. "What can I say? My daughter killed a man, and I'm comfort eating."

"They serve a mighty fine Irish coffee at the castle's café," Dottie added to me in a conspiratorial whisper. "It'll perk up Eda."

Shaking my head, I left the old ladies to their spiked coffees and sugary treats and headed for the museum. I needed to look for a replacement photograph for the exhibition, as well as dig through the RIC barracks papers Richard had mentioned. Part of me still clung to the hope that Nana was talking nonsense and Matt Sweeney was exactly who he claimed to be: a teacher from Donegal, newly arrived in Dunleagh.

I'd spent my life eschewing my mother's family's impractical lifestyles and wacky beliefs. I'd embraced my staid father's love for academics and immersed myself in facts and figures that I could back up with research. Suspension of disbelief had never come easy to me. While I was an avid reader, I preferred nonfiction to fiction, and TV documentaries to soap operas. The idea that I was some sort of guide for lost time travelers was absurd. What I needed was a good dose of research. Facts and figures that would disprove my grandmother's tale. The M. Slattery who'd been killed in the 1919 ambush must be buried somewhere.

Bodies didn't simply vanish. And dead men didn't time travel.

On my way across the courtyard, I spotted Cian, slumped on a bench holding a newspaper. I hailed him with a wave, but he was lost in his own world. I jogged across the cobblestones to join him.

"Hi, Cian." I took in the unshaven jaw and yesterday's clothes. "Are you okay?"

"Hardly. The play I spent years writing and months practicing is doomed." He shook out the newspaper, a national broadsheet that often crossed the line into tabloid territory. "My play's got a deadlier reputation than *Macbeth*. No one will come to see it now."

A blessing, in my opinion, but I didn't want to totally deflate the poor man. Besides, I was fond of Cian, even if I despaired of his skills as a playwright.

"The superstitions surrounding Macbeth have added to the play's popularity," I said. "Use the notoriety to your advantage. Make the next issue of the *Chronicle* epic, and focus on how *A Fighting Man* was used to facilitate a murder. Seriously, people will be lining up to see it when it finally opens."

He put his head in his hands, the picture of dejection. "*If* it ever opens. My leading man is dead, loathsome though he was, and my leading lady is the prime suspect in his murder."

"There are other actors," I said, opting not to enter

into yet another debate about Bliss's guilt or innocence. "Didn't you audition more people for their roles?"

Cian laughed. "The mayor wasn't Bliss's love interest when we started rehearsals. He got the part by picking on the guy who initially played the male lead."

"Whoa." An idea formed in my head. "Who played the role originally?"

"Charles Moriarty." Cian pulled a face. "To be honest, the mayor's bullying did me a favor. Hyland was no acting great, but casting Moriarty in a leading role was a mistake. He constantly fluffed his lines and missed his cues. The chemistry between him and Bliss was nonexistent. At least Hyland delivered his lines."

My heart thumped in my chest. "On the night of the dress rehearsal, Charles Moriarty had a further demotion. Is that right?"

"Not exactly. After I recast the male lead, I gave Charles a minor role. The drama on the night of the dress rehearsal involved him quitting the play. The doctor and the mayor got into a fight while the cast was getting ready to go onto the stage, and Charles stormed off in full diva fashion, vowing never to return."

"What did they fight about?"

"Oh, the usual. Hyland teased Charles about everything from his acting to his appearance. Charles got defensive and lashed out."

A thought struck me. "Wait a sec...I understood that *you* had a fight with Dr. Moriarty?"

"We had words, yes. I wasn't happy that Charles

wanted to quit five minutes before the curtain went up. Can you blame me?"

My brain was working overtime. "No, but you're saying the original fight was between Dr. Moriarty and the mayor, correct?"

"Yes. They were always making snide remarks to one another. Hyland never seemed seriously put out by Charles's remarks, but Charles often went off in a huff after one of their arguments."

"Wouldn't that give Dr. Moriarty a strong motive for killing the mayor?" I mused. "Maybe the argument on the night of the dress rehearsal was the final straw."

"Perhaps, but how did he find a suitable bullet at short notice?" Cian asked. "Richard kept them at home."

I considered this argument. "True, but his apartment is on the castle grounds. Dr. Moriarty wouldn't need to go far to find it. I'll ask Richard where he stores the bullets for the pistol."

"When I spoke to Richard at the police station, he mentioned he had a safe."

"Ah," I said, half laughing. "If the code to his safe is as easy to crack as the museum's alarm code, it wouldn't take long to open."

"I can't see Charles Moriarty breaking into Richard's apartment, cracking open a safe, and running back to the Great Hall to stage the murder." A faint smile broke through Cian's gloomy expression. "It's more outlandish than the plot of my play."

I laughed. "It's worth asking, though, and I need to go to the museum anyway."

"You do that." The corners of his mouth drooped, and he subsided into gloom. "I'll sit here and feel sorry for myself for another few minutes, and then I'll tackle the mountain of emails I've been ignoring since Friday."

"Good luck."

"Oh, hang on a sec, Dee. If you're going to the museum, will you do me a favor?" Cian rifled through his briefcase, eventually withdrawing three history magazines. "Can you leave these in Richard's office? I borrowed them for research and forgot I still had them in my office."

"Sure." I took the magazines and tucked them under my arm. "Take care of yourself."

He waved a hand in farewell. "You too."

On the walk to the museum, I flicked idly through one of the magazines. It was a special on the War of Independence. I'd ask Richard if I could borrow it. I stopped short when I turned a page to discover a missing section. I ran a fingertip over the ragged edges where pages had been ripped from the magazine, my mind a whirl of activity. Elaine claimed the anonymous letters sent to the mayor had consisted of magazine cuttings. It was out of character for Richard to tear pages, but what about Cian? Could his be the poison pen behind the threatening messages sent to Henry Hyland?

I tucked the magazine back under my arm and speed-walked to the museum, thinking over what I'd learned. If Cian hadn't sent the letters, who had? Richard? These were his magazines, after all. And had the doctor set up Bliss to kill the mayor in a fit of pique? Or had he done it in collusion with Mrs. Hyland? It was clear the men had issues with one another. Had Hyland pushed Moriarty too far and made the man snap?

The trouble with the snap-decision theory was the timing. The pistol only worked with a specific size of cartridge, one that wasn't easy to find these days. For the crime-of-passion scenario to work, Moriarty would've needed to know precisely where Richard kept his ammunition, plus the code to the safe. While it was true that Richard was lax about using secure codes and passwords, I knew the man well, and I was aware of his penchant for creating passwords using the names and birthdays of former pets. Would Dr. Moriarty know this? Probably not.

Taking the second scenario into consideration, collusion with Sally Hyland pointed to premeditation. This seemed the more plausible option. As an actor in the play, Moriarty had known that the final scene required Bliss to shoot the mayor's character. If he'd planned the man's death, either alone or with Sally, he could've stolen the cartridge weeks ago. The snag to this idea was the fight on the night of the dress rehearsal. Did Moriarty storming off make it more or less likely that he'd planned the mayor's murder? Was leaving the play a way to create an alibi? If so, how could he guarantee he wouldn't be seen if he snuck back at the interval? When I'd asked the audience if anyone had seen him, no one had.

I reached the museum more confused than ever. Nana and Dottie's mobility scooters were still parked next to the side entrance. When I walked in, the weekend staff was showing visitors the various displays. I waved to the girl on the desk and made my way to the back room where the storage boxes were kept. It was one of the few places in the castle that was kept locked at all times, but as part of the research staff, I knew the code. I keyed in the numbers and stepped inside.

Richard was already there, standing in front of a table strewn with old handguns and ammunition. He looked up, and our eyes met.

I sucked in a breath and scrambled backward. In his right hand, Richard held a revolver.

TWENTY-FOUR

Richard lowered the gun. An expression of relief washed over his face. "Good grief, Dee. You startled me."

I put a hand to my chest, feeling my rapid heartbeat slam against my palm. "Sorry, man. The sight of old guns freaks me out."

"We're all on edge this week," he said grimly. "You're safe among this lot, though. None of the firearms are loaded."

I closed the door behind me and noticed the woman seated at the table next to Richard's, leafing through a stack of old photographs. "Hello, Mary. I thought you two would still be at the library for the exhibition's opening."

"We stayed for the first two hours but then left the visitors to explore on their own," Mary said. "Our work for the exhibition is pretty much done. The exhibits should be self-explanatory, and the library staff has been schooled on potential questions."

I darted a glance at the table laden with old weapons. "Will your husband come to see the exhibition?"

Her smile was wan. "Charles meant to come to see the exhibition today, but he has to work late again."

That wasn't what Orla Tierney had told me, but I held my tongue.

Mary must've read something from my face, though. She straightened her spine and returned to her perusal of the photographs. "I'm looking for a nice picture to replace the one you borrowed."

"I don't mind taking care of that," I said. "I deprived the exhibition of one of its photos, after all."

"It's no bother." She squared her shoulders. "I like to keep busy."

"So do I." Richard held up an old revolver. "After the events of this week, handling antique weapons seems wrong."

"Why do you need to sort through them today?" I asked. "Is it urgent?"

He gestured to the open box on the floor beside him. "I need to double-check the contents of this box of World War II-era weapons before we send it to the National Museum. We persuaded them to buy part of our vintage weapons collection." Richard ran a hand through his curls. "Needs must and all that. I can only hope that the next mayor is more generous with the museum's budget."

"I came to look for a replacement photograph for the exhibition, but if Mary's taking care of that, I'd like to look through the RIC barracks files you mentioned, Richard, and perhaps the trench watches."

"Sure. They're right here." He hauled two large boxes from the corner of the room and stacked them on an empty table, and added a smaller box to the top of the pile and tapped it with his index finger. "The watches are in here. Help yourself."

I deposited my backpack and jacket beside the table and handed the magazines to Richard. "Cian asked me to return these to you."

"Oh, thank you," the man stammered, his cheeks leeched of color. "I'd forgotten all about those."

I stared at him for a long while, taking in the sudden pallor and tightening of his mouth. Had I been wrong? Had a hatred of the mayor driven Richard to do the unthinkable and defile his magazines? I swallowed a bubble of laughter. The situation was absurd. Even if Richard had penned those letters, it didn't necessarily make him a killer. On the other hand, he owned the lethal weapon...

A trickle of fear spread through my limbs. I took a deep breath. I was being ridiculous. With the drama of the last few days, it was natural to be on edge, but I had no reason to fear Richard.

I switched my attention back to the stack of boxes.

I checked the trench watches first, but neither shed any light on the murders. In any case, they were very different from Matt Sweeney's World War I-era watch and that was the one that had snagged my attention.

Putting the watches aside, I opened the first box of RIC material and removed an index card file. "By the way, where do you store the cartridges for your grandfather's pistol?"

Richard regarded me curiously. "In my safe. Why do you ask?"

"Do you mean the one in your apartment?" I vaguely recalled Richard mentioning it to me at one point.

"Yes, that's the only safe I have." He chuckled. "Everything else of value belongs to the museum."

I darted a glance at Mary, but she was absorbed in the box of photographs. I lowered my voice. "Apart from you, does anyone know the combination?"

Richard shook his head. "I'm not as security conscious as you'd like me to be, but I'm not stupid."

I fingered the index card, the words written on it a blur. "Is there any other way for someone to get hold of the correct ammunition for the pistol?"

The frown lines on his forehead deepened. "If they were knowledgeable about vintage weapons, yes. There are several special interest forums, for example. One can find just about anything online these days." He picked up a cartridge and revolver from the collection on the table. "My predecessor found this

Enfield No. 2, complete with a box of ammo, on an internet forum."

"Everyone involved with the play knew about the pistol," I mused. "Who among the cast and crew was interested in the time period and might've known what sort of ammunition it required?"

"Cian. Me. Paddy Patel—he takes an interest in old guns, but mostly those from World War II."

"And beyond the cast and crew? Anyone you can think of?"

"No. I've been over all this with the Guards." He sighed. "Do you want to see where I keep the pistol and ammo? The Guards took everything, but it'll prove it was secure."

"Sure."

Leaving Mary to continue her search for the perfect picture, I followed Richard upstairs to his apartment, once again marveling at how neat and tidy he kept his home.

"The safe is in my bedroom," he said over his shoulder. "It's behind the painting that hangs over my bed. A cliché, I know, but there's a limit to the number of places to hide a safe in an apartment as small as mine."

Richard removed the landscape painting of Dunleagh Harbour and revealed the safe. It was a modern affair and secured with a PIN code. He tapped numbers onto the screen, and the door sprang open.

"See? No one could get in here unless they knew the code."

I nodded. "Fair enough. Did you have any visitors in your apartment recently? Maybe at a time when the safe was open?"

"I showed Cian the pistol when he was planning the props for his play. I don't remember him following me into the bedroom while I was getting it. I'm sure he stayed in the living room."

I walked back into the living room and pointed to the mirror over the fireplace. "Could Cian have seen you open the safe in the mirror?"

Richard laughed. "With his bad eyesight? I doubt it. I'm always telling him to get new glasses, but he's too cheap."

The sound of creaking wood drew my attention to the door. Was someone out in the corridor, eavesdropping on our conversation? I gave myself a mental shaking. The events of the last couple of days had made me paranoid. "Apart from me on Thursday and Cian months ago, who's been in your apartment recently?"

"Not many people, to be frank." Richard glanced around his small living room. "It's on the snug side for hosting guests. I prefer to socialize elsewhere."

"What about work? Do you ever work with people in your apartment?"

He thought about it for a moment. "Mary and I

discussed the exhibition a couple of times over coffee, but never when the safe was open."

My gaze strayed to the coffee table. The neat piles of magazines I'd perused on my previous visit had vanished. The hair on the nape of my neck stood on end. My stomach performed a flip worthy of an acrobat. "Your magazines are gone," I said, observing him carefully and angling my body toward the door. "That's a shame. I'd have liked to borrow a few."

Richard ran an unsteady hand through his wild corkscrew curls. His eyes met mine. "You know, don't you?" His voice was curiously devoid of inflection.

My heart thumped against my ribs. What had I done? Was he about to confess to murder? And if Richard had killed the mayor, what would he do to me? I stepped back, putting distance between us.

The museum director deflated like a burst balloon. He slumped onto the sofa and stared into space. "You know," he repeated. "What are you going to do about it? Will you tell the Guards?"

"Wouldn't it be better coming from you?" Another few steps and I'd be at the door. "It would help your defense."

I had no idea if this was true, but it sounded good, and I wanted to keep him calm. *Five more steps...* My feet moved as though they were held down by invisible weights.

Richard's brow furrowed. "My defense? Do you think the Guards would take it that far?"

My steps faltered. Had I jumped to the wrong conclusion?

Realization spread over Richard's face. "Gosh, Dee, you don't think I killed him, do you?"

I released the breath I hadn't realized I was holding. "You didn't? You're just referring to the anonymous letters?"

"Of course," he said, horrified. "I know that giving in to the temptation to vent anonymously was terrible, but I didn't kill Hyland. I'd have confessed to sending the letters the moment he died, but with my pistol being the fatal weapon..." He trailed off, his cheeks burning red.

"So you decided to sit back and let my mother be arrested?" I snarled. "How gentlemanly of you."

He hunched his shoulders. "I've been on the verge of calling Lou ever since I heard about Bliss. I just can't find the courage."

Richard looked more like a forlorn little boy than a grown man. In spite of my annoyance with him, it'd be better for all of us if I persuaded Richard to talk to the Guards of his own accord. "Why don't I go with you? It's easier to be brave when you have company."

"Would you?" A note of hope rang in his voice. "I'm aware it looks bad for me, but I swear to you I never made good on my threats. I have no idea who tampered with my pistol, but I'm certain it wasn't me."

"The sheer number of people who disliked Henry Hyland doesn't make it easier to narrow down the list of suspects," I said dryly. "I'm relieved to know I can cross you off the list."

He looked abashed. "Writing nasty letters is about as violent as I get, Dee."

"I believe you, but someone arranged for the mayor to die, and I'm sure it wasn't my mother. Unfortunately, with her in the frame, the Guards are disinclined to pursue other leads." I went over to the sofa and tugged on his arm. "Come on. Let's get this over with."

Richard got to his feet without protest and strode to the door. "I don't know who put a bullet in my pistol," he said over his shoulder, "but I can't see Bliss doing it. The problem isn't *who* had an opportunity to tamper with the gun, but rather who *didn't*. Between the cast, the crew, and everyone else Cian got to proof his play, fact check, or otherwise add their two cents, most of the town knew the content of the final scene."

His words stirred a memory, still hazy but crystallizing by the second. I stopped midstep. "Just a moment. Cian was constantly tinkering with his play. I read several iterations. If I recall correctly, the scene with the pistol wasn't in the first version I fact-checked for him."

Richard opened the door and gestured for me to follow him into the hallway. "That's right," he said. "He added it in a later edition. All the changes drove me crazy. I proofread a couple of versions for him but gave up. What was the point in investing my time correcting words he changed in the next draft?"

I sucked in a breath. The hallway was empty, but I couldn't shake the sensation that we weren't alone. Paranoia. That was it. The whole business with Nana and her revelations had shaken me, and talking about the murders wasn't helping matters. All the same, I lowered my voice to the barest of whispers. "Mary also proofread Cian's script. Can you remember which version she saw?"

Richard was already descending the stairs. He looked up at me in surprise. "She was the proofreader *after* I quit. Sorry, Dee. That angle won't work."

And then it hit me, like a sucker punch to the solar plexus. The niggling doubt that had been at the back of my mind since Friday evening, nagging at me to pay attention. I exhaled in a whoosh and hurried to catch up with Richard. "Dr. Moriarty was supposed to play the male lead," I whispered. "Did Mary know he'd lost the role to the mayor?"

Confusion clouded Richard's face. "I presume so. Why wouldn't he tell her?"

"Because he's arrogant and entitled and had a bee in his bonnet about the mayor," I said, the scenario crystallizing in my mind. "He'd be too proud to admit to his wife that he'd been stripped of a leading role."

Richard frowned. "She'd have found out eventually, though."

"Yes, but did she know before the dress rehearsal?"

"Mary wasn't at the dress rehearsal, remember? She was one of the few people we know who wasn't in attendance."

"But she was at the castle that afternoon," I reminded him. "I met her when she was covering for Larry at the reception desk, and she mentioned she had a meeting with you."

He blinked. "Well, yes, but then she went home."

"Do you know for sure that she left the castle? Mary's a part-time tour guide here. She knows every inch of the building. She could've easily slipped into a room and hidden until she had the opportunity to tamper with the pistol."

"This is crazy talk, Dee. Mary wouldn't—"

We'd reached the bottom of the stairs and now faced the storage room. The door was wide open. Richard and I looked at one another for a loaded moment and then raced into the room.

"Mary's gone." I spoke the words out loud even, though her absence was obvious.

Richard ran to the box of weapons he'd been checking and paled. "So's the Enfield No. 2."

TWENTY-FIVE

I ran for the exit. "Call the police," I yelled over my shoulder to a stunned Richard. "Mary's going after her husband."

I barged past startled museum visitors and staff and burst into the museum's courtyard. Tourists poured through the Green Archway, led by one of the castle's tour guides. By the side entrance to the museum, Nana and Dottie perched on their mobility scooters and regarded me with unabashed interest.

"Did we miss another murder?" Nana roared. "Who's dead this time?"

"No one yet." I pointed in the direction of the archway. "Did you see Mary Yates?"

"She ran by a moment ago like a bat out of hell. Didn't even say hello." Nana sniffed. "And to think of the number of erotic romance novels I've recommended to her over the years. People have no manners these days."

"I need to go after her." Ignoring Nana's demands for an explanation, I broke into a sprint.

When I reached the Green Archway, I elbowed outraged tourists out of my way and battled through to the other side. There was no sign of Mary in the main courtyard. She had a few minutes' head start. Even if I ran all the way to the parking lot, I'd—

I hit my forehead with my palm. "Stupid. Stupid. Stupid."

In my haste to go after Mary, I'd forgotten that my bag was still in the storage room. The key to Bliss's car was in the bag. Without access to a car, I'd never catch up with Mary, and I had no idea if the police would reach her before she found her husband. I didn't know precisely where she was headed, but I could hazard a guess: Sally Hyland's house.

I bent over and tried to catch my breath. Behind me, more howls of indignation from the tourists heralded the arrival of my grandmother. Sure enough, Nana zoomed to my side on her mobility scooter. She was rocking the crazed-beetle look again with her goggles acting as a hairband over her wild purple hair. "Need a ride?"

"I think Mary killed the mayor," I gasped, "and I'm pretty sure she's about to kill her husband."

Nana pulled her goggles into position. "Hop on. I'll give you a lift."

Without stopping to think, I jumped onto the back of the mobility scooter.

Nana accelerated, forcing me to cling onto the back of her seat or risk falling onto the cobblestones. "I'll get this baby up to sixty," my grandmother shouted. "Just you watch."

"I thought you said it only went up to fifty kilometers an hour," I yelled over the roar of the wind.

"No. You guessed I'd had it doctored to go fifty. I didn't bother correcting you."

Nana raced over the drawbridge, forcing tourists to cling to the sides to avoid being mown down. The guard on the gate chased us part way down the road, but Nana was too fast for him. He shook a fist at us and shouted obscenities. Nana flipped him the bird and continued on her merry way.

We were halfway down the hill when Mary's red Toyota Yaris overtook us at a ferocious speed. "Follow her," I cried. "I bet she's going to Sally Hyland's house. We'll know for sure when we see which route she takes."

I was operating on educated guesses. The Enfield No. 2 had vanished, and so had Mary. Orla Tierney had said her boss was taking off early from work, plans his wife had known nothing about until I'd inadvertently clued her in. The last time I'd seen Moriarty, he'd been leaving the Hyland residence. If he'd lied to his wife about working late, he was hiding something. The logical conclusion was that he was spending time with Sally. Equally, I didn't know for sure that Mary knew about Sally, but Mary was no fool. If she'd figured out her husband was cheating on her, she was smart enough to find out with whom.

And that brought me full circle back to the antique firearms. Mary had a keen interest in history, and she'd worked closely with Richard to prepare the material for the exhibition. She'd had ample opportunity to quiz him about his grandfather's Smith & Wesson Model 1913 and to source a bullet that would work in the pistol. If I moved away from the spur-of-the-moment theory, it was an almost perfect example of a premeditated crime.

The mobility scooter reached the end of the hill. Nana slowed to a roll. "Any sign of Mary?"

"I see her," I shouted. "She went left."

Ignoring the red light, Nana swung left, forcing a turning tour bus to slam on its brakes. Oblivious to tooting horns and outraged shouts, Nana zoomed after Mary's car. We traveled through the town at breakneck speed, Nana yelling at anyone or anything in her way. I clung to the back, praying I wouldn't tumble into the path of an oncoming vehicle. Somehow, we made it to the beachfront alive.

Outside The Coffee Bean, Big Jim McElligott sat on his mobility scooter, eating an ice-cream cone.

"Do you have your air rifle?" Nana's booming voice made the man jump in his seat and slop chocolate ice cream down his shirt.

Big Jim patted the shopping basket at the front of his scooter. "It's right here. I never go anywhere without it these days. Not with crazed killers rampaging all over the town."

"Then get your backside into gear and follow me. Mary Yates killed the mayor and is on her way to kill her husband. We need backup."

Without waiting for her elderly friend to realign his jaw, Nana ramped up her scooter's speed. "Mary's turned onto the coast road," she shouted over her shoulder. "If she puts her foot on the gas, we'll never catch up with her."

I scanned our surroundings. "My running path." I pointed to the starting point of my favorite jogging route. "It leads directly past the Hyland residence. We can't beat Mary's speed, but this path is way shorter than the road."

My grandmother motored up the track, narrowly missing a dog walker and her irate poodle. Big Jim's mobility scooter followed suit, earning more squawks of protest from the woman and her pet.

"Are you sure involving Big Jim is wise? He's even older than you."

"Yes, but he's only eighty-one. Plenty of life in him yet."

"Only," I said dryly. "How well can Big Jim see to be firing an air rifle?"

"Oh, he has terrible eyesight, but he loves that rifle. He goes out every day, taking potshots at branches and the like. He accidentally blew up his neighbor's oxygen tank last month, the eejit."

"How...reassuring." I glanced over my shoulder. Big Jim had a near encounter with a tree before regaining control over the scooter and zooming after us. I'd often dreamed of being involved in a high-speed chase, but somehow none of these fantasies included rigged mobility scooters and geriatric sidekicks.

Nana covered the distance from the edge of town to the Hylands' house at an alarming speed. If she hadn't sworn the vehicle couldn't go faster than sixty kilometers an hour, I'd have guessed we were traveling at eighty. My perception was probably clouded by fear. When I was on Mavis, I was in control. Hanging onto the back of my grandmother's mobility scooter, I was anything but.

When the Hyland property came into view, I searched for an easy access point. "You can leave me here, Nana. I'll jump over the gate and run the rest of the way."

"Nonsense," she yelled over the sound of the surf. "I'll have us up that hill in no time."

With this confident pronouncement, my grandmother grabbed her cane from the back of the scooter, whacked the padlock off a gate I hadn't noticed this morning, and roared into the field. I was still wondering if I'd peed my pants when she took off up the hill.

I have no idea how she drove the scooter up the

steep incline. Every second, I expected to be thrown off and crushed by the falling vehicle. Either I'd underestimated my grandmother's steering skills, or we had incredible luck. At last, we crested the hill, and the ground leveled off.

Nana raced through the garden, narrowly avoiding taking out a newly planted tree. Big Jim and his air rifle reached the top of the hill a moment later and steered his scooter after Nana's. Once we neared the house, screams and shouts were audible through the open bay windows. Nana slowed her scooter, and I jumped free, landing neatly by the side of the swimming pool.

I didn't hang around for Nana and Big Jim to alight from their scooters and hobble after me. I legged it across the patio and over to an open window. Crouching beneath the sill, I took a cautious peek into the room. From my vantage point, the action was visible in all its ugly glory. Mary stood in the center of the room, aiming the Enfield No. 2 at her husband's chest. Dr. Moriarty cowered by the fireplace, his doughy face drained of its habitual haughty arrogance. Sally Hyland sat on the sofa, holding a large cushion over her body as a makeshift shield.

Nana and Big Jim's respective walking aids tapped across the patio. I jerked around and held a finger to my lips. For once, Nana took the hint. She and her friend snuck to the side of the house, careful to stay out of sight of the window.

"What's happening?" Nana whispered.

I made a gun symbol with my hand.

My grandmother pursed her lips in disapproval. "It's not nice to shoot people."

Behind her, Big Jim fiddled with his air rifle. Nana adjusted her goggles and edged along the side of the house, close to the window. She snuck a peek and drew back abruptly. "Give me that air rifle, you big eejit. I don't trust you not to blow a hole in my backside."

My grandmother's stage whisper blew our cover the instant she opened her mouth. Alerted to our presence, Mary adjusted her position and pointed the gun at the window.

For a horrible second, my breath caught in my throat, rendering me speechless. "Careful," I rasped. "Mary's aiming right at us."

"Well, now," Nana exclaimed, radiating indignation. "The cheek of that woman. First, she puts my Bridget behind bars, and now she wants to take us out. Not on my watch."

Before Mary had a chance to pull the trigger, Nana pushed the nozzle of the air rifle through the crack of the open window and let loose.

Proving his instinct for self-preservation was still going strong into his ninth decade, Big Jim hit the deck with an alarming crunch. I hunched beneath the windowsill and stuck my fingers in my ears to drown out the noise. The yelling, cursing, and gunfire seemed to last an eternity.

When Nana's last pellet was spent, she cast down

the air rifle in disgust and addressed her friend. "Sure, that's not much better than a water pistol. You need an upgrade, and then I can win it off you at poker."

"There's a lovely machine gun I have my eye on," Big Jim said from his position under a bush. "Maybe I'll splurge."

The comforting sound of approaching sirens persuaded me to remove my fingers from my ears and risk a peek inside at what remained of the Hylands' living room. Sally Hyland's mantelpiece ornaments had been pulverized. Sally herself sat on the floor, stunned, still clutching the now-shredded cushion. Dr. Moriarty had crawled under a table and curled into a fetal position, revealing a telling brown stain on the back of his pants. Mary slumped against a radiator, a dazed expression on her face. A trickle of blood trailed down her neck, and the Enfield dangled from her fingers.

"I should recommend Barney's incontinence pants to Dr. Moriarty," Nana said, leaning in to get a better look. "They've saved my dignity more than once."

"And mine," Big Jim piped up, still under the bush. "Do you remember the time I—"

Thankfully, I was spared the rest of the story by the arrival of law enforcement.

"Police," a male voice shouted from the other side of the door. "Open up."

No one in the living room moved. Loosening her grip on the Enfield was Mary's only acknowledgment that the game was up. It slid to the ground and she made no effort to retrieve it.

An instant later, the living room door's hinges groaned against the pressure, and it crashed to the ground. DI Bradley and his team tumbled in, accompanied by Lou, Eoin, and a couple more Dunleagh police officers.

"You blackguard." Nana whacked on the window and glowered at DI Bradley. "Let my daughter out of jail at once. That's your killer."

My grandmother pointed at Mary Yates, who stared blankly at the detective inspector. Whatever mad energy she'd possessed when she'd torn off to confront her husband was spent. Now she'd reverted to the tired, mousy-looking woman I'd thought I'd known. She was a sad sight, and I almost felt sorry for her. Almost, but not quite.

I got to my feet and helped Big Jim to his. We helped one another brush leaves off our clothes, but the dirt would have to wait for a shower. "Thanks for your help, guys," I said. "If we hadn't gotten here quickly, Mary would have killed her husband, and probably Sally too.

"It was no bother," Big Jim replied with nonchalance. "I'd nothing to do until tonight's poker game and no chance to use my air rifle. You and Eda livened up my afternoon."

"You can buy the poor man an ice cream to replace the cone he lost during the chase," Nana suggested, lending the story of Big Jim's lost ice cream a heroic touch. "And one for me, as well. And then we'll head to *Elaine's* and tell everyone we caught the Dunleagh killer."

We'd caught one of them, yes. Whether or not we'd ever find the men who'd killed Mr. Chuckles remained a question mark. I had a feeling Matt Sweeney had the answers, or at least knew where to find them, but that was a topic I'd address another day.

I regarded the crowded room on the other side of the glass. "I have a feeling we'll be busy for the next few hours, but I promise I'll treat us all to ice creams when we're free to go." I stepped away from the window and looped arms with my fellow crime busters. "I can't wait to see DI Bradley's face when he finds out who laid waste to the Hylands' living room. Let's go and make him squirm."

TWENTY-SIX

Two weeks after the air rifle throw-down at the Hylands' house, summer was in full swing. Dunleagh pulsed with tourists, and school children basked under the baking hot sun. In the aftermath of Mary's arrest, my mother had been exonerated of all blame in the mayor's death. The investigation into the clown shooting continued, but Lou'd indicated it was going nowhere fast.

Matt Sweeney, now released from hospital if not fully recovered from his gunshot wound, was recuperating at home. He'd sent me a text message the previous night to arrange dinner, but I had yet to respond. After the showdown with Mary, I'd thrown myself into my work and spent every spare moment on the beach, trying hard not to think of lost time travelers and my alleged duty to help them. Nana had emulated my ostrich-impression, and neither of us had referenced our conversation about Guides and Displaceds.

Into this bubble of peace, my sister decided to throw a wrench. River announced that a welcome party for Dunleagh's newest resident was in order, particularly after his first day in town had ended with emergency surgery. She had a point, but I was enjoying my head-in-the-sand approach to life, sometimes quite literally, and I had zero desire to face the madness that had overtaken my reality.

On the morning of the party, I was dispatched to collect a specially ordered cake from Amy at The Coffee Bean. I'd just wrestled it into the back of Bliss's car when Naido Lafferty appeared in front of me, sucking a lollipop.

She cast a mildly interested look at the cake box. "Celebrating?"

"It's for Matt Sweeney's welcome party. Are you coming?"

Naido shrugged. "Maybe. I haven't decided yet." She eyed the cake box again. "What flavor did you order?"

"Red velvet. I have no idea if it's Matt's favorite, but I know my sister loves it. Given that she's hosting the party, she might as well get to eat a slice of cake she enjoys."

The other woman sniffed, never taking her eyes off the cake box. "Maybe I'll pop in. Just for a little while. If I have time."

"You do that," I said. "I'd like to have you there."

A hint of a smile touched Naido's mouth but was gone so fast I might have imagined it. "I didn't stop to chat. I have something for you." She dug through her shoulder bag and withdrew a hard cardboard sleeve. "I enlarged the face in that photo you gave me. It's not a perfect job, but the quality of the original was lousy."

I opened the envelope and slid out the photograph. No emotion stirred in me when I saw the face staring back at me. I'd expected to recognize Matt Sweeney, even with the unfamiliar mustache.

"Is it okay?" Naido's question jerked me back to the present.

"Yes. You've done an excellent job." She truly had. "What do I owe you?"

Naido shifted her weight to her other leg. "An extra-large slice of the cake in your car. If I don't come to the party, save me a piece."

"Are you sure that's all you want? I'd like to at least pay you for your time and the materials."

"Nah, you're good. I did it off the books. I like a challenge."

"Well, thank you." This act of kindness by Aido's sister humbled me. I waited with bated breath for the catch. She was sure to follow it up with a sarcastic remark. To my surprise, she didn't.

Naido parted her fringe, giving me a proper look at the clear blue eyes that was the only feature she shared with her twin brother. "Funny you wanting an enlargement of that guy's face. His picture's at my aunt's place."

"What?" For the first time since she'd handed me the photograph, I felt my blood pounding through my veins. "Which aunt? Elaine?"

"Yeah." Naido sucked on her lollipop. "She's got pictures of old Republican heroes all over her café."

I tapped the photograph. "Including this guy? Are you sure?"

"Yes, times two. I worked at Elaine's place for years when I was in school, and her deco doesn't change. That guy hangs on the wall in her back room."

I slammed the car door closed. "Thanks again, Naido. I'll pay your aunt a visit. I'll make sure you get a massive slice of that cake. Hope to see you at the party."

She stuck the lollipop in her mouth again. "We'll see."

With the heavy traffic in town, the quickest route to Elaine's greasy spoon café was on foot. I dodged tourists and shoppers and made it to the café within a couple of minutes. Inside, the familiar smell of stale frying oil and sludgy coffee assaulted my senses. While a young man served customers, Elaine presided over the counter, her hairsprayed hair big as ever.

She raised one over-plucked eyebrow when I walked in. "Hello, stranger. Are you here for my Coronary Classic?"

The idea of Elaine's greasy breakfasts made my

stomach turn. I forced a smile. "No, thanks. I've already eaten."

She polished a glass with a worn cloth. "What can I do you for?"

"I'm interested in a photograph you have hanging in your back room. It's of a RIC officer around the time of the War of Independence."

Elaine cackled. "I don't think so, love. Most RIC officers were no friends to the rebellion, at least not in these parts."

I frowned. "Would you mind if I took a look all the same? Naido was adamant you had this guy's picture."

"If he wasn't a RIC officer, I probably do." She inclined her neck. "Come on and I'll show you. Ricky here can keep an eye on the place for a moment." She led me through the beaded curtains to the poky back room my grandmother and her friends so loved. Elaine waved a hand at the walls, which were covered floor to ceiling with old framed photographs. "Have a look around and call me if you find the man you're looking for."

It took me five minutes to locate the picture Naido had referenced. A young soldier clad in a World War I-era British Army uniform. I peered closer. With the grainy quality of the photograph, it was hard to be precise, but I guessed him to be an officer in the Irish Guards. Following the outbreak of the war, many members of the Royal Irish Constabulary had been recruited into or volunteered for the Irish Guards. I'd need to check the photos I'd taken of Matt Sweeney's RIC uniform to be sure, but I was confident he'd had military colors on the jacket. "Elaine?" I called. "Can you come here for a sec?"

Elaine reappeared, wiping her hands on her semi-clean apron. "Have you found your man?"

"I have." I pointed to the photograph of the man I knew as Matt Sweeney. "Do you know who he was?"

The woman regarded the picture and smiled. "Ah, sure I do. That was Mattie, my great-great-aunt's first love."

I sucked in a breath. "Mattie? Do you remember his surname?"

Elaine shook her head. "Sorry. I only ever heard him referred to as Mattie."

I swallowed past the lump in my throat. "What was your great-great-aunt's name?"

"Elizabeth," Elaine answered, as I'd known she would. "Elizabeth Randall. She was engaged to this Mattie fella, but he went away to war and died."

"Away to war, you say?" I stared at the photograph. Perhaps Elaine only knew part of this man's story.

"That's right. Broke Elizabeth's heart." Elaine snorted. "Well, for a few months at any rate. Then she ran off to Canada, got married, and had six children."

I pulled my gaze away from the photograph. "You know quite a bit about Dunleagh's history."

Elaine's shrewd eyes held mine. "What do you want to know?"

"Do you have any idea where the men killed during the 1919 ambush on the RIC barracks are buried?"

She whistled. "You sure have questions, girl. I can't say I've ever noticed one of the RIC lads' graves in the local cemeteries. Are you looking for a Catholic or a Protestant? The Prods are all up in the cemetery near the Rock Tower on the coast. Their graveyard's been in use since the nineteenth century. Burial quarters are a little more squashed for the Catholics." Elaine grinned. "There are more of us down south, don't you know."

"Does the surname Slattery sound Catholic or Protestant to you?"

"If you're talking way back, then definitely Catholic. It's much harder to say these days."

I shifted my gaze back to the photograph and the young man's serious expression. "Where did the Catholics bury their dead in 1919?"

"Try St. Malachy's Church on the outskirts of town. The church is still in use, but the graves in the graveyard are old. I'm pretty sure they stopped burying people there by the 1930s. If you have no luck there, talk to Father Quinn, your pal Suzie's uncle. He's a priest at St. Malachy's and interested in history. He'd know where to find the grave you're looking for."

I thanked Elaine for her time and left her café. Instead of heading back to my car, I kept walking along the main street, toward St. Malachy's Church. When I reached the church wall, I took a quick look at one of the graves—1845. Way too early. I scanned the yard and spotted a larger graveyard in a field beyond the churchyard. Taking a chance, I walked past the church and up a side lane. A turnstile gate marked the entrance to the larger graveyard. I walked through and continued up a gravel path.

It didn't take long to find the grave I wanted. In fact, I didn't even need to look. I followed the winding gravel path through the overgrown lawn and stopped in front of a simple granite headstone.

"So," I said to the man at my side. "Here you are."

Matt Sweeney and I stared down at the words etched into the headstone.

Matthew Arthur Slattery
1886-1919

"Here I am," he said softly.

"Thirty-three's no age to die. What happened to you?"

He raised his deep blue eyes and looked at me intently. "I was rather hoping you'd help me find out."

"There's red velvet cake in my car," I blurted. "For your party."

His warm smile sent a shiver of expectation down my spine. "I have no notion what red velvet cake tastes like," he said, "but I've never said no to cake."

THE END

A NOTE FROM ZARA

• I hope you enjoyed Dee's first adventure in Dunleagh Castle. Dee and the mysterious Matt Sweeney will be back in ***Fatal Front Page***.

• Did you know I have another Irish-set cozy mystery series? If you haven't read the Movie Club Mysteries yet, turn the page for a peek at Book 1, ***Dial P For Poison***.

• If you'd like to keep up-to-date with my books, sign up for my mailing list:
https://zarakeane.com/newsletter

Happy Reading!
Zara xx

MOVIE CLUB MYSTERIES

Dial P For Poison

The Postman Always Dies Twice

How to Murder a Millionaire

The 39 Cupcakes

Rebel Without a Claus

Some Like It Shot

TIME-SLIP MYSTERIES

Deadline with Death

Fatal Front Page

ABOUT ZARA KEANE

USA Today bestselling author Zara Keane grew up in Dublin, Ireland, and spent her summers in a small town very similar to the fictitious Whisper Island and Dunleagh.

She currently lives in Switzerland with her family. When she's not writing, Zara loves knitting, running, unplugged gaming, and adding to her insanely large lipstick collection.

zarakeane.com